Kilbaddy

Meg Woodward

ISBN – 13 978-1533552587

ISBN – 10 1533552584

Published by Tulloch Books

Dedicated to all farmers struggling against the odds

In particular my thanks go to the singing farmer, Colin Campbell, who wrote the modern ballad, 'Kilbaddie's Bonnie Quine' and who years ago gave me leave to include phrases from the song as building blocks in this three generation love story. This I have set against the background of Banffshire, no longer a political county, overlooking the Moray Firth.

My Kilbaddy Farm does not exist. It and all the characters are generic and fictional but I hope they reflect the types of personalities and values which can be found in all North East Scotland's rural communities. Most Scottish farmers are tenants, not owners as Jock Wishart was, but like them, according to custom, he is still identified as 'Kilbaddy', the name of his farm rather than by his given name. Whether a new owner will be awarded the soubriquet will depend on whether he earns it in the eyes of the local community. Many fail, especially those from gentler climates.

This story is set in 1990/1, before the horrific Mad Cow Disease (BSE/CJD) struck Europe's cattle industry, before Foot and Mouth Disease led to the destruction of thousands upon thousands of cloven hooved stock all over the country – almost before the existence of properly mobile phones (which changed the art of plotting forever) and the double-edged intrusion of computers and the internet into farm management.

Chapter One

'What d'you know about Kilbaddy's Bonnie Quine?'

'Which one?' I little realised what lay in front of us all.

'Are there more than one?' Surprise strengthened the girl's New Zealand accent. I smiled at her sitting beneath my open window, her mop of short, dark curls stirred by the breeze. The wind was soft and warm, whiffling north from the Grampians which had baked quietly since early in the morning, a true fruit pickers' day. The raspberry crop would be the first harvest for the new incumbent at Kilbaddy Farm. Above the humped green hills of Banffshire the cooling sky was now washed with mauve and dove grey. In a couple of places dying storm clouds blown up from the Lowlands were tinged with almond pink promising more good weather, though no doubt my neighbours would still find fault with it. Farmers always do.

'Of course. Every time a new man takes over the farm there's a new quine too. If he marries. Or if he has a daughter. And a farmer who doesn't take a wife is in a sorry state. - You did know the man is named after the farm, didn't you? Few people around here would know your grandfather as Jock Wishart, but everybody knows Kilbaddy.'

'But I met a clot in Dumfries yesterday who insists a quine is a cow.'

'Ah. It is in Galloway. There they mean a heifer, but up here in the north-east, well, I suppose it means the same, a young woman who is not yet a mother. A girl. A lass. Is it your grandmother you want to hear about, Katherine? Or your mother?'

'Oh, call me Kit. It's less of a muddle with Mum. And Grandmother too. There must still be folk around here who knew her. Whoever thought of calling three generations of females all by the same name? I ask you! - You knew my grandmother, didn't you, Mr. Cryckiewicz?'

'Bruno.' My face must have shown delight at the perfect pronunciation. Kathy, the middle of the three Katherines, had built well on the smattering of Polish I had dropped in her young path. By adding Russian, German and French she had created for herself a hedge against an ill fortune which none of us had anticipated. How she had needed that hedge. It pleased me that she had also thought it worth passing on her skills to this wandering, chattering daughter of hers, this Kit, or Kitty, who looked so uncomfortably like her grandmother Kate. Now she had been Kilbaddy's Bonnie Quine. Most certainly she had been bonnie. 'My neighbours gave up trying to pronounce the unpronounceable forty years ago. Which name does your mother use for me?' I couldn't resist the question.

'Bruno. Always. She's not into feelings much, not speaking about them, I mean. But I'd guess she's pretty fond of you. She talks as much about you as she does about Kilbaddy. - Only, I suppose he's not Kilbaddy any more, is he?' Her voice was sad. 'Not since he sold the farm.'

'Ah, there you're wrong. He'll be Kilbaddy till the day he dies. Maybe Old Kilbaddy,' I mused further, 'if the new man shows signs of doing well. But that'll take time. In the beginning your grandfather was Jock Wishart longer than he wanted.'

'He had to prove himself before he was considered worthy of the name of Kilbaddy?' '

'It's a good farm, after all.'

'An accolade, then?' She laughed, throwing her dark head back with a slow, sensuous shake. The sudden familiarity of it squeezed my heart with shock and drove me to the privacy of the kitchen. 'I'll fill up the pot again.' Before I had recovered she was there behind me, standing a sturdy five foot five or so. In stockinged feet and jeans and a man's checked shirt she looked more like a boy as she picked her way among the damp debris she had dumped on my floor. The storm had caught her in Dumfries and her journey north had barely dried her out.

'How did you know we drank more tea than coffee in New Zealand?'

'Your mother said so in one of her letters. She also mentioned that I would have a fight on my hands to teach you tidiness.' She had the grace to look abashed for a second. Then she bent and picked up the rucksack, tattered maps, severely unfeminine cycle boots heavily spattered with mud, and the black leather jacket and crash helmet. The wide smile knew very well that it would win her a place in paradise and she raised an eyebrow. 'Into the back lobby,' I nodded, prising open the old tin tea caddy with expert stiff thumb and bottom teeth. 'The wet things can go on the line. And make sure you leave a clear path to the door. With no straps reaching to grab me in the night, if you please. If I trip and break a bone, it could be days before anybody thinks to check up on me.'

I turned just in time to see the blue eyes darken. 'I'm sorry, my dear! That isn't altogether true. The new man at Kilbaddy has taken to stopping off every time he passes. Sometimes twice a day. And as you'll have seen, he can't go off the farm without passing.'

'That's nice of him.' Sounding doubtful she picked up the teapot and headed back to the living room. My cottage is very small, just a but and ben tucked into the breast of the brae away from the gales, all that a solitary, elderly misfit of a scholar has needed for more than four decades. All too often the winds lash southwards off the Moray Firth bringing the stinging chill of Arctic rain. A hunch of geans and alders and a thick holly hedge protect me from the east and from the huddled slopes to the west a tiny stream rattles down from Kilbaddy Farm, side by side with the winding cart track which incumbents are obliged to use every time they come and go. Below my ragged little garden the track leaps the stream over a wooden bridge. We had barely sat down again when it rumbled.

'Prophetic! The devil himself summoned to hell?' The landrover screeched at the gate and impatient feet stumped up the path and in through the door.

'Bruno! Your prescription, sir. And I'll pick up your grocery list tomorrow about nine.'

'Come and meet Kilbaddy's granddaughter.' I had to get it in quickly or he'd be away again.

'Oh!' He came two inches into the living-room to look at her, square and harassed and wearing an abstracted frown. 'Studying at Christchurch, aren't you? Seen him yet?'

'Yes, early this afternoon...' But the man was gone, banging the door in what I knew was more haste than ill manners. 'Well! If that's what you get for a visit ...'

'He's very busy just now, my dear. I'm glad he bothers to look in at all. Maybe he'll stay longer next time.'

She pouted. 'Has he ever stopped long enough to tell you his name?'

'Matthew Grey.'

'A bit young to afford a farm, isn't he?'

'Twenty eight. I gather the purchase was helped by a recent inheritance. He did have experience as a farm manager before acquiring a small stock farm of his own.'

'Oh, I remember. Didn't you tell Mum he'd run one of the royal farms somewhere? And did I detect an accent? Foreign to Banffshire, I mean?'

'You did. He's a white settler.'

'A what?' Laughter began to defeat her annoyance.

'It's what the locals call people from the south, people who sell land in England for a good price then come here and buy a farm for a lower sum. All too often they underestimate the differences in climate and conditions. Whether they do it to pay off debts or to escape the rat race I wouldn't know. There are probably as many reasons as there are settlers. They don't usually come alone, though.'

'So no family? Huh! Doesn't surprise me.'

'Why don't you wait until you know him better before you judge? Tell me instead how you found your grandfather. How was he?'

'Dottled.' I hadn't expected the doleful old Scottish word, but her mother was a Banffshire lass after all. Why shouldn't the children have picked up some of the dialect? 'Just rambling. On and on about things I hadn't a clue about. I don't think he'd any idea who I was. I - wish I'd come sooner.'

'Could you understand him? He does speak very broadly.'

'Oh, yes! We've plenty Scots in Kiwiland. It was just that he seemed to be in another time. And back in Kilbaddy.'

I sighed, regretting her distress. 'I think I know why. My dear, you are disturbingly like your grandmother. Did you know?' She shook her head. 'She wore her hair longer, mind you, to her shoulders most of the time. Not a, um, - an urchin cut?'

That brought the grin back. 'Mum warned me you'd be with it!'

'Not bad for a man turned seventy? You have quite a number of your grandmother's gestures too. I didn't expect that.' It was spoken before I had thought.

'Why?'

'Hm. Because your mother didn't have them. Or very few. I had forgotten about them, the gestures I mean, till I see them in you again. It's nearly forty years since she died but your grandfather must be seeing them too.'

'And thinking she's come back to him?'

She sat frowning at her hands for a little while and I watched her, my head burgeoning with reawakened dreams. 'Shouldn't I have come?'

'Of course you should.' Somehow I'd known that question would come. It was uncanny how we were slipping into a familiar companionship, an elderly, disfigured Middle European exile and a girl of twenty he had met only an hour before. The precognition in our meeting disturbed me. 'He's been alone a very long time. Your mother was only four when Kate died in 1952. Kilbaddy had to bring her up on his own and when she left to marry your father in 1966 - I expect he returned to his dreams.'

'He wasn't alone,' she pointed out. I was uneasy about the old-fashioned glance she gave me. She had her father's atrociously long, curved lashes, glinting gold at the tips. Kate's had been thick and velvety giving a slight sleepiness to her eyes which this lass had not inherited. 'He had you as a friend. Mum often said that instead of having a father and a mother she'd had two fathers, and was never sure which of them had given her more. - Didn't you stay friends after she left?' That came out sharp with suspicion. I was waiting for that too, thankfully.

'Of course we did. Why do you think there's cake on the menu?'

'You've seen him?' She was startled. 'Since I did?'

'I just missed you at the hospital. He told me all about you so he's not so dottled after all. I can't describe how much your coming has meant to him.'

'You think so?'

'Yes,' I insisted. 'I do.'

11

'Then I'll visit him every day. You don't mind me staying here, do you?'

'I am honoured. Be welcome.'

'Oh! That's exactly what Mum said you would say! She says it too, you know, but nobody else I know.'

For a moment she remained solemn then I watched, almost bereft of breath, as the laughter trickled across her features. Oh Kate! I'd forgotten that too, the laughing, loving gaze that starts far back in the blue eyes, your eyes, the sparkle of that quirky, sideways glance and the twitches at the corners of the lips just before they curve in wide delight. This Kiwi girl even has your throaty chuckle that is just a shade more of a gurgle than a giggle. Oh Kate. This is going to be hard.

I didn't dare ask how long the girl proposed to stay. 'So which Kilbaddy quine were you asking about?'

'The one in the song. Dad often used to sing it but he never said who the girl was. I wondered if she'd landed herself in the club and that was why she had to go away.' I felt the blood leave my face but this time the dreadful child rattled on without noticing.

'I've never heard of the story,' I said lamely, 'or the song. Perhaps I can help you to find out.'

'Good. Mum said you would. Seeing you're a researcher by profession, I mean. You see,' she chattered on, 'there was this girl, the daughter of the farmer at Kilbaddy. I suppose all the men fancied her and one of them wrote the song. I imagine it's quite old, from a nice romantic time like the Forty Five, and I don't suppose she was any better than she should have been. Maybe she was summoned to do penance for adultery, or fornication or whatever it was. You

12

know? Sit in the middle of the kirk and have everybody preach at her for hours on end? Like Robert Burns did with - was it Jean Armour? Well, I know he didn't have to but he thought he ought to since he was the father of her baby, though I don't know what his wife must have felt. Just think of the shame of it!'

'Er, Jean Armour was his wife, if I remember rightly. Eventually.' What a peculiar mixture of doubtful literary knowledge and wild nostalgia.

'Oh? Oh, well, I digress. But this other girl...'

'What was her name?'

'Somebody Wishart, I expect. I call her Jeannie.'

'Wishart!'

'Yes, my grandfather's name. So that I'm a descendant of hers if she turns out to be real. It's a nice name. Seems a pity that it has to die out because my grandfather just had a daughter. I tried to get Mum to change back to it when Dad lit out but... Oh damn!' She looked horrified at herself. 'You're not supposed to know that, are you?'

I stood up abruptly. 'Am I not?' So he had remained true to his spots after all, the young hooligan who had carried off our innocent Kathy. 'Perhaps it would be better not to mention that to your grandfather.'

'He's definitely not meant to know. I know Mum felt that he might just think it served her right. - Might he?'

He might. And I might. But neither of us would dream of saying so. And in merely thinking it our hearts would shard more sharply. 'It would distress him immensely, my dear. Shall we take care to say nothing?'

'You mean will I kindly keep my pestilential blabber-mouth shut. Oh, Bruno, I'm sorry. Truly I am. I feel I've let Mum down dreadfully. And you. I'm not normally so indiscreet.' I wondered about that.

'Then forget it, my dear. Why do you think it slipped out now?'

She was examining her hands again, then she looked up with her grandmother's solemnity passed down across decades. Coming to me from the settee she collapsed by my chair and took my withered right hand in hers with a natural ease I found touching. Apart from Kate and Kathy nobody had ever failed to stare in covert curiosity, only to look away in embarrassed aversion. Even more warming, this girl had also looked without discomfort on my poor, patched face and had greeted it with warm recognition. Instead of the shifty flicker of the eyes before unfailing politeness she, this fine, lovely lass, had greeted me instantly with a broad, shining smile, reaching out both hands to me sure of her welcome, kissing my damaged cheek in unique warm spontaneity. I was feeling the absence of her smile now.

'I don't know what it is, but I - think you have X-ray eyes or something. Even if I hadn't said a thing I just know you'd have guessed soon that my father wasn't around any more and started probing.'

'I've no intention of probing,' I protested to cover my own moment of truth. 'And certainly not into other people's private matters.'

'I don't know why she didn't want you to know. It doesn't make sense. Everybody knows at home, of course. You can't spend years as a single parent without...'

'Stop.' Her brow furrowed and I went on more quietly, putting my other hand, the better one if not as good as other people's, over the clasping she had made. 'Are you sure you won't be compounding a felony by telling me more?'

'Would I?' How young she was, less mature than she liked to think and much in need of reassurance.

'If you don't know the answer, my dear, it might be wise to say no more for the moment. Take time to think about it. Since your mother has kept it from us then she must have a reason. She wouldn't necessarily have told you everything. You don't want to feel you have betrayed her, do you?'

'No, of course not. But - I have already, so what does a bit more matter?' I raised an amused eyebrow and she dropped her face to hide her flush. Then there she was, laughing again. 'Okay. Mum warned me about that too. You'd never let me get away with anything, she said.'

'Certainly not loose logic,' I agreed. 'Not from a young lady half way through her history degree.'

'I'm not.' This time the flush was thoroughly uncomfortable and in dismay I let the silence lengthen. 'I've chucked university.'

'Have you now?' A sudden shaft of rosy light set the dust motes dancing and I concentrated on the intricacies of their cavorting. 'And you haven't told your mother yet?'

'N-no. - You have a phone, haven't you?'

'You want to tell her now?'

'No fear! It's just that... Oh, Bruno,' she wailed, 'when she finds out, she'll do her nut. If she knows I'm here she's going to hammer your phone till I back down. She will! I know she will. And she'll drive you nuts till you agree to make me.'

'Now, then, calm down. Kit... You know, I don't like that name much. It reminds me of your back-pack. What about Kitty?' That was a step farther from Kate. 'No, that's like a two-faced puss pestering me for milk. I shall call you Katherine. If I may?'

She gave me a small smile. 'Yes. Because you're not going to let Mum bully you. Are you?'

'Your mother knows better than to try. Nobody makes me do anything against my will. Nor would I make, or try to make, anybody do anything against her will either.' It was only when she put her head on top of the pile of clasped hands and began to weep softly that I realised how much tension and weariness was in her. I let her cry, releasing one hand to stroke the curly head. Later, I went to fetch a damp face cloth and towel, wiped away the tear stains then tipped up her chin. How often had I done just the same with her mother?

'Katherine, I don't know how you come to be suffering jet-lag on a motorcycle, but this is my recommended remedy. Your bed is made up and your room is all ready. I'm really quite a handy housewife, you know. Or would you call it a househusband? While I prepare a meal, you can bathe and dress in fresh clothes. After we've eaten you may have a glass of my very best port and when you've drunk it, and maybe another, you may go straight to bed.'

'But - no talk?'

16

'No talk. Not yet. You are not ready. Your mind is in knots. When she was small your mother used to say that when she was confused about something. When you are ready, just let me know.'

Before she moved away her soft lips touched my cheek and I felt like weeping too.

Chapter Two

Katherine didn't appear at the dinner table. Her bath over, she must have flopped on to her bed for she was sound asleep when I went to summon her, her towel still around her. Only just. With less embarrassment than I should have felt I covered up her near nakedness with a quilt and returned to read memories in the fire I'd just lit. Kilbaddy did without us that night.

Next morning we were both wakened by a raucous chorus above the rumbling on the bridge.

'What in the blazes was that?' she stuttered from the living room doorway, clutching the quilt around her. She was probably still naked beneath it.

'The raspberry pickers. Matthew has a couple of fields contracted to the jam factory.'

'Grief take us. A bus'll never make it up that road.'

'It has a dozen times already. Now, do you want to spectate at my levee?' After breakfast, which she tackled with youthful ferocity, she announced that she herself was going up to the farm to ask for a job.

'There's no need,' I said, although I approved of her wish to be independent.

'I'm not battening on anybody, least of all you.'

'Why not me?'

'You've obviously done so much for Mum already. And Kilbaddy. I know he'd never have managed without your help, either with bringing up Mum or with keeping the farm going.'

'You're wrong.' I felt comfortable this morning, at ease and, yes, curiously happy. 'They may not be right on the doorstep, but there are many good neighbours nearby. Marvellous, kindly folk. He may not have had a wife but Kilbaddy's larder was never short of baking and his shirt was never minus a stitch or a button. Your mother had more clothes than she could possibly wear right up to the time when she started providing her own.'

'All second hand, though.' Was I hearing resentment born of a heard complaint or personal experience? 'Or home-made. Who taught her to sew?'

'Mrs. McKenzie from the Post Office. And Mrs. Allen at Balbeggie Farm insisted on teaching her knitting and crochet, determined not to be outdone.'

'Rivals were they?'

'In a way. Not for Kilbaddy's favours. - Nor mine, so you can remove that smirk. A patched, plastic face like this put paid to any such pretensions.' That was careless of me for she was instantly dismayed.

'There's nothing wrong with your face. Anyway, there's a mountain more to a man than that.' She heaved a careful breath. 'Mum said it was a bomb.'

'Did she?' I prepared more toast for her and waited. When she remained subdued and silent I said, 'I was trying to defuse it when it went off.'

'Oh. How did you get on to that kind of job?'

'When I escaped from Poland I offered my services to the British Army and that is what they asked of me.'

'Were you an expert of some kind? I mean - they wouldn't give a job like that to just anybody.'

'I expect they gave it to me because I had particular control over my hands and fingers.'

'Why?' I hesitated, then looked at the frank enquiry on her face. She knew, I realised. At least she knew something was hidden inside me, wrapped up away from ghoulish human inquisitiveness, shrouded in distant pain. I had never told Kathy. Just as I had known that there was something about this girl's father, I knew that there was more to learn about her studies and this unexpected, as yet unexplained visit to her roots against which she was cushioning herself. We truly were on the same wave length. 'No,' she rushed in. 'It doesn't matter.' I rescued the toast before sitting down again.

'Perhaps it does, my dear.' She pulled down the edges of her lips. 'Maybe we're not meant to deceive each other, you and I. I was training to be a concert violinist.'

The breath was forced out of her with a crack of disgust. 'Oh, the dirty buggers! The mean, mindless, uncaring... What a horrible, horrible thing to do!' She was out of the room before I could defuse that particular missile but she returned again immediately, rubbing tears from her eyes with the back of her hand. 'Sorry,' she sniffed. 'I'm good at swearing. I learned it at my father's knee.'

I ignored the defiance and leaned over to butter her toast. 'Raspberry picking is hard work and the pay is aimed at schoolchildren.'

'Anything's better than nothing.'

'There might be better jobs available, if you really are determined to work.   And don't you need a work permit or something?'

'Only if they catch me.   Do you?'

'I'm British now.'

'You've still got an accent.   It's lovely.'

'Nonsense!'

'Yes, you have.   Very slight but - posh.   And you speak very proper English.   Mum used to say I ought to come and see you in the hope some of it would rub off.'   I sat bemused, as much at the new perspective on myself as the information that Kathy had encouraged her children to make contact after all.

'My father used to bash my mother, you know.'

It burst out of her and she put down the toast, glaring at it with loathing although the previous bite had gone down with relish.   Was she suggesting this as the reason for Kathy's withdrawal from us?   Again she looked up, anguished.   'I'm sorry, Bruno.   It just won't stay inside me.   Not any more.   I - seem to have come to the place where everything stops.'

'Or starts?'   Why was I unsurprised at the sad revelation?   And why, in the name of heaven, was I still feeling happy?   Can you explain that, Kate? 'Katherine, my dear, are you ready to talk yet?'   She sat and looked at me mutely.   'Not yet awhile?   Then shall I talk?   It's time we took our conversation in hand, you know.   It's becoming so disjointed that it's almost meaningless.'

'No it's not.'

'Well, ...'

'Not to us.' She was right. 'I want to go and see Kilbaddy.'

'Alone?'

'No, with you. Come on the back of my bike if you like. A lot handier than buses.'

'My dear girl, I've never been on a motorcycle in my life!'

'You'll nivver learn younger.' That gem came straight from Kilbaddy's store of wisdom.

'I don't have a crash helmet.'

'Borrow mine.'

'You need it.' She shrugged. 'It's a legal requirement in this country, my dear.'

'In New Zealand too. But same as before. They have to catch me first. And there's not another machine can catch up with mine.' The thoughts conjured up by that comment were not pleasant. 'Anyway you don't have a car, do you? Mum said you never learned to drive. Would the new Kilbaddy man have a helmet, d'you think?' It was my turn to shrug. 'I'll go and ask. Back in half an hour.'

I was left wondering if she wanted to escape from me or the washing up. Freed from her presence my illogical happiness drained into irritation. So far the girl had not lifted a finger to help, unless I counted the clearing of her luggage from the kitchen to the lobby and the back green. And the monkey had left a strap lying loose because I had tripped over it, nearly flying headlong through the glass door sometime around five in the morning. My sleeping had been even more sparse and disturbed than usual, since my mind would not stop whirling. Was she more of Alistair Sanderson's daughter than Kathy Wishart's? For her own sake I hoped, prayed she was not.

It was all so different from what Kilbaddy's gentle Kate would have wanted, both for the merry little Kathy she had adored so deeply and for this unknown grand-daughter she may never even have imagined.

Angrily I shook myself out of the malaise and set the house to rights. By the time Katherine returned, it was how I liked it - and it comforted me to see her grimace. 'Mum said you kept things ship-shape. So do I usually, only I don't always get around to doing it straight away.'

'Kilbaddy thinks a left job's a lang job,' I returned, more sharply than I wanted. 'You found a helmet, I see. Matthew's?'

'No, his foreman's. Absolutely not Matthew's. And he was such a boor about it I came damn near to braining the bugger with it.'

'That's enough!' She winced, making me drop the carping note. 'Please. I am old-fashioned and pedantic, but I do find it distasteful to hear anybody being foul-mouthed, particularly women. Particularly young ladies who are my guests and of whom I wish to feel proud. Apart from anything else it's so - unintelligently unimaginative.' She came dangerously near to snorting and my voice sharpened again in spite of my resolve. 'Well? What did Mum say on that score?'

She glared. Then that devilish grin came surging back, knocking the sides of my heart out. 'She said you'd be my match if anybody was.'

'Did she now?' I growled. 'Then that must be my cue. As I said last night, be welcome. You may stay as long as forever if that is your wish but...'

'On your terms,' she broke in, still grinning. Before

23

I could continue she did, ticking off the points on her fingers. 'Leave things tidy. Don't walk away from household jobs. No swearing. Be polite to your friends and neighbours, no matter how much their rudeness chokes me. And I suppose I'll have to keep decent hours and respectable company and not ride around the countryside at speeds above twenty miles an hour.'

'Unless you know how to deal with acute coronary failure in the elderly. - I think I'll go in by bus after all.'

'Chicken.'

'Absolutely. Bravery never was my ...' Oh, how crass could I be? Her eyes filled with tears and she reached out for my withered hand, lifting it to her lips. How very, very fragile was her bravado. 'Let me try the helmet, then,' I suggested gently. 'Just to see if it fits.'

'I'll come by bus with you,' she whispered. It was my turn to laugh at her, carefully. We went on the motorcycle. I hung on in terror, shivering in the rush of cool air and shuddering each time the great black and silver beast tipped off the vertical when rounding a corner, leaving my lurching stomach trailing along the roadside. The wind set off the neuralgia which plagued my brutalised face but that I was used to. We parked just outside the geriatric ward where Kilbaddy was living out his last days, none of us having any real idea of how many or how few those might be. By the time we reached his bedside a small knot of men and boys were already admiring the cycle by his window, deep in discussion about this and that contraption on it.

'Belongs a curly headed laddie,' Kilbaddy muttered. 'Cam tae see me yisterday an' all.' Katherine caught my eye and swallowed hard. It was not one of the old man's better days.

'And here's Katherine,' I said. 'Kit. All the way from New Zealand.'

'Kathy took her ain road,' he said despondently. 'She had the right. It was nane o' my doin'. Nor yours neether, Bruno lad.'

'Quite right,' I soothed him. He looked at Katherine, both disturbed and comforted.

'Hullo, Grandfather. I was up at Kilbaddy a while ago,' she tried. 'They're getting on well with the raspberries. Matthew Grey thought they'd be finished by the end of next week.' Kilbaddy frowned at her.

'Nae rasps. Nae at Kilbaddy,' he said firmly. I caught Katherine's eye again. The doctor had told me the previous week that the old man was a difficult patient, restless and ill at ease in the hospital but in good physical condition. But he often refused to eat, occasionally throwing the dishes on the floor with unexpected violence. That I found disturbing because he had always been a peaceable man, grumpy often, frighteningly depressed in the very early days after his return from his equally unpleasant war, but never violent. His huge bulk had shrunk and the big frame now curved to create a prominent dowager's hump below the nape of his neck. What looks he ever had were gone with the sinking of the flesh from the bones, leaving a cadaverous skull with a great hook of a nose, incongruously more noble now than I could remember. A nurse bustled in with a spouted mug and a cheery smile as she chattered at us.

25

'Ready for tea, Jock?' I saw how the intrusion of the given name jarred with Katherine as it did with me, used as it was by a lassie so young to address a man so old. However, Kilbaddy responded and drank, spilling a little. Before he had finished, a bell jangled and the nurse laid down the cup before hurrying out. Katherine picked it up.

'May I? Will he take it from me, do you think?'

'There's one way to find out.' And if he wouldn't, he would from me. By now I was fairly well practised. At first he turned his head away, dashing at the cup with first one hand, then both. I half expected Katherine to exhibit the volatile impatience I'd glimpsed earlier but she waited for a few seconds then tried again.

'Jock,' she said, barely glancing at me as she dared to use the intimacy. When he turned to look at her properly for the very first time she put out a gentle hand and stroked his brow, smiling into his puzzled grey eyes. Did she guess? Could she possibly know how like Kate she was in that moment? Kilbaddy gazed and gazed like a child at a Christmas tree. 'Jock,' she said again, firmly this time. 'Your tea's getting cold. Shall I prop you up a bit?' And he took the drink just like a baby.

'Ayrshire's best,' he confided to her. 'Mair milk even when there's less cream.'

'Yes,' she said, completely at sea. 'Do you want some more?'

'No, but the laddie'll need some. The laddie wi' the big bike. Cam in yesterday.'

'I know.' Wiping her face clean of despair she laid the mug on the bedside trolley before turning and clasping the old man's hands in her own, as she had done with mine the evening before. Watching instead of receiving I realised that, once again, this was Kate in her. To Kilbaddy she was Kate, his own bonnie quine, Kate come back with her comforting gentleness, her soft words and soothing hands. The laughter was missing, but it is hard to laugh when there is nothing to laugh about.

Later, after a long hour of non-communication between us on the one hand and Kilbaddy on the other, we left heavy-hearted. Aware of distress squashed inside her I took Katherine for lunch before daring to let her loose on the roads again, with me at her tender mercy. 'Did you understand him?' she asked.

'Some.'

'That about more milk and less cream?'

'Ah, yes. Early on, about a couple of years after the war when he was recovering from his leg wounds and growing stronger, he switched from beef to dairy cattle. Kate was unhappy about it. Dairying is a job for a young, fit man. Kilbaddy's ten years older than I am. He was already well on in his thirties when he returned from the war and his wounds had been in the pelvis and upper leg areas. They talked of amputation at one stage, but he was adamant in refusing. I think it was sheer will-power which brought him back to health but it took years.' Years of constant pain, depression and the unfailing tenderness and patience of the finest of women.

'Was Grandmother much younger?'

'A few years. She was twenty nine when he returned.'

'Weren't they engaged at the beginning of the war?'

'And she had waited, helping his aunts to run the farm,' I nodded. 'Not many women did wait in those circumstances. They were married a week after he came back. That was a few months before I crawled into the valley more dead than alive.'

'What brought you here?'

'Serendipity? Sheer chance, I think. When I was released from hospital in Southern England I could not bear to be among people. Staring eyes and over-patient courtesy I knew were wearing thin because everyday human beings already had too much pity demanded of them. That was more difficult to tolerate than the constant pain of my face and hands. I climbed on a train which pointed north and kept changing at stations, each one smaller than the one before, always searching for a quieter corner, a more solitary place, until I came to a station so small that there was nowhere else for which I could change.'

'The end of the line?'

'It turned out that way, yes. They closed the station many years ago and pulled up the tracks. Where it ran is now part of a long distance walk.'

'And you got off and - then what?'

'I walked out of the station into the rain and the darkness. My face was still sensitive after all the repairs done to it and it stung, but nevertheless I felt comforted by the privacy in the night's misery. In the village I remember standing for a very long time trying to gauge which direction I should choose next in my running away. I knew that the sea was due north, perhaps a dozen miles away, and I could sense that there were mountains to the south. Which would allow me greater solitude? Where could I bury myself, a poor, broken man with a ruined face and ruined future with a new abhorrence of his fellow men that was unlikely ever to leave him?'

Katherine's blue eyes grew wide with compassion, then darkened with intelligent doubt although she used no words to take me to task.

'Because I imagined my fellow men would abhor me, of course. Fool that I was. It was Kilbaddy and his wonderful wife who taught me, not without difficulty, I can assure you, that I was placing far too high a value on myself. I was no more than an ordinary man, like so many other ordinary men put on this earth to live their ordinary lives fulfilling ordinary purposes. - It's strange how I remember that night more clearly than almost any other occasion in my life. Certainly more than any of the war-time happenings. More than anything from my childhood,' I mused.

'Come back.' Her hand covered mine and sadness lay behind her smile. 'You're here with me in the New Age Nineties. Haven't they got something to offer?'

'I'm sure they have, my dear. You, especially. All the good in my life today stems from the decision I made that night. I walked south into the hills. But you are right, my dear, that was all a long time ago.' A tiny quirk at the corner of her mouth told me she knew that nothing was forgotten for all that.

'And the dairy cattle Kilbaddy was talking about?'

'Ah. Kate wanted him to buy dual purpose animals like Shorthorns to be on the safe side but he chose Ayrshires. Little, boney, red and white beasts they are. Their carcasses are no use to the butcher but they give a very high yield of milk and take less feeding.'

29

She frowned, facing a new idea to her.

'They lost popularity,' I added, 'because the butterfat content is very low. - Look how fashion changes. That's the very stuff the housewife wants today, now that farmers have all moved out of Ayrshires. Holsteins are fine, I suppose, but the Channel Islanders are anathema.

Her smile was wan.

'And the rasps? Did Matthew Grey put them in?'

'No, no. Matthew took over only in February. Kilbaddy planted them right enough, two seasons ago. When the set-aside scheme came into force it offended him grossly and...'

'Set-aside?' I wondered what a New Zealander would make of the idea, but her grunt at my explanation reminded me she was a town child. 'As you can imagine, after a lifetime's struggle to win every last ounce of yield and every last penny of profit from his land, he couldn't bear the thought of leaving acres to become infested with weeds or revert to hill heather. He opted to diversify.'

'Into raspberries.'

'It was a good enough idea. If he hadn't retired he was going to plant ten acres of blackcurrants. There's a big cannery and jam factory fifteen miles away that would take every last berry he could produce.'

'But?'

'Well, Kate would have said no again for precisely the same reason as before, and with infinitely more justification. How was a man of nearly eighty to hop from one saddle to another? I'm not saying he couldn't adapt, just that he was physically less able than he was mentally.'

I answered her surprise. 'Then, I mean. Apart from the labour involved in preparing the fields and planting the bushes and erecting the stakes and wires, he also had the expense of buying in disease-resistant stock to meet the factory specifications, and he spent a small fortune on sprays and fertilisers. There was just Holly to help and he's, hm, a fraction doltish, I'm afraid.'

'His head's not very big,' she agreed, 'if his helmet fits me. But why call him Holly, for God's sake?'

'His name's James Holland. Don't misunderstand, he is an excellent worker. Kilbaddy managed to programme him to do all the routine jobs well enough and Matthew probably did the right thing when he asked him to stay on. But he can't rely on him for advice and may have some difficulty in changing his ways, if he decides he wants things done differently.'

'He's not that old.'

'Early fifties, but neither bright nor adaptable. The raspberries flummoxed him. He had to be instructed at every step and in the end Kilbaddy had to hire two extra workers to help with the planting and wiring. All in a time of recession, too, with farming profits plunging as never before.'

'Aren't farmers always saying that?' she grumbled.

'True. But this time I think it might be more justified. It was all too much for Kilbaddy, the stubborn old fool.'

'You're very fond of him, aren't you?' Her eyes were intent on my face.

'I suppose I am. But I've talked enough. It can be your turn when we reach home.' If we get there, was my grim thought as we headed towards our transport.

31

One last admirer was still gazing in awe at the big machine. When he saw a slip of a girl throw her leg over the seat and an ancient gargoyle climb on behind her, joints creaking, his face was a study in disgust. My spirits jolted upwards.

'Is po-faced the word we want?' I spoke into her ear and her throaty laughter whisked across the car park as she swung the motorcycle round towards the exit. The trip home was just a trifle more enjoyable. Um, I mean, less petrifying.

'Well?' she demanded. 'Wasn't so bad, was it? Mind you, it's a crying shame to trundle along at thirty when this baby can do a ton before the cat licks her whiskers.'

I thought of the tortuous lanes we had traversed. 'Where exactly?' She opened her mouth, caught my caustic tone and decided to leave the thought unuttered. 'I hope you won't,' I declared. 'Other folk use these roads too. Including children. And old cripples like me need to take a walk now and then.'

When the worst happened, however, it was ten minutes later right outside my own door. I was preparing tea while she rode down to the post box with a letter she had forgotten earlier. With all the windows open in honour of yet another scorching day, the sound of the machine never completely disappeared from my hearing, just faded to a quiver from the bottom of the valley where the main road ran through the village, fluttered for a moment while she did her posting then came buzzing home again on a surging roar which soon masked all other sound. Till the crash.

32

When metallic screams and screeches reverberated round the garden I dropped the cake, plate and all. Sick with fright I rushed outside into a sudden, water-plashed silence, broken a moment later by the brief tinkle of glass fragments trickling on to the pebbles of the baked cart-track. Dear God! You wouldn't. Couldn't! Not so soon after I'd found her again? No, found another like her. Oh, Kate. Even the confusing of them seemed a wicked tempting of Providence.

That didn't last long. By the time I had reached the gate I could hear muffled swearing in a manner Kate never had, never would have used. Matthew Grey was answering in equally royal fashion although, remarkably, he was managing to eschew the richest of her epithets as he stood at the top of the bank scowling downwards. The cycle was on its side down by the burn, its front wheel frothing the water in its slow spinning. From its position I surmised Katherine had been dumped unceremoniously among the nettles on the thick sward of the bank with little but her dignity damaged. And her pocket, I amended, looking at the broken glass and badly bent, er, sprockets did she say they were? She was claiming a twisted chassis too, in between richly selected nuggets of offensiveness. It sounded serious, but not enough to stem my growing anger at her behaviour. At first sight the land-rover seemed to have fared better, although Matthew did not agree.

After a couple of vain attempts to douse the flames of fury I gave up. Neither seemed aware of my existence.

Indoors I sat down with a sudden thump, my knees useless. It took several minutes for the surging inside my ears to settle but I still felt nauseous - and they were still castigating each other.

'... damned well you're in the wrong!' That was Katherine. 'Just look at where your jalopy is right now, stopped on the wrong side of the road.'

'Insufferable woman! I had to swerve. You came round that bend right in the middle...'

'Come off it!' She swore again, out to aggravate as much as she possibly could. 'Just look at the skid marks! ... Oh, go on then, bully boy! Hit me. How like a man. Can't accept you're wrong, so use your fists. Yaah! Too chicken even for that.' Her taunting was so outrageous that it did in fact silence Matthew. I looked out and saw him gripping on to his wing mirror, his face chalk white, while Katherine spat at him like a wildcat.

Shaking more than ever, I banged the door shut then the windows and sat down again to await some kind of resolution.

Twenty minutes later I heard the land-rover start up. After some shunting it was driven off up towards the farm from which it had come only to return a few minutes later. By then I had cleared away the mess of cake and felt up to returning to the scene. Matthew threw down a heavy rope at Katherine's feet and she bent to collect it, tying one end to her cycle saddle and the other to the tow-hitch of the land-rover while Matthew sat drumming his fingers on the steering wheel. One hand, I noticed, was laced with blood. The one with which he had held the wing mirror when the girl had taunted him? If so she was lucky indeed

34

that this was not a man like the one her mother had chosen. Now that they were verbally silent I had my turn.

'When you've brought up the motorcycle, put it into the garden for the meantime. Then pick up the glass. Every last sliver. I don't enjoy the idea of a tyre exploding and sending your bus careering under the bridge with thirty berry-pickers on board. I'll have tea made by the time you've finished.' Matthew opened his mouth but decided to close it again when he saw the look in my eye. By the time they came in he at least was beginning to look sheepish.

'Now let me see your hand, Matthew. How did you do it?' When he flushed I knew my guess was right. 'Can you feel any glass in it?'

'I'm sorry, Mr. Cryckiewicz,' he mumbled, mangling my name. 'You must've had a dreadful fright.'

'One way or another I've had more excitement in the last two days than I have in the last twenty years and I don't think it's very good for me.' I knew my voice was peevish. 'Katherine, are you hurt?'

'No.' She hid her stung hands behind her back and let her eyes slither away from my unsympathetic nod.

'Before either of you begin again with your recriminations, that accident was most definitely not nobody's fault. Since both of you were on the move, I'm inclined to think the police would consider both of you culpable. Just be thankful that neither of you came out of it dead or maimed. Or any innocent creature who might have been standing at the point of impact.'

I bent to pick up some last crumbs. 'It's plain enough to me,' I grumbled on, sure by now that my own signs of shock must be obvious, 'that neither of you could stop in time. Let that be a warning to both of you. Now, drink this. Every last drop.'

Chapter Three

There was no serious talking that night. Very subdued indeed, Katherine spent the time tinkering with her machine, listing what she would need in the way of repair items. I walked down alone to the main road to catch a bus in to visit Kilbaddy. I had done so a couple of times a week since he had left the parish, maintaining a lifetime of companionship and its habits.

'How was he?' the girl had the grace to ask when I returned.

'Better. Fairly lucid.' I sat down, glad to accept the tea she offered. He had remembered about her visit, but I kept that to myself because he had persisted in calling her Kate.

'I'm glad. Is it just me, do you think? Does my presence upset him?'

'No. It doesn't. I think it does him good.' I had no idea whether that was true or not but I was too tired to care. 'Do you mind? I would like to retire.' The disadvantage of my sleeping in the living room was that she had to go to bed first.

'Oh, - yes, of course.' She tidied away the supper things, picked up her lists and headed for the door. There she hesitated, turned towards me then away again before addressing the doorknob, 'I'm sorry. Really I am.'

'It is over.' It was not my intention to make it sound unforgiving.

'But I am! - Oh, Bruno, I was so disgusting!'

'Indeed you were.' I waited for a moment before retracting a little. 'But I think from the marks on the road and the position of the vehicles you may have been less to blame for the accident itself than Matthew was. Just a little.' She swallowed. 'I expect it was fright which made you, er, lose control.'

'And the same with Matthew.' That was generous in the circumstances. 'I'll - go and apologise tomorrow. Though he might take a shotgun to me sooner than...'

'There are no guns at Kilbaddy! Now go to bed and let me go to mine. Goodnight, Katherine.' There wasn't an ounce of warmth left between us. The hideous incident had shown me that she wasn't at all like Kate. I lay in the over-warm discomfort of the night wondering why I had ever thought she was.

By morning I was the one feeling ashamed and there was a black mood on me. I doubt if the girl had a good night either and left unfed for the farm before the pickers arrived. I thought it a bad sign when she returned within twenty minutes, but she did swallow a mug of tea then and a slice of toast.

'I'll have to take a bus into town to find a garage that sells bits for my beastie,' she said quietly. 'Shall I call on Kilbaddy?'

'He would like that. Do you need any money?'

'I - No thank you.' I sensed it was untrue, but now was not the time to upset her equilibrium. Heaven knew my own was unstable enough. 'I'll have lunch in town. Need any shopping?'

'No thank you.'

Around ten Matthew arrived on my doorstep. 'Mr. Cryckievicz, about yesterday...'

'Bruno,' I corrected. 'Please, Matthew, it is over.'

'But - don't blame the girl. It wasn't really her fault.'

'Mm?' I tempered my sour response with an offer of coffee. 'She has, er, an unexpected turn of phrase, I'm afraid.'

That did nothing to divert him. 'When I saw her disappear down the bank, bike and all... My God, I thought she'd bought it.'

'Shall we say that so did she? That explained much of what happened afterwards. Please, my boy, it really is better forgotten. All of it.' At last the dryness of my tone penetrated his worry and guilt. 'You saw her this morning?'

'Yes, she said she was going to see Kilbaddy. I - thanks. Two sugars. - Oh, heck. It really was my fault. I was in too much of a hurry and I cut the corner without thinking.'

'You've been in too much of a hurry rather often recently, haven't you?' I said. 'No, I'm not criticising your driving on other occasions. But - you seem to be a little short of hours in the day.'

He sighed, glad to sit down for a few minutes. 'You can say that again. To be honest, I'm beginning to wonder if I've bitten off more than I can chew.'

'In what way?'

'Phfff. For a start, I'm really a stock man and I don't know the first thing about rasps. If you hadn't stopped me spraying at green fruit stage I'd have had the lot condemned for commercial purposes. Holly never gave it a second thought when I started him off. Then there's the barley. If it doesn't make the grade for the distilleries I'll be badly in the red with no cash

39

reserve to pay for next year's fertilisers. I know I'll have to get the buyer to look at the crop in the next fortnight, but I daren't let him see it in the dirty state it's in right now and ...'

'...you haven't any time to spare to it because of the rasps? Well, it might not be much of a comfort to you, but Kilbaddy met with the same problem. I can help, you know.' The astonished look he gave me was hardly complimentary. 'I've been living here for forty years and many a time I have lent a hand. There's little about the farm and its working I don't know something about, even if I don't have Mr. Wishart's skill and innate knowledge. I can tell you this. You have four or five days in hand. The buyer for the distilleries is extremely regular in his habits. Since this farm is higher than those on the coast the barley will ripen here at least a week later, which means that you will see him only after he has done his first rounds along the Firth. Probably at the end of next week. You won't need to call him. Kilbaddy is already on his rota. What I suggest is that you catch up with all that you can, apart from the barley, between now and this weekend - and I'll see what I can set up for you for next Monday.'

'I don't want to go begging for help,' he objected. 'That's hardly likely to put me in a good light.'

'You'll be a fool if you don't. Your neighbours will know very well what your problems are - the same as theirs. It's not a competition to see who gets the best price or the best yield. It's survival that matters up here and you would be very unwise to forget it, young man. There have been all too many incomers who have, and have paid dearly for it. Local men too.'

He bristled but kept quiet.

'Besides, if you are willing to ask them for help and advice you will be stroking their fur in the right direction, showing that you recognise their superiority. It will also suggest that in the future you might be willing to help them in return. Believe me, Matthew, without help from others Kilbaddy would have gone under a dozen times. He's not alone. It certainly doesn't mean thar he didn't know his business.'

Mind you, Matthew had no winsome, persuasive wife to do the asking, which might make a difference. Kilbaddy had been just as unwilling in the early days, but Kate had had no scruples. While her husband had limped over his fields in black, towering frustration she had quietly gone next door and explained the problem to Balbeggie, or Kindrum, or whoever would listen. I had heard her do it. I smiled as I remembered that she had never actually asked for anything, except in dire emergency, just mentioned the need. It was enough. With no fuss at all the need would be supplied, all for the cost of a lovely, gentle smile. Repayment in the form of other favours came later.

Suspicious of the unexplained blip of amusement which invaded my bad humour, Matthew scowled at his coffee, not in offense but in anxiety and near exhaustion.

'Matthew, when Kilbaddy sold out to you it was because he thought you could make a go of things. Yours wasn't the highest bid, you know. Just the best one. That's the advantage of a sealed bid system. I agreed with him when he asked me, and I wouldn't want to see you let us down, would I? Won't you trust me? Kilbaddy did.'

He looked into his cup for guidance. 'I suppose so. Oh, sorry! I mean, yes, thank you. Thanks very much indeed.'

'One more thing. The field by the conifer plantation needs attention. The bullocks have been leaning against the wires to get at Kindrum's clover and they have pulled up a couple of posts. I'd have seen to them myself but...' I spread out my miserable hands with a shrug.

'Certainly not, sir!' He jumped to his feet. 'I'll see to it before lunch.'

'Dinner,' I corrected.

Suddenly he smiled. 'Aye! I'd better get in tune.'

'Are you still having trouble with the raspberry squad?'

'Cheek, but nothing else. Sending that Bertie character home with no pay stopped the rot.'

'I thought it would.'

'Thanks for the tip. I half expected an angry dad on my doorstep but instead I got a teacher from the school phoning to say great stuff. - Bruno, I'm so glad I've fallen in with you.'

I walked him to the gate. 'No vehicle?'

'I needed the exercise.' His answer was dry, leaving me to wonder why.

It was mid-afternoon when Katherine arrived back, hot and weary. I had been at my books for several hours.

'Have you had any luck?'

'Not much. It's a specialist job, you see, a very special beastie. Not many of them were made and I can only get spares from the manufacturer.'

'Vintage, too?'

'And quite valuable, so I might even have to get bits specially made. Tea? No, I'll make it. You carry on.'

However, she chattered nervously as she pottered in the kitchen, making sure I couldn't concentrate.

'It's a real pain, just when I could do with it. Oh, and the hospital want me to go down again and feed Kilbaddy at tea-time. With the bus journeys and all it'll take three hours.'

'Why?'

'Well, I went in just as they were dishing up dinner and got the job of feeding him. Apparently he ate more than at any meal since he went into hospital. I even got him to feed himself a bit. How long has he been in?'

'About six weeks.'

'Where was he before that? I thought he'd got himself a house in the village.'

'He simply couldn't cope on his own. He had managed while he was at Kilbaddy, but once away from familiar surroundings he lost interest. He became severely run down then he had a touch of pneumonia. His removal to hospital was intended to build him up but once there he simply stopped trying and has gone steadily down hill ever since.'

'It's so sad.' She came and sat on the corner of my desk then straightened in guilt as her hip dislodged a couple of books. 'Sorry.' I was beginning to find her anxiety to atone for her sins amusing, fairly certain that meekness was out of character. 'Er, what are you doing?'

'Looking for a recipe.'

'A what?'

It was a medley of borrowed gardening and pottery books which I had before me. The library and postal services were my occupational lifelines. All my clients now came by recommendation. With many more enquiries for researching than I could deal with I could choose the tasks which interested me most, a gratifying position to be in. If I had wished, I could have asked higher fees, but I had no need. My expenditure was small and over the decades my bank balance had grown steadily. From it I had purchased a tidy, well-balanced portfolio of shares which would survive all but the worst winds of stock market ill fortune.

'For the patent office.' She looked suspicious at that. 'Have you ever seen the words 'patent applied for' when you buy something?'

'Yes.'

'Well, somebody has applied to patent a recipe for a particular mixture of clay, cement and ceramic powder; one which can be fired so that it is porous but relatively leak-proof, won't crack in frost, does not leach undesirable chemicals, is very much more difficult to smash than ordinary earthenware and is light in weight. It's my job to ensure that nobody else has found the recipe first. If that has happened, I must then find out if a patent was granted to that discoverer. If so, that is the end of my job. If not, it might still be over because the reasons for turning down the last application may also apply here. If neither of these cases pertain, then I shall have to check that the recipe works by asking a specialist to try it out and have the necessary tests run to ensure the product meets the promised standards.'

'Sounds complicated. - And interesting. Is all your work for the patent office?'

'About a third. I do less and less now I'm growing old and am finding the scientific side in particular is expanding too far beyond my reach. I prefer literary searches, or history and genealogy. This patent is an exception.'

'So Kilbaddy's Bonnie Quine is right up your street?'

'She might be, if she ever existed. Why do you want to find out?'

'Well, I - er - I don't really. Not any more. I thought it might make a good research exercise for my degree, but ...'

She dried up and I put down my cup, turned a firm back on the desk and stood up. 'Would you like to come for a walk, Katherine? On neutral territory?'

'I would, yes, but I ought to try and get my bike back on the road. And I'll have to leave in less than an hour to get to the hospital...'

'Hm. Why don't you go down with the raspberry pickers? And Matthew mentioned he might visit Kilbaddy in the early evening,' I added, prepared to lean on the young man to amend my mendacity. 'He might give you a lift home. You wash up and I'll give him a ring.'

I closed the door between us before telephoning but Matthew was out, predictably I realised. Then I made another call.

'The bus goes by at ten past five,' I told her a few minutes later. 'Another friend of mine will collect you from the hospital at seven. Will that do?'

'Marvellous!'

'That leaves us an hour and a half for our walk.' She looked away then back again. 'You still don't want to talk?' The shrug came again. 'Katherine, tell me this at least. Are you in trouble? I mean trouble with the college authorities, or...?' There was definitely something wrong, but I had nothing but confused signals to follow so far.

'No.'

I led her across the bridge then sharp right on to a narrow path among the heather. 'This is an old drove road. The cattle and sheep were driven south over the Grampians to the markets in the Lowlands. - Are you running away from something?'

'Yes. Me.' That was clear enough.

'Why?'

'I'm a mess. Or - I'm in a mess. All kinds of a mess.'

'Tell me.' I kept my voice as impersonal as possible, a disinterested alter ego.

'Well. I've no money. I - can't afford to mend the bike.'

'That's a simple, practical problem. We can discuss it later. Why have you no money?'

'I spent it all, er, getting the bike over.'

'You mean you didn't buy it here in Britain?'

'No, it's - it was my Dad's bike. That's why...' I heard her gulp hard several times. 'That's why I had to have it.'

I looked closely at the gorse bushes hugging the fence we were following and narrowed my eyes. 'Had to have it?'

'Yes. He meant me to have it. He told me so lots of times. He said the boys would just slog the guts

46

out of it within a month and he was right.'

I said nothing. Her older brothers, Brian and Jock, had never bothered to make contact with either Kilbaddy or myself, apart from duty letters, and I imagined them more like their father than their mother. It was Kathy and her daughter, this Katherine, who had kept the correspondence going. But now I was wondering just how much news was being passed back to Scotland and how much edited out - and wondering why my previous suspicions had been so shallow. On the few occasions when Kilbaddy and I had mooted the idea of a trip to the Antipodes our plans had been withered by a polite lack of enthusiasm. Offers of assistance to any or all of the family who might like to visit Scotland had come to nothing. There had been nothing but the cold written word till this girl turned up three days ago, after one brief telephone call to tell me she was already in Dumfries and on her way. It was only Matthew's mention that somebody had telephoned him to ask for Kilbaddy that had given me any pre-warning of trouble because it told me she had not known that the farm had changed hands. Kathy had been told months ago.

'You want me to shut up?' she asked, as I turned over my thoughts.

'No. How long have you had the machine?'

'Since Dad died.'

I gasped and turned to face her. 'Your father is dead? - Why was I not told?'

She screwed up her face and shrugged. 'There are a lot of things I don't know the reason for. I'm sorry. I can see you care and... I just don't know.'

'When did he die?'

'February. It was sclerosis of the liver. You know,'
she gave a lugubrious grimace, 'the drunkard's curse.
That was why Mum threw him out in the end. She just
couldn't cope any more with never knowing what he
was going to do to her next, or to us. Or whether
there would be enough money around for the next
meal. Pretty pathetic really.'

'And still he owned this machine?'

'Called it his hedge against inflation. He bought it
on my eighth birthday. - It was the most exciting day
of my life, Bruno! He was sober for a start. He could
be fantastic fun, you know, when he wasn't drunk, and
he took me, just me, to this rally. Just him and me
and his guitar, and in one of the intervals between
races he met a guy who needed some cash. Dad had
been betting on the races and won a packet for a
change. And so he bought the bike. I suppose that
was why he stayed sober, because he'd spent drinking
money and all. Anyway, he bought me a crash
helmet, a little one that fitted, and sat me on the back
of this thing all securely strapped in and the guitar on
my back and away we went.

'We rode for miles and miles, for hours and hours
and the sun shone all the way. And we stopped for
ice-cream, then for hot dogs, and went for a paddle
beside one of the geysers - it was the time we lived in
Palmerston - and then we went to a circus show with
the geyser mud still sticking to the insides of our
socks. When we got home it was pitch dark and Mum
was nearly crazy because he hadn't told her he was
taking me out for the day and she was just about to
phone the police to say I'd gone missing. I suppose
she was scared he'd taken me off while he was blazing

drunk.

'Poor Mum. She had such a rotten time. He'd put the mortgage just in his name, you know, and it wasn't insured so she got nothing when he went. Except debts, because he even managed to re-mortgage the house. It was quite fraudulent and she copped it because he drank it all away and ran off and left her with the responsibility because he'd done it when she had been living with him and she hadn't declared herself not responsible for his debts, or whatever - She's still in second hand clothes, you know,' she said sadly.

I bit so hard on the inside of my mouth that the salt taste of blood appeared, but she was too distracted to notice. 'She never wanted you and Kilbaddy to know how bad things were. Do you know why? I'd have thought you might have been the very ones to help. Wouldn't you?' Any answer was beyond me then.

'Anyway, when Dad left she got a job as a full-time translator. She'd been doing it part-time ever since I could remember. Did you know? She's good, isn't she? What a shame she never got to college. Still she's got what she needs. She doesn't get much English-French, but her Polish and Russian and German are always being asked for now the Iron Curtain has gone.' She reached for a twig of alder and began ripping the leaves off, twisting and tearing in absent-minded frenzy.

'And now? Is she still in debt?'

'Oh, she didn't go to prison. Dad might have done if they'd caught him but he just disappeared off the face of the earth, him and his bike. We think he was in Oz for a while. She just slogged and slogged till enough of the repayment was made to let her stay on in the house, and the building society who had the first mortgage agreed to let her renegotiate. But of course the terms were shocking, especially when we moved to Wellington, and she's still hardly keeping her head above water. She wanted the boys to go to college but at the time when they should have gone she was desperate for money and they just had to leave school. Then when they did get jobs they just moved out and didn't give her a penny.' She stopped to wipe her nose, daring me to suspect tears. 'I really hated them for that. So I got a paper round and gave her the money, and I got a Saturday job in a garage across the road. I think they gave me it because they were sorry for her. Never thought I'd be any use, but when I'd learned a bit they began to see sense and let me do simple jobs on cars and bikes. My pay went up too. Not much but it helped. By the time I sat my exams she was beginning to see daylight and she decided at least one of her kids should get on. - Oh, phooh, I'm puffed.'

'Walking? Or talking?' My head ached slightly with the pace I had unwittingly set. 'In a minute we shall come to the top.'

'Oh boy!' she exclaimed when we arrived. 'That's worth a puff or two.' It was the clearest part of the day and there before us were the uphills of Banffshire rolling one upon another, heaping ever higher towards the Cairngorms which cut clear across the pure, cobalt blue of a perfect, unblemished sky. 'Better than the Alps or the Himalays even. And much, much better than the piddling little Cumbrians.'

'You've seen them?' I was startled when the stream of words suddenly dammed up. 'Katherine? Is this your first visit to Scotland?'

'Yes.' The answer was reluctant.

'Britain?'

She sighed. 'Yes, and Europe. And Asia. First visit anywhere except New Zealand.'

'You said you sent your cycle ahead. I assumed you meant to Britain.'

'Uh, no. Couldn't afford that. I sent it to the farthest point I could afford.'

'Which was?'

'Er, Madras. I'd just to ride it from there.'

'Dear God! There's fighting round every second corner.'

'Oh, that was okay. I just went north of it, up through the Hindu Kush into Afghanistan where it's okay if you know where to avoid, and on into Russia.'

I struggled with my astonishment. 'It's as well you took the chance while you could,' I murmured. 'Who knows what politics will bring tomorrow?'

'I thought I'd have no end of trouble getting into Russia, but when I could tell them in Russian that I wanted to get to Scotland before my grandfather died, they just opened up. Same when I wanted to get through Poland and East Germany. Not once did they even check my rucksack, just poked it now and then. They were much too bothered about their own spate of new little wars and about gawpers from the West come to see the mess the Commies had made to pay much attention to a scruffy kid on a motorbike.'

'A somewhat noticeable motorbike,' I mentioned, bewildered at the wild effrontery of the child.

51

'I never imagined he was really dying,' she said in a small voice. 'When I phoned Kilbaddy and an English voice told me to f... Well, no, I mean when he said Kilbaddy was in the geriatric hospital, honest to goodness, that was the very worst moment of all. It was! I was so glad when I got through to you and you sounded normal and precise and sensible and brisk in your beautiful English, so exactly what Mum said you were. - I just sat on my bike in the rain and grat. I howled with sheer relief. Then I came straight here to you, just stopping at the hospital on the way.' I felt her looking at me but I kept my eyes on a high north corrie still patched with blinding snow despite the heat which bathed us. There were truths in my head that I did not want her to read. Not just yet.

'Your father must have died around the time Kilbaddy gave up the farm.' Did something else happen around that time? 'Didn't your mother tell you he was retiring?'

'No.' Her voice was so small that I did finally look at her. 'I - we fell out.' She gulped. 'I never meant it to happen,' she complained.

'Tell me.'

'I - Well, he said I could have it. In fact he definitely said I *should* have it and I've got a letter to prove it. I'd never have been able to change the registration to my name otherwise.'

'Ah. You mean there is some argument about the ownership of the motorcycle?'

'No!' That was angry. 'I've got Dad's letter saying it's mine. That's surely good enough?'

'I would have thought so. But wouldn't it depend on the law? And the state your father was in when he

52

wrote that letter?'

'You're as bad as the rest of them. A girl can be just as good...'

To prevent her from ranking me an enemy I broke steadily into her resentment. 'If he thought you would look after it best there might be a way of proving that it was his intention that you have it. Do you mind if I ask some questions. Firstly, you said your father had left home years ago. When did he come back?'

'Never. I - fell over him at a Hogmanay scramble. I'd gone with friends from college, the biking gang. I've always been keen on engines. There was this guy there, blotto in an elegant, controlled sort of way with a bike that everybody wanted to see. Well, as soon as I saw the bike I knew who the man had to be underneath the beard and the old-fashioned hippy muck. You see, I knew he would never ever give it up, no matter how bad things got. He loved that bike.'

After a lengthy silence I asked, 'What did you do?'

'I - lit out. Just backed away and went home.' She kicked at the stones at her feet, angry and upset. 'I'm not proud of it. But I couldn't face the possibility that he might recognise me...'

'In front of your friends? But later?' She looked startled. 'You must have seen him again if he gave you the bike.'

'Well, on New Year's Day I borrowed a scooter and went to the race-track. Just to ask if anybody knew where Dad was, that's all. Well, the bike was still there. It was chained to the guard-rail and when I checked it had been immobilised.'

'Mm?'

'I knew he always did. I always do.' She took a

53

metal lump out of her jeans pocket and showed it to me. 'Then the only way it can be stolen is by cutting it loose and carting it away on a lorry. And it's f..., er, hellish heavy. Because it's old, you see.'

'Presumably if the bike was there your father was somewhere near.'

'Under the hedge to be precise. Dead drunk. In fact for a minute I thought he *was* actually dead. It was disgusting. But pathetic too. He looked so ill. But there was nothing I could do but leave him to sleep it off so I went home again. When I went back he was gone, bike and all. God only knows how he managed to keep legal, but not once was he done for drunken driving. Not once.' She plucked another twig which she proceeded to pulverise as she fought with herself. 'I wanted to say that was that, but I just couldn't walk away. It was Burns Night when I finally found him. You've guessed it. Dead drunk again. No sign of the bike though. Just as well because he was an absolute down and out. He was really bad too. I took him to a hospital but they took one look and said, not again. They'd dried him out so often that their patience had gone. I got so angry they got the police to throw me out.'

I took her hand and she turned to me instinctively, leaning her head on my shoulder. How on earth could an ignorant, unworldly, old man help in a situation like this?

'There was one young doctor came out to the park after us. He told me Dad couldn't expect to live more than a few months. So I went home to ask Mum if she'd let him come back just - to die. She said no. She was livid with me for getting in tow with him again, said he'd conned me like he'd conned everybody else who went near him. Except you and Kilbaddy. Said she wished from the moment she'd left Scotland that she'd listened to you... I'm sorry, Bruno.'

'Don't be.' My plastic patches were not rendering me immune to her perceptiveness. 'It's best to get everything out now, don't you think? That will give us a better chance of rehabilitating ourselves. And putting right what we can. - Now, time is growing short. I've just seen the bus go up the road. You'll have to run if you want to catch it on its way down. Take care, my dear.'

She turned back, gave me a big, spontaneous hug then flew down through the heather.

Chapter Four

Katherine arrived home shortly before eight in the passenger seat of a neat, red sports car. She glared at me as the driver wriggled his short, plump body from behind the wheel.

'Evenin', Mr. Bruno, sur. My mither says how's the newralja.'

'Fine thank you, Lewis. Except when I travel by motorcycle. Do give her my regards.'

'Noo, whaur's this crock?' He turned in at the gate and went to inspect the damage.

'You didn't tell me a mechanic was coming!' hissed Katherine. 'I do my own repairs. Besides I can't possibly afford it.'

'One step at a time,' I advised and went to see what Lewis was doing. Or not. He was standing stock still, scratching the beginning of a bald patch and staring in surprise at the sorry sight.

'Guid sakes, an auld bike ye cried it?'

'Isn't it?'

'Oh, aye,' he drawled, his voice dry as the desert, 'it's auld enough. Whaur the divvel did it come fae?'

'My young guest rode it here.'

'The divvel she did!'

The devil in me added, 'From Madras.' He tut-tutted about taking it over the Grampians, assuming I meant Madras College, and I added with satisfaction, 'Madras, India.' Watching his reaction, Katherine's hilarious expression registered glee and apprehension while Lewis made a great play of, 'Damn the bit!'

'It didn't break down once,' she said defensively.

'Whaur did ye get it?'

'It was my father's.'

'Registered, is it? Hive ye had time?'

'Of course it's registered.' An edge of panic sharpened her voice. 'I'll show you...'

'Na, na, lassie. I mean wi' the veteran club. Ye'll get cheaper insurance.'

'Oh.' Her tone made me ask sharply if she had insured the thing at all.

'Of course I have. - Well, I got the cheapest international insurance. I'd not have been allowed to cross borders otherwise. But - it's only third party. I'm sorry Mr, er, Lewis but I, er, can't afford to pay you. I'm afraid you've had a wasted journey.'

'Send the bill to me, Lewis. Katherine,' I shut off her argument, 'there's a telephone message for you on the table. While you are indoors, please put on the kettle. Lewis needs coal black tea to charge his batteries.'

'Phone call?' She didn't like that. 'Who...?'

'It's on the note. Lewis, is there something special about this machine?'

'Is there something... Guid sakes, Mr. Bruno, it's a real tiger, this ane, rare and royal. Worth a bomb.' He knelt and fingered various parts of it with tenderness, almost as if it were alive, and would indeed bite or explode.

'How much would that be?' Anxiety nipped me.

'Ah, noo.' He wagged a sage head, picking up a dented mudguard which Katherine had removed.

'That's nae sae easy. Depends on the market and the market in auld things is fickle. Hereaboots - forty, maybe?'

'Tens or hundreds.'

'Na, na. Thoosands. If she sent it doon south she might get nearer a hunner thoosand for it. Aye, aince I've straightened it oot, like.' The cold round my heart grew icy. Quite apart from the craziness of riding such a vehicle half way across the world, and the unbelievable luck in bringing it safely through some of the world's most deprived communities and most inhospitable terrain, did she really own the machine? She was, after all, the youngest child and had two older brothers, both of whom would no doubt long to own it. 'My, but she's a bonny machine this, for a' the bumps. Been weel looked aifter. How lang has the lassie had it?'

'I gather she took possession of it when her father died in February. Since then she has driven it, or is that ridden it, across Asia and Europe. As she appears to have no money I presume she did her own maintenance. How she paid for fuel I have no idea.' The entire escapade filled me with an awesome horror.

'Worked,' she announced coming up behind us. 'Dead easy - a morning's garage work for a fill of my tank, even where petrol was scarce. They were so short of mechanics that most folk threw in food as well. Tea, Mr Lewis?'

'Weel, there's mair damage here than a mechanic can put right. And I doobt if ye'll get spares noo. The factory shut doon thirty years sine. They'll hae tae be custom made.'

'Any idea where?'

He grinned. 'Aye. Joey Matheson doon at the smiddy would give his eyes tae get a job like this.'

'No deal. Sorry, but I want it properly done by somebody who knows what he's doing. Otherwise...'

'I can vouch for Joey,' I interceded. 'He is a fine craftsman and does a good deal of specialist work for the owner of the local Motor Museum.' She frowned at me for a full minute.

'I'll think about it.'

'If ye wanted a buyer,' Lewis suggested, 'ye could dae worse than go there.'

'I've already got a waiting list, twenty at least in as many countries, but no deal. It's not for sale. Ever. Not at any price.' For the first time I heard something gravel hard in her voice. Lewis must also have caught it for he turned back to the bike and began checking on the scribbles she had brought out with her.

'Aye, ye've been pretty accurate. If ye get Joey tae dae these,' he ticked half a dozen, 'I can maybe find the rest. It's nae as bad as it looks.'

'Is he accurate?'

'Aye, sure. Gie him the bits and he'll copy.'

'A spitting image,' she fretted.

'Tae keep within the spec. Dinna you worry. Joey kens a' aboot that. Ye're wrang aboot the chassis. Straight as a die. Look, I'll show ye.' He demonstrated with a technical terminology which soon lost my interest.

'See me when you've finished, Lewis,' I said, withdrawing. 'Would you have a look at Matthew Grey's land-rover as well, please?'

'Aye, fine that, Mr. Bruno. Noo, you tak' care.' He wagged his finger with his usual odd solicitude,

59

sending me indoors with a faint smile.

The cycle absorbed Lewis and Katherine until dusk when I heard the sports car head uphill. I wondered how Matthew would receive Lewis at that time of night.

'Did you phone back?' I asked the girl, knowing Kathy would be in her office.

'No. Did you tell her I was here?'

'Yes. She asked outright so I couldn't very well say no, could I?'

'Suppose not,' she sulked. 'What else did you say?'

'That you were tense and unhappy. If she wanted to know more she should ask you.' I had also promised to look after her daughter and nurse her through the grief and confusion Kathy was sure she was suffering. 'Katherine, when she heard you were here she was so relieved that she began to weep.'

The girl looked ready to cry herself. 'I - did write to her just before I left. Said I'd be away for a bit and she wasn't to worry, and I'd be in touch when I got to where I was going.'

'Then do that, my dear. Now. It isn't fair to inflict needless suffering, is it?'

'But - what do I say?'

'Whatever is the truth.'

'I can't,' she confessed in blunt misery. 'It would only make things worse.'

I sighed. 'Is there more you haven't told me?' She admitted there was and I wondered where this wayward grand-daughter of Kate's was going to lead me next. 'Then perhaps we should talk again before you speak to her. Sit down. You never did try that port, did you?' I poured her the drink, daring her to retire without my permission. 'Try that. Ever tasted port before?' She shook her head, tasted then tasted again.

'That's nice. I thought port was the hooker's turn on... Er, sorry!'

'Much too good for the average hooker,' I grimaced. 'Probably too expensive as well. Now, shoot. Is that what they say? And this time I want the whole story.'

'Mum said you always knew when you hadn't got it all. She could never get away with a thing with you, whereas Kilbaddy was much easier to wangle. - You really are getting fed up with 'Mum said', aren't you?'

'Slightly.' I concentrated on my own glass.

'You shouldn't because it means she talked such a lot about... Oh, all right, I won't put it off any more. If you must know, I - kind of stole the bike. That's what they'll say anyway.'

My heart plummeted, but with disappointment rather than surprise. 'I really do have Dad's letter saying I was to have it. It even says he's giving it to me because he knew he would never be able to ride it safely again and it says where he had it locked up. And he was the one who made me send off and change the ownership documents to my name. But...'

'It was part of his estate?'

'No,' she said miserably, 'it was his estate. He hadn't another bean. When the medics wouldn't take him on again I had to get a room for us to get him out of the junk yard. We have a cardboard city too, you know. And I nursed him until he died. It lasted three weeks.'

I sensed that pity was the last thing she could tolerate, so deep was her devastation at the

61

experience, breaking swiftly and suddenly as it had done into the sunshine of college youth. 'I spent ages agonising about whether to interfere but in the end I couldn't just leave him to die on the streets. Mum was mad with me. I could understand that after what she'd been through. I don't think I saw the half of it. I'm - sure there was sexual violence as well.'

'I hope I am wrong,' I said, blinding myself with severe practicality to the hideous images flashing into existence, 'but you seem to suggest that she forced you to choose between your parents.'

'N-not exactly. I wanted to borrow money for the room, but she wouldn't help.'

'How did you manage? If you were nursing your father you couldn't have worked.'

'No. I - used my college grant.'

She put down her glass because she was shaking so much. 'I couldn't go back to Mum after that. I couldn't have told her. She'd have flipped.' Oh Kate, how do I handle this one? Paying the debts would be easy, but how can I readjust the child's values without completely crushing her undoubted spirit and ingenuity? I can't condemn the brave compassion either, can I, for surely that came from you, dear girl? I must never underestimate the character and courage of this grandchild of yours. Underneath the wildness, the downright amorality of her there must be...

Yet, I didn't know you at twenty, did I? What were you like then, in the frenetic, incoherent thirties when the storm clouds were lowering over Europe? Were you wild and uncontrollable, driven by the whiplash of your emotions and dominated by an erratic power of reason, as Kathy was too at this age? What turns of

62

fate tamed you, I wonder, into the gentle, wise creature who nursed Kilbaddy and me, coaxing us back to sanity? Or was it the very caring for two broken men which taught you the hardest lessons of your life? Post trauma stress disorder, that was our affliction. Whoever had heard of it then? Even now it is a strange, incomprehensible weirdness, a horrific disemboweling of the mind and knotting of the spirit causing a man to revolt against loving and caring in a welter of inexplicable self-destruction.

And yet you healed us. Both of us. One would have been enough of a test for any woman. Yet you took two of us on. You protected each one of us from the black viciousness within ourselves, driving us towards the light in spite of our lack of interest, our malign ill will even.

I sighed. How often did you cry in the night my dear, dark girl? What was it that enabled you to go on when you were at your wits' end to know what to try next, knowing the black dog could still settle on one shoulder or the other? For that matter, what Grace of God protected you from the destructiveness of depression? Why did it never, as far as I could see, settle on your overburdened shoulder? And what premonition urged you to bind us together, Kilbaddy and me, for our own sakes as well as Kathy's?

'I will pay it back.' Katherine's desperate voice drew me out of the reverie. 'Just as soon as I can. And the cost of repairs to the bike. And the land-rover if it...'

'We'll talk about that tomorrow. Hm, how much do you think the cycle is worth?'

'I'm not selling,' she flared.

'I'm not suggesting that,' I soothed. 'I just wondered if you had it sufficiently well covered by insurance.'

'Oh. Well, about fifteen, twenty thousand, I suppose. Enough for the boys to want to cash it in maybe.'

'How did that figure come about?'

'Dad said.'

'It's what he paid for it?'

'No. He paid eight thousand three hundred. Cash. New Zealand, of course.'

I nodded. 'You said your father had written a letter stating he gave the machine to you. When did he write it?'

'When he came into the flat with me.'

'So it could be said that you had influenced his decision.' She stared, her face becoming even paler. '*I'm* not saying it, my dear. But perhaps others will. Or have they already done so? The machine could become the subject of a probate wrangle. After all, your father had three children. Legally the others, and your mother, are entitled to part of his estate. Most countries have rules about that.'

'I'm in Scotland now,' she said rebelliously.

'We have rules too. And an extradition treaty.' She leaned forwards, took another sip of port then laid down the glass again staring at it with an expression of profound distaste on her face.

'You don't like it?'

'I - Do you mind if I don't drink any more? It's lovely but - well, I'm not exactly sure that I'm not my father's heir in this as well. You know the song, one drink is one too many?'

64

'A thousand not enough?' Her admission shook me. So young?

'You are with it! - Only don't go thinking I'm a dipso already, will you? It's just that - the stuff makes me feel funny and when I feel that way I actually want to feel funnier still.'

'And you are afraid. In that case you are wise to leave it alone. Very wise.' The flush this time was one of pleasure. 'When did you send away the papers to register change of ownership?'

''Bout ten days before Dad died. I wanted to wait but he insisted. They came back the day before his funeral. Even then the boys were after the bike, so I - just took the papers and vamoosed with it. I went to Auckland. I'd no idea how I was going to hide the damned thing, and then I'd a brill idea. I went straight to the docks and booked it on to the first cargo ship that was sailing somewhere that wasn't Kiwiland. I'd meant to send it to Australia but it was actually cheaper to send it to Madras and the Indian ship was sailing sooner so I plumped for that. It was due to arrive in April so I went and booked a cheap flight with the last of my grant money and hitched a lift home for the funeral. Of course, since I'd absconded with the college cash I had to keep my head down for the six weeks till I flew out.'

'You mean you had to hide?'

'We-ell, I got a job as a mechanic in Auckland. It gave me just enough money to keep me afloat. And in the evenings I was able to raid the university library for books on Polish and Russian to give them a bit of a brush up.' She gave a nervous laugh quite unlike her usual gurgle. 'Anybody asking for those was bound to be a bona fide student, don't you think?'

'You stole the books too?'

'No, of course not. Just borrowed them. Nobody else was after them because they were inches thick in dust.'

'Where did you stay?'

'Dossed in the parks. Easy enough to hoodwink the attendants, and it was quite an adventure.'

'And early autumn,' I pondered. 'And your mother?'

'I phoned her every weekend. Didn't tell her where I was, just that I was fine.'

'And are you going to phone her now?' Her eyes widened with apprehension. 'Or is there more?' The eyes slid away from mine. 'Are there any more debts?'

'No,' she said firmly.

'No police trouble?'

'No.' Was that marginally less direct? 'There are other things I might tell you later but... That's all my real troubles.'

'Very well. Now if you will allow me, I at least shall phone your mother. I love her too much to leave her fretting.' It took us some time to make contact with Kathy at the work number she had left with me.

'Bruno - she hasn't vanished again?'

'No, my dear, she's sitting beside me right now, and I am going to chase her off to bed in a minute. Kathy, please be patient with us. Your daughter is "muxed up and middle" - you remember what you meant by that?'

'Yes. Oh, don't I just! And you want to unravel her before she speaks to me?'

'If you don't mind. Will you trust me?'

'Oh, Bruno. Dear, darling Bruno. I'd trust you before anybody else in the world. But - she's a handful, you know. She might run off again.'

'She won't run off again, dear. I promise you.' I caught the girl's woebegone look across the room. 'She has got to where she was going. But how are you? Are you in touch with your sons?'

'Sort of. I'm afraid they're blaming me for aiding and abetting Kit in... Oh, one thing and another.'

'I've already had a confession from her, so you may speak plainly.'

'She's being blamed for absconding with her father's motorbike, if you must know. She'd better know that Brian has reported it to the police.'

'What do you think?'

'It's nowhere in sight. And if she's got as far as Scotland I guess she sold the thing to pay for her passage.'

'Hm. Do you now?'

'You mean you know otherwise?'

'I do and I don't. My dear, I don't want to be uncommunicative. Let me have more time with her and I think I can persuade her to phone you herself in the next few days.'

'When she can be uncommunicative too, I suppose,' she said tartly. Poor Kathy. I could hardly wonder any more at her loss of trust.

'We'll see. I hope otherwise. And, my dear,' I offered a crumb of comfort, 'when you do hear what she has been up to I think you will be surprised. Very surprised. Maybe even proud.'

'Oh, Bruno!' I heard the break in her voice. 'What did we ever do to deserve you?'

Suddenly, I found myself speaking words I had held back for long, grey years. In spite of all my restraint, they burst out and spluttered across the ionosphere. 'Kathy dear, - why don't you come home?'

My reward was utter silence, broken eventually by a sniff. 'I'll be waiting to hear from Kit, then.' Miserably I listened to the harsh words and the final click. It was all a stupid, tactless old fool deserved. When I sat down again Katherine must have realised how disturbed I was. She came and knelt in front of me, folded her arms across my knees and laid her head on top of them. It was so exactly what Kathy used to do that it finally sent a couple of tears down my cheeks. I leaned over and switched off the lamp, glad to sit in the glow of the bright July night. For my own comfort as much as hers I stroked the girl's soft, springy curls. Her mother's hair had been thick and heavy, like a fleece of dark gold silk. It had always felt warm, I remembered.

'Tell me about my grandmother,' Katherine said then looked up as my fingers jerked involuntarily.

'I will,' I said. It was futile to hide my distress. 'But not tonight, my dear. I think we've both had more than enough for one day. Hm?'

When she had prepared for bed she came back to me. 'Is Kilbaddy having money troubles? I meant to ask you earlier.'

'Not in the least. I suppose he could have sold his farm for a better price ten years ago, in relative terms, but nevertheless he has more than he'll ever need. Why?'

'He's worrying about an account he has to pay. I couldn't make out what it was, and he doesn't seem to have any details. But I had the definite impression that payment was due any day.'

'Odd. Did the staff know anything?'

'They said he'd been fretting all day about it, but he hasn't had any mail except a get well card, and the only visitors have been us, and Matthew and Lewis. - Could it be something I've said?'

'I've no idea. Let's go in together tomorrow and see if we can get to the bottom of it. Did he eat for you?'

'Yes, very well. They want me to go in again tomorrow.'

'Are you willing to?'

'Yes, of course. I - even thought he was a bit stronger already. Silly, isn't it?'

'Perhaps not,' I smiled. 'Now, off to bed. You look tired out.'

Twice in the night I heard her crying. On the second occasion, thinking to help, I went through only to find that she was not in fact awake, but sobbing in bitter, child-like despair in her sleep.

After all that had happened, it was little wonder that I spent the lonely hours with Kate. The girl was so like her. Several times that evening my heart had stopped still as I saw Kate in the twitch of an eyebrow, or the swift, light gesture of expressive hands. The girl's intelligence was much more developed, sharp and self aware and her rapid speech delivery was deceptive, but behind it the low pitch and the faint, humorous echo of Banffshire intonation brought Kate alive again uncannily. She was there the room, listening, with her head a little on one side, dark curls tumbling on to one shoulder. My inner eye even watched a forgotten gesture which had once aroused me wildly, the raising of one slim, lazy hand to lift the tresses and throw them backwards to free her slim, white throat. That was not one of Katherine's movements because, of course, her hair was short.

There was so much to tell Kate, so much to explain about this vagabond made in her image, to worry at, tease out and reassess, so many things I could do, should do, should not do, and so little about which I felt sure. I tried to see Katherine through her grandmother's eyes. How would she have handled things? Would there have been a bond of understanding? Could I possibly be the conduit between them even now? Could I, should I be the channel for her utter good sense and her strong, quiet support? In my more foolish moments I used to imagine I had served in that capacity with Kathy. But then Kilbaddy had always been around to help. And he had been much closer to Kate, knew more of the secrets of her heart. He may even have understood the source of the wells of hope and courage which had watered us all during the brief years we had her. He had been her husband, after all.

But with Kathy we had failed in the end. She had fled from us to make her own life in her own way, beyond our reach and beyond any risk of our unwanted interference. Or was that really the way of it? It seemed that she had talked of her childhood and background, because Katherine knew a startling amount about it and in startling detail. The memories were kindly too, for Katherine had intentionally come to me, or at least to Kilbaddy and me, as if to find sanctuary. Surely that instinct had been nourished in her by her mother, even if only subconsciously? If so, was that something I could build upon? And how, Kate? What would you have done? What should I do now?

Chapter Five

When morning came Katherine again slept on. She was still sound asleep when Matthew arrived, again at ten. 'She's not ill, is she? I mean, she wasn't hurt in the accident after all and didn't admit it?'

'No, no. She's just exhausted,' I reassured him. 'Coffee and commiseration?'

'Yes, please. So Lewis told you about the land-rover? That I've bought a pup?'

'He did. He even suggested that the steering column was already cracked before the accident, and it was sharp braking which sent the vehicle out of control.'

'Mistress Kit won't like that,' he said ruefully.

'To see you exonerated?' I smiled. 'I think you might be wrong. But now you have no transport, hm?'

''Fraid not.'

'And - forgive my being inquisitive - no money to buy something else?'

'Uh, I'll manage.'

'May I buy something suitable?' His head reared.

'You don't drive.'

'You can drive for me. If ever I need to be driven. The rest of the time you can have the use of it.'

'No! Look, I don't mean to be rude. I'm really deeply grateful but - it's not on, you know.'

'Call it a loan.'

'I'm sorry sir,' he said emphatically. 'I've got an appointment with the bank this afternoon and I'm sure I'll be able to organise something.'

I refilled his cup and said no more. A man is entitled to his pride. And this was a young man I had grown to like and respect.

'That motorbike of Kit's,' Matthew slewed the conversation aside, 'is quite something, isn't it?'

'So I believe.'

'A bit big and heavy for a girl, though. How did she acquire it?'

'The story of that, my boy, is almost as surprising as the bike itself. It was her father's before he died. Not very long ago,' I added quietly. 'I think that explains a good deal.'

'Her behaviour, you mean? I see.'

'I'd be grateful if you would bear it in mind. She is grieving deeply, if my guess is right, and a good many other things have gone wrong in her recent life, things she is not able to manage very well just yet.'

'I see. I'll remember that. Would she like a lift down to the hospital with me? I've booked a taxi for two thirty.' I explained our plans and he generously changed his bank appointment to twelve. It barely gave him time to detail a few jobs for Holly. The stirks had broken out again into Kindrum's silage field and would have to be moved to the opposite end of the farm till their triumph had been erased from their memories, and Kindrum's.

At eleven I went to waken Katherine with the news and a cup of coffee. She was sleeping like a curly headed baby, her limbs splayed out over the bed.

'Oh dearie, dearie me!' she yawned. 'I slept like a log last night. A very, very dead one. First time for months.' As I bent to lay down the cup she reached up and put her arms around my neck. It was so natural that I responded with a hug, glad that there was no memory of the weeping.

'Good. It probably means you have decided not to run away from yourself any more, hm?'

'And I've got to where I was going,' she agreed, coming fully awake and realising with embarrassment what she had just done. 'I'm sorry.'

'For arriving here?'

'No. Oh, no, of course not. Though you might be.'

'Never.' The slow smile began at the back of her eyes, and I sat down on the edge of the bed and enjoyed it. Yes, my instincts were right. Kate would have told me to show her she was wanted. I was sure of that now. 'You asked about your grandmother last night. I think she would say my job is to provide you with somewhere secure and calm where you can begin to piece your life together again.' I hugged her once more and stood up, all too conscious of the proud young breasts beneath a distinctly tatty vest thing. 'And sooner than you think you may even want to let go of your teddy-bear.'

'Teddy-bear?'

'It's substitute, then.' Had I risked it too soon?

'What...?' She propped herself up on her elbows, beginning to scowl. 'You mean the bike?'

'Don't be cross with me, my dear. Last night I thought for a long time about all you told me. Isn't it possible that your passion for the bike is - a kind of grieving?'

'Probably.' Her chin stuck out. 'All the more reason for not selling it.'

'I'm not suggesting that. But it might be better for you if you were to begin to nudge your attitude to it

74

towards something, ah-hum...'

'Less psychotic?'

I eyed her, realising that, bright as she was, she was having to work hard to keep her temper up to heat. 'I think I've said enough. Hm?'

'Hm?' she mimicked. Her grin flashed out, totally different from the earlier loving smile, and she pulled me down to hug me again. 'Oh, Bruno, I feel I've known you all my life. Or more alarming, that you've known me!'

'Good,' I said briskly. 'In that case, get up and get dressed. Right now. I'll have your breakfast ready in fifteen minutes. Haven't you something better to sleep in than that rag?'

'A bonnie nightie, you mean? That wouldn't half have given the game away!'

'What game?'

'Oh, come on! For a brainbox you're being a bittie slow. You don't think I went bike-riding alone through Moslem countries as a girl, do you?' My jaw dropped and she gurgled, wiping her hand down over her short haircut. 'Meant one or two problems when it came to ablutions and effusions but at least I was allowed.'

'Crazy girl!' I breathed. 'Didn't your passport betray you?'

'Nope. My name really is Kit, you know, not Katherine. And nobody seemed to notice the sex bit. Just looked at the photo then at me in my leathers then at the bike. Once they'd seen that they couldn't take their eyes off it.'

'Which is probably why you succeeded. But, my dear, you could so easily have been murdered for the sake of that piece of machinery.'

'Easily. But I took the required precautions.'

'What precautions?'

'Always slept in crowds. You know, with big groups of camel drivers and the like. Or with nomadic families. Or in temples or church hostels. And I always had the immobiliser in my pocket. If I hadn't anywhere safe to leave the beastie I slept on it. I mean leant against it on my rucksack with straps tied right round me and through the wheels as well. There are always ways and means.' She bobbed her head on one side and said cheekily, 'So Mum says.' I put my hand beneath her chin and kissed her brow soundly.

'Get up. Or we'll be keeping Matthew waiting. I don't like discourtesy.' She had my poor brain reeling again and I wondered how much longer this was going to continue. Surely there must be very few surprises left for her to spring?

All the way down to town she sparkled and chattered, mostly to Matthew, sometimes to me. It was when she turned her nonsense on the taxi-driver for a few moments that I chanced to notice something. Matthew was utterly entranced by her. A shaft of sudden, searing jealousy turned my face to the window. I sat astonished, ashamed at the unlikeliness of it.

'Bruno?' Katherine had been silent for several seconds, I realised, and was looking at me anxiously. 'Are you okay?'

Suddenly I laughed, wholly recovered. What a fool I was. This wasn't Kate. This was quite another bonnie quine, dark and lovely and soft-hearted like Kate it was true.

I glanced at Matthew again. She had her own highly individual light to shed on the world and it was not a light she could hide beneath a bushel.

'Of course. Just dreaming.'

Reassured she turned to Matthew. 'Why the taxi?' she asked bluntly. 'Is the land-rover out of sorts?'

''Fraid so. - Oh, no, nothing to do with the accident.'

'Convince me.'

'It appears I, er, made a bad buy.' I was perversely amused at his discomfiture. 'It turns out it was in a bad crash months ago. Fell down a cliff and...'

'...got hiss-sself written off? And some greedy b...' She blew her cheeks out then exhaled, which amused us all. '...blighter patched over the cracks and waited for an idiot to come along?'

'And an idiot did,' he said gloomily, giving up the pretence.

'Tough. Seriously, I'm sorry. Really I am. So now what? You can't run a farm without wheels.' When I repeated my offer, sure now of an ally, Matthew glared.

'I'll manage.'

'Don't be a stupid b... blighter!' Katherine said smartly. 'You want to go under, do you? Well, think about it, idiot. For the want of a nail, you know.'

'Enough, my dear.' Her help was proving devastating and Matthew stalked off towards the bank. Unrepentant, she slipped her arm through mine.

'We don't need his permission to buy a land-rover for ourselves,' she suggested maliciously. 'Do we?'

'We? But you are quite right. Could you drive one?'

77

'No sweat. We, um, could have a look around after seeing Kilbaddy.'

'We could,' I agreed solemnly. 'But first things first.'

Kilbaddy seemed amazingly improved and was happy to do Katherine's every bidding, his old eyes bighter than I had seen for months. He did indeed look as if he had put on a little weight, or at least stopped losing it. But his gaze never left her face, which sent a tiny trill of disquiet tingling down my spine. About the unpaid account, however, he seemed completely ignorant.

'You've no idea what it could be?' Katherine asked as we left, promising to return in the evening.

'None at all. I have the key to his house. Perhaps we ought to go and check there.'

'On the way home,' she frowned. 'But first let's go and buy some wheels. - If you really don't mind. Mum said, er, sorry, but she had the impression that you - oh, heck.'

'I can afford wheels,' I said calmly. 'This way.'

She made an impressive customer. In the garage I was recognised and the salesman looked vaguely familiar to me. He probably knew I could not drive and kept darting curious glances at me throughout Katherine's sharp questioning. She insisted on checking everything, finishing with a test drive of the vehicle she eventually chose. 'I shall be arranging for a professional second opinion before Mr. Cryckiewicz signs anything,' she announced. 'But if you sell it to anybody else in the meantime we shall buy elsewhere. Always.' It might have been the perfect Polish pronunciation which made the salesman and his

78

manager agree to the impudent restriction without a deposit. It could have been her surprising technical knowledge. On the other hand - she really did look bonnie that day. A good night's sleep, however disturbed, and perhaps her delight in seeing Kilbaddy's improvement, had brought a sheen to her and a bubbling cheerfulness which spilled over into the world around her.

'Come on, Bruno,' she finished rather loudly. 'Let's have a fling before we meet Matthew.' She linked arms with me and marched out to the street before giggling and whispering, 'They think I'm your floosy!'

'What! - You shocking monkey. Well, if that's the case we are going shopping. I prefer my floosies to be well dressed. I can't take you to church on Sunday in jeans.'

'Church?' she said cautiously.

'Church,' I said firmly. 'If you rebel at a Roman Catholic mass you can go to the village kirk in the evening with Mrs. Allen.' To my surprise, she didn't argue, merely reminded me when the taxi reached the village that we were to check on Kilbaddy's house. Matthew dropped us off, knowing that the walk back to my cottage was one I frequently took. We found nothing, just an empty, cheerless building with some sad, deserted sticks of furniture and mementos left over from a lifetime of solitude, and a pile of highly inappropriate junk mail. I always took Kathy's letters in to him.

'He won't ever come back here, will he?' she demanded. 'It's so cold and lifeless.' I felt accused.

'He wouldn't come to me. He said it wouldn't be fair on Matthew having him looking over his shoulder all the time. And he knew I wouldn't move from my cottage. I - need it,' I added lamely, 'its familiarity and security.'

She frowned, leaving me wondering how much she knew about my medical condition but all she said was, 'That doesn't sound like a dottled man.'

'He wasn't then. It was only when he came here that he began to go downhill.'

'I'm not surprised,' she muttered.

I took her arm gently. 'Katherine, while we are in the village...'

'I was going to ask,' she said uncannily. 'I want to see my grandmother's grave. Mum said...' She kissed my cheek very deliberately to convince me that this really was something important to her mother. 'She told me a story. Would you tell me your version, please?' The witch in her was standing back watching my expression closely, unnerving me.

'About how she planted a rose bush by the grave?' I waited. So did she, her tense chin held high and her eyes registering every twitch in my parchment face while we locked Kilbaddy's bleak house and walked the few yards to the old churchyard. 'It was when she was nine,' I sighed. 'As a birthday gift she asked for the sweetest smelling red rose bush in the world. Nothing else would satisfy her.'

'And? She told me how you and Kilbaddy took her to several nurseries during the summer to smell all the roses there and it took her weeks to decide on which one she liked best. And that when her birthday came you took her down to plant it in the very corner where her mother had been buried. I'll know where to look. It's in the north-east, isn't it?'

80

Where the sun shines on it from the south-west. It wasn't on her birthday,' I said, more roughly than I wanted. 'It was eleven days earlier, on the anniversary of her mother's death.'

Kate had known she would die that late November day. It wasn't the dying against which she had rebelled. That she had encompassed with a remarkable serenity which had contrasted fiercely with the bewildered despair and rage Kilbaddy and I had harboured in our hearts. The dying she accepted and handled, when it came, with an amazing gentle peace. It was missing her daughter's birthday which she had regretted. Dear God, why could You not have given her that one small remission? Eleven short days.

Strangely, at that particular time the little girl had seemed almost oblivious of what was happening, something which seriously disturbed us, Kilbaddy and me, then and for months afterwards. It was only during the following spring and summer that there had been sudden isolated storms of unexplained weeping With aggravating perversity we had been even more anxious about those because she had refused to accept comfort from anybody at all and run off to hide till the storms had passed. Twice she had ended up right here by her mother's grave. The villagers and neighbours, especially the women, had desperately tried to console the unhappy little girl but she had rejected them all, finally returning to her two inadequate fathers when she had recovered. I tried to explain this to Katherine.

'It undoubtedly disappointed our two particular neighbours.' The memory was embarrassing as well as painful.

'Mrs. Allen of Balbeggie, Lewis's mother, has just her two boys. Tom, the older son, has taken the farm now that his father is gone and neither of them has married. I doubt if they will now. We all wondered at one time if Tom might end up courting Kathy,' I remembered. 'On the other side at Kindrum Susan Patterson had three sons and was desperate for a little girl to mother. But Kathy wouldn't have it.'

'That was just the way it was. Mum couldn't have done anything else about what was inside her, just learn to live with it.' How did the girl do it? The voice might have been her grandmother's. And certainly the quiet good sense was. Firmly she turned my ragged attention to matters present. 'My, what a show! Who looks after them? You?'

'I am no gardener,' I disclaimed. 'The most I can do is keep my own patch mown. But recently I've been weeding this corner.'

'While Kilbaddy's been away?'

'Yes.' My throat was too congested with emotion to allow me more just then. Perhaps later I would be able to tell her how the little birthday girl had fretted all that winter, coming to this corner on her way home from school to look at the apparently dead twigs which, week after week during a particularly unpleasant season, had shown no sign of life. Only later did I learn that she had stubbornly knocked on one door after another seeking advice. Where she knew an able gardener lived, and there were quite a number in the area, she went to complain of her father's lack of time and her godfather's lack of skill, totally unprepared to leave regeneration to nature and spring. Would they tell her what to do, please, and

82

she'd do it? I guessed that ever since then every able gardener for miles around had been keeping a surreptitious eye on the bush. Certainly it had flourished gloriously now for thirty years and more, clambering over the high wall to tumble down the other side and along the bank by the roadside.

'Voluptuous, that's what it is,' Katherine pronounced, inhaling deeply at the fragrance. 'What a super choice.'

'She insisted on its being dark red and "smelly". She also wanted one that bloomed until winter but at the time it was quite difficult to find a perpetual variety which was hardy enough for here. She finally accepted this one when Jimmy Matheson told her it had big, red hips which lasted almost until spring.'

That day was a turning point, the first of several. Kilbaddy grew more placid, less irritable with the staff at the hospital and totally submissive when Katherine was with him. Within days he was visibly filling out and the weighing machine soon confirmed an increase of several pounds. He had never been bed bound and now he began to show more interest in his surroundings, taking himself off for walks around the hospital and its grounds, occasionally appearing in areas where he was not supposed to be. His inbuilt diurnal clock brought him back for meals which he ate without help now. In addition, although his lucidity was not constant, I understood almost all of his references and could explain them to Katherine.

'Undressed airman?'

'No, he's not becoming a dirty old man. Airman is the name of a cereal and undressed simply means the grain has not been treated with protective powder before storage.' It occurred to me then that the old man had not lost touch with the seasons. Seed corn was just the thing that should have been on his mind at that time of year, although the variety his random memory had chosen was long out of date.

The day she took delivery of our new land-rover, however, Katherine went in alone and came back decidedly worried. Matthew was with her and they were arguing as they came in.

'...no protection rackets in farming. It's a crazy idea. Oh, hello, Bruno. Mm, yes, please.' Matthew nodded as I raised the coffee pot.

'Well, why is he so scared?' Katherine fretted. 'Something must have put it into his mind.'

'Tell me,' I said.

'He's convinced that there are rogues about.'

'Rogues?'

'Mm. And he's still on about that bill.' Matthew suddenly began to laugh.

'What are you two grinning at?'

'Bill? Rogues?' I checked. 'Roguers, he meant, my dear. And I think he means Bill Anderson. He's the barley buyer due on Friday.'

'But...?'

'You saw those lads in the field this morning?' Matthew asked her. 'They're pulling out all the 'rogues' in the barley crop.'

'Rogues?' she asked stupidly.

'Any grain that shouldn't be there,' I said. 'Wild oats, or even barley of another variety that has seeded itself from a previous crop.'

'Oh,' she murmured then added in disgust. 'Oh, shucks! All that worrying about nothing!'

'But the point is, my dear, that Kilbaddy has been worrying and now we can put his mind at rest. Are two boys going to be enough, Matthew?'

Peems Patterson from Kindrum had sent over his youngest son, Gareth, and a friend, son of another farmer, both of whom were keen to earn pocket-money before starting college in October.

'They're all I have.'

'I'll come up,' I offered. 'It's boring, but it's not difficult. I use the time for thinking.'

'Could I do it?' Katherine offered. I looked at Matthew, half expecting him to offer to teach her the basics. He had been showing an increasing interest in being around wherever she was but when he looked straight back I wondered if he was not yet ready to make a declaration.

'I can show her the ropes if you like,' I suggested.

'Well, thanks very much. It would make a heck of a difference.'

'You'd better have these an' all,' Katherine drawled, dangling a spare set of car keys impudently in front of his nose. We had had several tussles with Matthew before he finally agreed that he might, occasionally, make use of the vehicle. Even now he glared at them before reaching for them. Katherine winked at me before whisking them away and skipping out of reach. 'Mind, you've got to promise never to cut corners. And always drive within your braking distance.

Otherwise...'

'Katherine!   Hand them over and stop your nonsense,' I commanded. She had judged her man correctly, however, for at last there was an unwilling smile struggling across Matthew's rugged features. 'Will it be convenient for her to use it tomorrow to go to the hospital?'

But the next day proved to be the second turning point. It began while we were finishing the morning coffee Matthew was now taking regularly at my table, a rushed fifteen minute break which he certainly needed. Katherine and I had already spent an hour in the barley field right next to the cottage and it was she who answered the phone, returning with her face transparent with shock.

'He's disappeared.'

'Kilbaddy?' My disquiet surged to the fore. 'Tell us.' Matthew pulled her to the chair from which he had just jumped up, holding her arm with infinite tenderness.

'He's gone from the hospital. Oh, God Almighty, what the bloody hell were they playing at?'

'Perhaps God Almighty is looking after him perfectly well,' I said firmly and she bit her lip. 'Now, don't panic. We know he is not depressed, just anxious. And he is probably reacting in the way he has always done.   If something is bothering him, he does something about the situation. In the past it has always been something sensible.'

'What, walking out of hospital in his slippers?' she snapped, and Matthew put a firm arm round her shoulders.   'Where to?   He's got no money or anything.'

'How do you know that? I left money with the staff for him.'

'How much, for G... heaven's sake?'

'Enough for newspapers and fruit and the like.'

'That's not going to get him far.'

Matthew soothed her. 'Isn't that a plus? I'm sure the police will soon pick him up. The weekend rain has cleared up and it's a nice day. He can't come to any harm, can he?'

'How would you know?' she muttered miserably, but her panic was settling into disgust at the way her wits had deserted her. 'Oh, hell. I'd better phone back and ask all the questions I should have.'

She discovered that the police had already been informed and that the hospital staff were not, in fact, unduly worried. Occasionally elderly patients did wander off and it was very rare indeed for them to come to harm because most of their life-long instincts for self-preservation and social intercourse were more or less intact. Kilbaddy himself had revived remarkably since Katherine's arrival and as well as being stronger he had become more lucid and purposeful, all of which were encouraging. They would, of course, want him to be returned when he was found.

'Just to check that all is well,' she mocked. 'Good God Alm... ' She swallowed the rest as if it were a lump of molten lead. 'What else do they think we would do? Abduct him?' I returned to the roguing, but Kathering couldn't bear to leave the authorities to do the job of looking for Kilbaddy on their own. Wryly I noted that she was just like Kathy in this respect.

87

Matthew shrugged at me, already suspecting as I did that she would make an utter nuisance of herself when in all likelihood Kilbaddy would turn up sooner or later right where we were ourselves. He did. It was Matthew who saw him first, at the far end of the top field on the western march of the farm, carefully swishing his long legs through the barley and systematically, perfectly happily yanking out plant after plant of rogue corn until he had gathered a great armful which he dumped at the edge of the field. The two boys accepted his arrival without any surprise, not aware there was anything wrong with a situation they had known all their lives.

'It was always the field he began with,' I told Matthew, 'because it was always the dirtiest corner. How is he?'

'I didn't go near. - I wish to heck Kit hadn't gone chasing off. She's the only one who can handle him. - Unless you are willing to try?'

'Come on, then. Don't think too badly of her, Matthew. I think she might normally be more stable than she appears now.'

'It's too soon after her father's death, you think?' As we walked up I told him a little about the problems she had faced and he was immediately sympathetic. 'Poor kid.'

Then he laughed awkwardly. 'I hope you won't mind me saying this, but if she's had half the reassurance I've had from you she must have been blooming glad to get here.'

I looked at him in surprise.

'I - can only say I was, am, profoundly glad I was here for her to come to. I shudder to think what would have happened if she had found me, er, gone.'

Kilbaddy did no more than give us a wave when we reached him. By common consent Matthew and I simply joined in the job, the three of us striding in a diagonal phalanx across the field, while the boys moved off to the field we had begun. In no time Kilbaddy was away ahead of us, selecting, plucking, shaking the sandy loam off the roots and adding the weeds to the armful he already carried, all with a rhythmic efficiency I had never been able to match. He had an unerring eye too, for several times he pointed out a rogue one of us had missed. At mid-day I tried to divert him.

'Dinner time?'

'Aye.' He stretched his shoulders backwards and glanced at the sky. 'Then right back. There'll be rain afore night.' To my consternation he set off for the farmhouse, but when I made to head him off Matthew touched my arm and shook his head.

'You go with him,' he said quietly. 'There's not much in the house but use what you can find. I'll go and see if Kit's back and bring her up.'

Even she was unable to persuade Kilbaddy to leave the roguing to the rest of us, and the hospital, when contacted, suggested we return him in the evening when his mind would be at rest - and his out-of-training body thoroughly exhausted. The rain did come, which helped to convince him, though the last of the rasps might be lost. It would only be one or two hundred pounds but I thought Matthew could ill afford even that, if his store cupboard was any indication.

'Maybe he just hasn't had time to do his shopping,' Katherine suggested on the way back from returning Kilbaddy to the hospital. Once off the farm he had begun to ramble again. 'Being without transport I mean. Will I offer to do it for him? And maybe do a bit of cooking for his freezer?'

I looked at her doubtfully. 'Hm. I suppose an offer is permissible. But be careful, my dear. Don't offend. In any case, I don't think he has a freezer.'

'Well, could he...' Suddenly she blushed an unbecoming beetroot. 'This'll sound an awful cheek but...'

'Could we feed him at the cottage?' I asked blandly. 'I don't see why not. It's just as easy to get to as the farmhouse is.'

'And he seems to like to come for coffee.'

'Yes,' I said my face as blank as a plastic face should be. 'He does, doesn't he?'

Chapter Six

Within eighteen hours Kilbaddy had given the hospital the slip again, much to their chagrin. He disappeared just before Katherine arrived to give him his dinner, walking off into driving rain, and this time I worried considerably more about his well-being. Towards the end of the afternoon, however, we had a call from Mrs. Allen of Balbeggie.

'Aye, soakit tae the very skin, but, my, he's eatin' a gran' tea. Did they nae feed him at yon hospital?'

'Mrs. Allen! Bless you a thousand times over. Katherine and I will come immediately.'

'Na, wait a half hour till he's eaten. He mightna' be sae keen when he gets back.'

'Hm. As always you're thinking ahead. Seven o'clock?' I was curious to see how the old lady would react to Katherine. She had known Kate well and I was not disappointed.

'Losh, it makes me feel queer! She nivver wore troosers but - ach, ye could be Kate coming in the door, lassie, ye really could. Anither Kilbaddy's Bonnie Quine and nae doubt about it.' She smiled broadly at our astonished reaction. 'There's a sang about that. Did ye nae ken, Mr. Bruno?'

'Yes.' Mrs. Allen turned away from us and began to look as if she regretted mentioning the fact. 'Do you know who wrote it?'

'Aye. - Weel, it was young Alistair. Your Daddy, Katherine. Lang afore you were born. And of course he wrote it aboot your Mam. She didna look at a' like you, nor yet like Kate, but she was a real bonnie quine for a' that.' I gritted my teeth with annoyance at myself. Of course it had to be Alistair! He had always had a tune in his head and a guitar in his hands, charming the birds out of the trees. And the girls out to the cornfields. I knew Kathy had by no means been the only one. It was only Kilbaddy's fury and, I suspected, Kilbaddy's hard won cash, which had made the scoundrel face up to his responsibilities.

'It's a nice song,' Katherine said lamely, aware of the undercurrents in the conversation but not understanding them. Mention of her father had set her trembling. 'My - father died a few months ago, you know.'

'Oh, lassie! I'm that sorry.' Mrs Allen was in the process of embarrassing herself again, not knowing how much Katherine knew of the past and entirely unsure of how the marriage had gone. Her predictions at its inception had been as pessimistic as ours, in spite of being not untouched herself by Alistair's charm, but we had respected Kathy's privacy and said nothing about our guessing. 'And is your Mam coming back home, do you think?'

'I don't know,' Katherine said stonily, longing for an end to the topic. 'How is Kilbaddy?'

'Come awa ben and see.' In the living room the television was blaring. On one side of the empty fireplace sat Lewis snoring his head off. On the other sat Kilbaddy in equal tune, his chin slumped on his chest. In the middle sat a third man, Lewis's older brother Tom, also unmarried though well on in his forties and now the farmer at Balbeggie. The lady of the house, prideful but pernickety, had looked after her sons all too well since neither of them showed any inclination to leave her apron strings. Tom stirred from his slumbers and scowled at his mother who shook her head fondly. 'Things dinna change, eh, Mr. Bruno?'

I smiled, my heart aching. Kilbaddy had sat down for forty winks after almost every dinner and tea time of his life. 'Indeed not, my dear lady.'

'It's a pity he has tae go back,' she murmured. Again I felt accused.

'He won't come to the cottage. I tried that yesterday but he was adamant. Besides, I have only one bedroom and Katherine's using that.'

'Aye. - He could aye come here.'

'I think we both know he wouldn't,' I told her gently. Tom nodded, now more awake, and watched keenly as Katherine put her hand on his mother's arm.

'Mrs. Allen. He seems to be quite happy in the hospital as long as I am with him. I'd spend all day there if it helped. And they do know how to look after him properly.'

'Aye,' the good lady said doubtfully. 'Aye, I suppose so.'

Her doubt proved justified, not an uncommon occurrence. Katherine's efforts were not enough. Early on Thursday morning the old idiot absconded again, this time taking less than two hours to reach Kilbaddy. How we never discovered. He arrived, in fact, before we heard from the hospital because all of us were out among the barley again. How he knew I never understood, but he was fully aware that Bill Anderson was due the next day.

93

'We'd better git a move on,' he said anxiously and strode off to inspect the top field we had finished in his absence. Matthew turned to Katherine.

'Kit, could you run up to the house and ring the hospital?'

'What are we to do?' she exclaimed, shaking her hands forwards and open-palmed in anxiety. 'It can't go on like this... All right, all right! I'll be back in ten minutes.'

In fact it was nearly an hour. Kilbaddy pronounced himself satisfied with our work and we began again on the big thirty acre field we had started the day of his first perambulation, leaving Holly to check the beasts and finish some calf boxes he was making. The two boys were not available that day. While the old farmer was at the far end of the field I saw Katherine waylay Matthew who was an entire stint behind and working next to the road. At first it seemed that there was a fierce argument under way, then they both nodded and Katherine disappeared into my cottage before returning to the farmhouse where she remained for some time. At noon she shouted from the gate. Automatically Kilbaddy made for the farmhouse kitchen and we followed, Matthew warning me with his eyebrows to go with the tide. Katherine had prepared a scratch meal for us all and we sat down quietly and ate together as if everything were completely normal. Kilbaddy ate in typical farmhouse fashion, at choking speed and more or less silently, then retired to the living room for his forty winks.

We looked at each other uncomfortably. 'Please, Matthew,' Katherine begged, 'Don't be offended. If we can get him through today things might settle down.

94

Once this Bill Anderson has been, he'll have nothing more to worry about.' I was not entirely sure of that. Farmers always had something to worry about. Worry was part of their wallpaper. They worried all the more if the worry wasn't there. So might Kilbaddy.

'He's a Godsend in the field right now,' I murmured. 'By tea-time he'll be thoroughly tired and perhaps more manageable.'

'I don't mind,' Matthew murmured, looking genuinely upset. 'I'm just desperately sorry for the old fellow.'

Kilbaddy drove himself very hard that afternoon. It didn't help that the air grew thundery. When Matthew tried to call a halt around five, having sent Katherine off to prepare a meal half an hour earlier, Kilbaddy became angry and unpredictable. When she called us in to eat he insisted we all continue, and not even she could calm him enough to stop.

'Oh, well,' she shrugged, more placidly than I had thought was her nature. 'I'll take the toad out of the oven and we'll eat it later. See you in ten minutes.' Matthew rolled his eyes at the unexpected acquiescence then headed off across the field again, accepting the inevitable. It was well after eight when we finished, with the rain already begun, but only when the last square yard had been covered would Kilbaddy stop. His face was grey with fatigue and Katherine had her second failure with him when he flatly refused to eat.

'What about a glass of milk, then?' she pleaded with him. 'Please, Jock.' Without thinking she stroked his brow, brushing his sparse hair back, the very gestures Kate would have used. He gazed into her eyes, frowned in slight puzzlement, then nodded and drank a glass and a half. He still would not take solid food, but at least the milk would keep starvation at bay. She led him through the house to an easy chair where he sat down and fell asleep instantly.

'I'll give him an hour then take him back,' she said wearily, inspecting her hands where yavins from the barley had burrowed their way under her skin in spite of her care. 'You two can turn in.'

'No!' Matthew spoke sharply, startling us both. 'I'm not letting you take him back alone. What if he grew wild while you were driving?'

'Oh, he won't be wild with me,' she said calmly, totally sure.

'I don't care. I'm coming.' He glanced at me when she looked askance and handed him a tea towel. Then he flushed, and I began to wonder if he wanted time alone with her on the way back. Later when she went to wake Kilbaddy I took the chance to speak to the young man.

'Don't rush her Matthew, if that's what is in your head. She's playing a complicated double role here and is having to feel her way. Remember she never met her grandmother, and her mother was only four when Kate died. Katherine has to reach a long way back over desperately empty years with nothing but instinct and my shaky memories to help her.' Only slightly embarrassed, he looked at me keenly, perhaps realising for the first time what was happening.

'I'm sorry, sir,' he nodded. 'I've been slow.'

'Indeed you have not. But when the dust settles I think perhaps I should tell you some more of the background. Well, Kilbaddy,' I added heartily, and he slapped me on the shoulder, hardly taking any notice of me, so much part of the fabric of his life I was. 'You're off, are you?'

'Aye. We'll nae be late. Will ye shut up the hens for Kate?'

'I'll do that,' I promised him solemnly. It was thirty years at least since the wretched creatures had plagued us with their wanton habits.

Matthew dropped Katherine off at the cottage gate shortly after ten, taking natural possession at last of the land-rover. They couldn't have stopped anywhere even for a quick drink.

'He's nice,' she said, flopping into a chair. 'Must admit, I was glad of somebody else there.'

'He has sense,' I agreed. 'But he's not much of a housewife, is he?'

'Yuk. - Didn't you notice the bloody difference?' she came alive as Kit.

'I smelled the bleach,' I smiled, almost glad to hear the expletive. 'I do realise there's a limit to what you can achieve in a couple of odd hours. Was it your idea to offer the meals in the farmhouse instead of here?'

'Well, Kilbaddy just goes there automatically. There was no sense in breaking the string he was hanging on to, was there?'

'No, but it could reinforce an idea we don't really want reinforced.'

She heaved a sigh. 'They're drugging him tonight. I hate that.' I got to my feet to bring in the supper tray I had prepared, stumbling as I laid it down beside her. 'Are you okay, Bruno?' she demanded immediately, her white face anxious all over again.

'You're not supposed to get overtired, are you?'

'I'm fine. My dear, have you thought again of phoning your mother?' During the upheaval over Kilbaddy and the barley, not a word had been said about her troubles, except that I had asked how much she required to repay the university. I had made out a cheque and written a letter, explaining on her behalf that she had been nursing her father during his last illness and asking for forgiveness for her in her time of distress. When I had handed it to her to read she had looked thoroughly ashamed, then had kissed me soundly on the cheek before handing it back to me and retiring to indulge in a storm of weeping.

'I still don't know what to say,' she mumbled now.

'But you would like to make contact all the same?' She looked at her hands as if they had lives of their own. 'Why don't I speak to her first and explain what has been happening?'

That's how we did it. First I told Kathy about the grant and pushed it into oblivion where it belonged. Then I outlined the position on Kilbaddy, trying to deal lightly with the seriousness by repeating one or two of the humorous confusions. 'Katherine has been wonderful with him. The difficulty is that he seems to think she is her grandmother. It's putting quite a strain on her, as you can imagine.'

'Isn't she too young?'

'In what sense?'

'Mam must have been ten years older when she married Kilbaddy.'

'But weren't they engaged before the war began? She could not have been much older than Katherine is now.'

98

'Yes, I suppose so. Well, that might give her some security aga... Is she there? Will she speak to me?' I raised my eyebrows at Katherine, ignoring Kathy's hasty change of direction, and she stood up reluctantly to take the instrument from me.

'Yes, she's here. But...'

'Don't fuss, Bruno,' Kathy said testily. 'I won't ask her to say anything she doesn't want to.'

I handed over and left the room, shutting the door firmly behind me. Within two minutes Katherine came into the kitchen, straight up behind me and put her hands around my waist. Laying her head on the back of my shoulder she just hugged me. I was sure she had been crying.

'She doesn't really mean it,' I said quietly. She astonished me by giggling and I turned. She had been crying, still was through the giggling.

'That's what I came to say to you,' she protested, scrubbing her eyes with the dishtowel. 'I heard her snap. She was just trying not to cry herself. We - couldn't say much,' she admitted. 'Just sorry, and I love you, you know?'

'That sounds enough to me,' I said gruffly and hugged her, finding a huge amount of comfort in it myself, and a sneaking delight. 'Come on. Supper and bed. And while Matthew and I are tackling Bill Anderson tomorrow, you can do some shopping and cleaning for him. If you don't mind?'

'I don't. But, er, won't he be bl...blooming affronted?'

'Probably, but he'll recover.'

That night was atrocious. By morning the track from the farm looked as if the burn had taken it over. For that reason as much as any other Bill Anderson knocked on my door first, handing me a bundle of music tapes, new classical productions he had bought in Edinburgh. He shared my deepest passion but I had so far resisted his penchant for expensive compact discs.

'Bruno. Good to see you again. How's Kilbaddy?'

'Ah, come in out of the rain and I'll tell you. Leave your car here. I'll phone Matthew to bring down the land-rover.'

'Fine.' He turned as Katherine entered, in a skirt for the first time since Sunday, when she had elected to join me for mass. She had fetched some very curious glances. 'This must be Kilbaddy's Bonnie Quine? I heard she was here.' He smiled a charming smile. 'Lewis Allen's taken quite a fancy to you, my dear.'

'What! But he's...' She stopped, realising Bill was about the same age as Lewis, old enough to be her father, and was also bestowing on her an admiring glance that was somewhat short of being paternal. 'I've hardly met him,' she said coolly, and I hid a smile at the unexpected adroitness. She was growing up, or pandering to my wish that she be polite to my guests. Whatever it was the touch appeared again when Matthew arrived. In spite of the polish acquired from a public school education somewhere in England, he was surprisingly awkward and ill at ease in the presence of a man on whose approval he was desperately dependent. I would have reassured him quite openly, well aware that the crop was likely to pass inspection at reserve grade at least, but

Katherine intervened, carrying the conversation along smoothly and sweetly, keeping Bill's attention on her rather than on the young farmer. Illogically it annoyed Matthew.

'Charmed the socks of his big feet, didn't you?' I heard him mutter as he took the coffee pot back to the kitchen for her. To my mind he deserved more than the arch look she gave him. A few days earlier he would have received more, I suspected. Interesting. It was at that point that the door opened and Kilbaddy walked in.

'Oh, Grandad!' Katherine exploded in utter exasperation. Every stitch he wore was sodden, including the slippers.

'Aye, Bill,' he announced, shaking himself to shed some of the moisture all over my carpet. 'Saw your car come in aboot. Ye've picked a gie weet day, eh? I doubt some o' the crop's been flattened, but it'll do, I think. Are ye ready?'

'Grandad, you can't go out again like that! You'll catch your death...'

'I'm fine,' he said irritably. 'I'll just borrow Bruno's jaiket.' I handed it over and gave Bill a resigned nod. Understandably he was bewildered.

'You've nothing to worry about,' I murmured, trying to reassure both him and Matthew. 'Bring him back pretty soon, though.'

'But Bruno...' I gripped Katherine's shoulders to reassure her.

'Half an hour won't matter, my dear. We'll switch on the immersion for more hot water, hm?'

Ten minutes later Matthew ran back. 'Look, we've got to talk. The old fellow's never going to be happy

101

anywhere except at Kilbaddy. I think he should come and stay with me.'

'But he needs looking after,' I ventured.

'And your place is like a tip,' Katherine said bluntly. I winced with shame at it. The boy was making a tremendous gesture.

'Well, do something about it,' he snapped at her. 'I haven't the time to...'

'Right, I will!' she snapped back, and then they stared at each other as the false rage drained away from between them. I couldn't define what remained, but it was certainly highly charged. 'Oh, heck, I'm sorry.'

'No, I am,' he countered, frowning.

'And so am I,' I broke in dryly. 'Or I soon shall be if you don't get a move on. Matthew, go and join Bill and bring Kilbaddy back as soon as you can. Back here, I mean. We must thaw him out soon. No, never mind Bill. He knows the place even better than you do and I fancy he'll come looking for a plate of hot soup before he leaves. Katherine, there's central heating up at the farmhouse. If you look behind the green door in the pantry you'll find the switches. Don't put it all on, just the kitchen wing. Kilbaddy used to sleep in the bedroom directly above. Turn the heating to maximum for the time being, and make up the bed. I'll give you linen.'

'There is,' interrupted Matthew. 'I mean - I made up the bed last night. I had a feeling he'd be back. Poor old blighter.' A tear trickled down Katherine's cheek and Matthew reached out a tender finger to catch it. 'It's all we can do, Kit. But maybe it'll help a bit.' She nodded, licked the tear off his finger with a twisted smile, and went to change for a morning's housework. Matthew turned, reminded by a slight movement that I was still there and watching. 'Am I on the right track, sir?'

'I'm not sure what you and I get out of it, my boy,' I said gratefully, 'but it's the right track for Kilbaddy. And I imagine for Katherine.' It would be a big boost for him in her eyes, as I was sure he realised. 'I will cover the financial side of things. Now, please don't argue this time,' I added with irritation, my head beginning to pound with the sheer pace of life. 'If you take in a lodger, and that in effect is what will be happening, then you are entitled to the fee. Kilbaddy and I have lived in each other's pockets for forty years, as you well know.'

Bill passed the barley for malting which meant the top price. He held my eye for a moment, confirming my suspicion that the crop had scraped through because of an extra dressing of compassion. Perhaps he realised what we were planning for old Kilbaddy. He certainly shared my guess that Matthew was going to need every penny to keep his head above water this year. I walked him to his car after lunch.

'Not a bad lad that, eh, Bruno? Got a hell of a fight on his hands, though, trying to break in at this time. Did ye hear Corrievrack has gone bankrupt?'

'And Westside.'

He nodded gloomily as he started up his car. 'I've even heard rumours that Easter Millton's selling up his dairy herd'

'Good heavens! Things must be bad for that to happen. It's been pedigree since the thirties, hasn't it?'

'Aye, it's bad. Mind, he has been spending a lot more o' the banker's money than he should have on pursuits outside the matrimonial home, if I've heard right.'

'You,' said Katherine tartly over my shoulder, 'are a pair of old gossips! Can I pinch this anorak, Bruno?'

'Keep it.' She noticed Bill was laughing at her, and she finally laughed back over her shoulder as she splashed away up the hill again, festooned with my buckets and brushes.

'My, but that's a grand lass. Mark my words, Bruno, she'll make the song come true again if our young Mr. Grey makes the grade. Now that would be a fine asset for him.'

'Kilbaddy's Bonnie Quine?' I was beginning to hate the sound of the damnable ditty. 'Who knows?' I growled. 'It sounds as if Matthew has got Kilbaddy out of the bath. He'll need help.'

'You're sure you don't need me?'

'Quite sure, thank you.'

'Well good luck to you all. And Bruno, my friend - watch your own health, won't you?'

'See you next year,' I answered, forcing the edge out of my voice. I don't think he was duped.

We began by tucking Kilbaddy up in Katherine's bed where he slept for almost nine hours. When called, his family doctor suggested it could have been partly due to the effects of the drugs he had been given the night before. He also offered to arrange for Katherine and myself to speak to the geriatric specialist who should have seen the old man that very day. Eventually it was decided Kilbaddy could go home to where he wanted to be, at least for a few days. If we could manage, if Matthew would permit, the implicit promise was that he could stay there. I thought Katherine was near to hugging the doctors.

'I'll spend the days up there,' she planned, 'and come back here after tea. It'll give me a chance to clean the place up. Will you come up to eat? I'm no Cordon Bleu but I can keep your belly from sticking to your b... Er, sorry.'

'I've fed myself for forty years,' I answered. 'I can manage a little longer, thank you.' It sounded churlish which prompted me to add, 'I have work to do here.'

'Oh, - yes, of course.' My ill temper had subdued her most sadly and I made a determined effort for the rest of the day to push away the dark tentacles which were reaching out to engulf my spirits. A fit of depression I could well do without at this stage, but even Kate had not been able to eradicate the black dog from my shoulder. Not completely. She had from Kilbaddy's, as far as I knew. After those first years I had never seen his eyes grow dead in that tell-tale fashion. There had been Kathy after that, of course, first as a thrilling, swelling dream, then as a growing, developing, laughing child who learned and loved with equal vigour and who always seemed to carry the sunshine with her wherever she went, lighting up our lives from morning till night. How Kate had adored her. How we all had. Kilbaddy and I had continued to worship her after Kate died, would have done even without the promises Kate had extracted. It was beyond us to do otherwise.

There was still Kathy, even though she too was gone from us now and had been at the other end of the earth for half her lifetime. For Kilbaddy and me

105

there always would be Kathy. Often enough I felt we had failed Kate in allowing her daughter to go her own way, for failing to protect her from her own wilfulness. In that instance alone we were aware of making a major mistake. We had mishandled her, misguided her; even misadvised her, that was for sure. Moreover, it had been the only occasion when our advice had differed radically, the only time when Kilbaddy and I had diverged so violently that we came near to hating each other. For weeks our friendship had teetered on the brink of destruction.

How would Kate have handled us then? I wondered again and again over the years. Would she have understood our instinctive, tactless reactions to the young bounder bent on ruining our bonnie quine? Had we over-reacted in our double, distinctive paternal fear? If somehow we had managed to give parallel advice, as we had always done in the past, would we have won our daughter's trust instead of destroying the security we had spent nineteen years building up? Would Kate have done any differently? To put it bluntly, if Kathy had had a wise, understanding mother instead of two doting but decidedly unworldly fathers, would she have been spared her suffering?

Kilbaddy got up around eight in the evening. 'The rain's gone,' was his only comment. Katherine had been to his spiritless house in the village and fetched a good selection of clothing. It hung on him still but he dressed at her suggestion, ate a few mouthfuls of omelette and set off up the hill.

'Warn Matthew,' the girl whispered as she followed him out. She returned almost two hours later, escorted by Matthew who would do no more than look in to reassure me Kilbaddy was sound asleep again, this time in his own bed and completely at home.

'It's funny,' Katherine frowned, joining me for a snatch of music before retiring. 'He knows Bill Anderson was here today. Remembers the rain, and what I have given him to eat. Yet he doesn't remember a thing about not being Kilbaddy any more and gives Holly all his orders. Poor Holly doesn't know what to make of it, but the orders seem rational enough. Matthew just nods to him to get on with it. Kilbaddy looks at Matthew in a puzzled kind of fashion. I think he thinks he's a student or something.'

'Is he puzzled about you?'

'Not usually. He just accepts me and treats me as if I've always been there. Just now and again he looks at me as if he's seeing me double, or something. Suppose he is, in a way. Spooky, isn't it?'

I sighed. 'Is he happy? That is the real question.'

'Too early to tell. If he's not I expect we'll find out soon enough.'

'Because he will become morose?'

'N-no. He gets a bit wild, though, if he can't get his own way. - He wasn't violent as well, was he?' The moment she said it she looked alarmed. 'I shouldn't have said that!'

'He was never a violent man,' I assured her flatly. 'Whatever violence may appear now is more likely to be of the tantrum variety.'

'Reversion to early childhood like the specialist said?' I nodded. The visit had been well worth making but it had not helped my peace of mind. I sat forward.

107

'Katherine, may I give you a warning? I am certain beyond any doubt that Kilbaddy would never offer you any deliberate hurt. You must believe that.'

'But a tantrum in a man of his size and strength could make him hurt without meaning to? - Sorry to interrupt. I - Oh, Bruno, I didn't want you to have to put that into words. I know how you're hurting, over Kilbaddy's state as well as Mum's... well, you know, her miserable past. I do understand. Matthew and I were talking about it earlier. - I hope you don't mind about that, but he's a caring sort of character. If it'll put your mind at rest we've rigged up a few ways in which I can fetch him in if it ever becomes necessary.' She began picking at the yavin scratches on her hands. 'Will Matthew be okay with him, do you think?'

'Of course he will,' I said loudly. 'The medical people would never have allowed Kilbaddy home if they had had any doubts on that score.'

'They were falling over themselves to get shot of him,' she muttered rebelliously.

'Hm. Aren't you being a little unreasonable? I thought you approved?'

She heaved a great sigh. 'Sorry, I'm just bug... shattered. - And so are you. And Mum says that's not at all good for you.' She came and hugged me goodnight. At the door she looked back uncertainly, but said nothing. In a startled moment I realised that 'Mum' had also said that when I reached a certain stage of depression I disliked being touched. Katherine had sensed that the hug, for once, had been unwelcome.

Chapter Seven

I left them to it. There was no alternative. When the mists take a hold on me I am totally unfit for human consumption. In a way I was glad Kathy had warned Katherine about that, although it made me feel chillingly exposed at the time. She left in the morning, avoiding all but a brief touch of her fingers, always wisely on the back of my hand, and stayed up at the farm till early evening. On the first day she returned for two minutes to check up on me while Kilbaddy was having his after-dinner nap, dressing it up as a visit to keep me informed about his progress. I made the mistake of snarling at her that I knew perfectly well what she was doing. Thereafter she left me to spend the evil hours alone, deluding myself that I was working. As always the pace was leaden and I knew from past experience that I would jettison almost all of the poor stuff I did manage to produce.

Kilbaddy, by contrast, was placid and happy. It had happened so often that way and, as in the past, he wandered down to my cottage a couple of times for a game of chess in the evenings. I had a notion Kate had been the first to suggest this as a therapy long ago. On the first occasion Katherine followed him everywhere, worrying whether this was an aberration and hovering annoyingly until we were settled in silence over the board. Music was intolerable for the moment. At these times Kilbaddy almost invariably won, but at least it involved no physical contact and no conversation, no emotional demand to drain my impoverished reserves, just a mechanical intellectual concentration which shifted my attention briefly to something other than my sorry self. Even in his current mental state he recognised and accepted my disfunction and I loved him for it.

'A game?' was all he said as he entered. And, 'Nae bad,' when we had finished. 'I'll look in the morn's night.' He did. It was exactly what I needed as he well knew. After the first visit, I learned later, he had told Katherine on the way out that the blackest spell would last for just a few days. 'And dinna worry. He'll come a'right. He aye does.' She took the hint and kept to her room or the kitchen until he set off for home. Straight away she would lift the phone and with a single ring let Matthew know that the old man was on his way home. Only then would she come and sit quietly with me, near but not touching, a silent, comforting presence.

About a week later I took myself out for a day to walk my feet into the hills. Again it was part of the pattern. When I arrived back at dusk Katherine came to the door, her face ashen. She took one look at me and exploded into a tirade of fury, lacing it liberally with Kit's favourite words and stripping the skin from my conscience as her anxiety and relief spilled into the night. '...and where the bloody hell have you been?'

'I'm better,' I said lamely.

'I can see that! Why didn't you say you were going out? I had to ring Mum to find out what to do next. D'you know that?'

'And what did "Mum say"?' I asked grimly.

'She...' The rage deflated like a popped balloon. 'She said not to worry. But I couldn't forget...' Tears of shame began to glisten on her cheeks. 'Can I hug you?' she pleaded, realising I was ready again. I hugged her instead, feeling wretchedly guilty at my lack of consideration.

'You couldn't forget what, my dear?'

'Oh, nothing,' she snuffled into my shoulder. I tightened my hold, rocking her a little, and she finally blurted it out. 'I couldn't forget how sharp your voice was when you said, oh, early on, that there was no shotgun at Kilbaddy farm. I wondered if...'

'Your imagination ran wild, did it?' She pulled herself away so that she could look at me properly. I was foolish enough not to turn away. 'As far as I know there hasn't been one for decades,' I managed. 'How is Kilbaddy?'

'Fine. He's out on the farm every day. I think Matthew's learning an awful lot from him too. He's almost normal, you know. Kilbaddy, I mean.'

'So Matthew doesn't feel his privacy has been invaded?' I nearly said something about his style being cramped but remembered in time that that could have a different connotation these days.

'Don't think so. He hasn't said anything anyway. Bruno, I'm sorry I screamed at you just now. Honestly, I would never have done it if your eyes had still been empty.'

'Forget it, my dear. I should at the very least have left a note.'

'You are okay now, aren't you?'

'Just very tired physically. It was to induce it that I went walking.'

111

'I changed the beds today while Matthew took Kilbaddy in to the hospital. - Oh, just for a check-up. They think he's wonderful. - And I think you should have your own bed. I'll take the bed settee. Please, Bruno. You need it. Maybe...'

'It would have made no difference,' I interrupted. 'The black dog arrives and departs when it wishes. It seems to bear no relevance to anything else in my life.'

'None at all? Not even getting so tired with the barley roguing?'

'None at all. I've been tired often enough with no ill effects afterwards. Now, what can I smell?' After eating we sat in the firelight talking quietly together, with Katherine again at my feet and her head on her arms on my knees. It was very soothing and comforting. In a benign sense it was tenderly intimate. We were drawing very close, Kate's grand-daughter and I, and there was no doubt in my mind that this was the way we both wanted it.

'Bruno?' she asked sleepily. 'Are you gay?'

'Not particularly. Just pleasantly happy.' The stifled giggle made me jerk awake. 'Oh, you mean in the corrupt sense, do you?'

'It's not corrupt to be gay!' she exclaimed, looking up to examine my expression. 'Not nowadays.'

'I meant the corruption of a very lovely word,' I countered. 'Why do you ask?' It surprised me a little that she was not embarrassed by asking such a blatantly personal question. Her acceptance of the condition as natural I assumed to be reasonably healthy, normal perhaps in her generation.

'Just that - well, you are very close to Kilbaddy. Are you? Have you never, er, had women? I think you'd be super at it,' she added pertly, just slightly nervous at her own daring.

'You, young lady, are shockingly immodest and intrusive. If you must know, I am not - gay, as you call it.' I sat for a while then began to tell her about my life before the outbreak of war. Naturally I avoided the coarser details but she assumed correctly that I had been a bit of a lady's man.

'You were an aristocrat, weren't you? It must have been a wonderful life, all those parties and everything. And the literary gatherings and the concerts and the freedom to do what you liked.'

'You mean being forced to join a crack cavalry regiment with wild young blades measuring themselves against each other with rapiers and vodka and strings of female conquests? Oh yes. As well as all of those, every man was obliged to be proficient in some military skill. Remember the Nazi shadow was enormous over the land and we walked every day with fear in our hearts, however much we pretended otherwise.' She sat back and waited, frowning. 'All I wanted to do was to play my violin, but by the time I had done my military service, and learned all the lessons that my exceedingly literary mother insisted I learn, there was little time for me and my wishes.'

'Was he titled? Your father? What happened to him and the rest of your family? Did you ever go back?' Her curiosity had a tension about it.

'No. I never returned. Nor will I,' I added, seeing her about to point out that the border was no longer closed to me. 'I know what happened to them all.

113

More or less. My father died in a massacre of Free Polish forces, along with all his junior officers. My mother was most certainly dead before I left Poland, perhaps even before my father met his fate. You see, she belonged to a very rich and gifted Jewish family and they were exactly the kind of people who aroused the envy and viciousness of the Nazis and their collaborators. I'm afraid there were many of those in Poland.' I sighed pensively. This, for me, was so old a story that it now felt unreal, someone else's. 'Not all of Polish blood. The Poles themselves suffered under the German yoke, of course, and even those who were prepared to tolerate the Jews were able to do very little for them.'

'That's guilt by inaction!' she said, horrified at my tale. 'Guilt by bloody laziness!'

'Hush. Any action on their part would have brought disaster on them and their own family. Besides very, very few actually knew what was going on. There were stories of atrocities, but those stories were also spreading abroad here and in America early in the war. Few believed them till years later, not until the first of the camps was liberated. They couldn't bring themselves to accept that such disgusting tales could possibly be true. Even now you can find the odd German who still insists it is all no more than a smear campaign.' She had withdrawn to the edge of the hearth and was sitting curled up in a tight crouch. I felt I had said enough but she kept asking more questions, at first about my childhood and then returning to my mother.

'You think she went to a concentration camp?'

114

'Yes. I know my three sisters did and that two died almost immediately.'

'The final solution?' She looked sick. 'And the third?'

'The only information I have is that someone saw her about a year later. When the camp was opened up, however, she was no longer there. I have no reason at all for thinking she survived. If I had I would have gone looking for her.'

We watched as the fire burned low, then she asked, 'What were they called?'

'Marguerite, Dominique and Louise. My mother liked all things French.'

'You - don't know why the third sister survived longer?'

'I don't let myself think about that,' I said briskly, ending the conversation. 'My dear, you are going to find it hard to get up in the morning.'

'Mm.' Then she stood up and shook herself like a puppy before struggling to grin at me. 'No matter, there's an ogre in the next room who will lend a hand.' My past was not mentioned again.

Late summer proceeded very pleasantly, contented far beyond our expectations. It began with a quiet dinner out, which I organised to celebrate Katherine's twenty first birthday. Once primed by me, Kilbaddy ordered a bunch of flowers to be delivered to her and I found a necklace of rare seed pearls which delighted her, though I was less delighted when she decided to lodge it in the bank for safety after wearing it for the dinner. It meant she guessed - or Kathy might have warned her - that I had spent a good deal on it. I was surprised when Matthew produced a gift, knowing how short he was of money. It was a simple gold neck chain, very fine and therefore probably not too expensive. The first time she elected to wear it she looked guiltily at me, then grew chagrined and embarrassed when I smiled broadly, not in the least offended. Kilbaddy noticed not a thing. In years gone by he would have teased her blatantly, but only I was left to observe the sad omission.

On the farm things were startlingly different. Kilbaddy advised Matthew when the last silage crop was at its maximum vitamin count and ready for cutting. It was he who judged when to begin harvest - though he caused difficulties when he wanted stacks built in the corn-yard, which had been turned into a cattle court a good fifteen years earlier when the dairying had given way to beef stock. At the same time he knew by heart the telephone numbers of the contractors who came and did the cutting and bagging of the grain. He organised the baling of the straw then the ploughing and harrowing which followed, ending up with the sowing of the winter barley and a field of 'neeps' to bulk the store cattle's winter feed. Matthew left him to make the arrangements which worked to perfection.

'I did check up with the contractors after he'd called them,' Katherine confessed. 'Was that an awful cheek?'

'Of course,' I agreed, 'but not entirely foolish. By now everybody knows the score, I should think.'

'Everybody's been ever so kind as well,' she murmured, not aware that her own sweet approach was more than likely to be part of the explanation. I had found that touching and unexpected, so like Kate,

116

so very unlike the hoyden Kit who had first arrived. The black dog kept its head down as we drifted into a glorious golden autumn. I was able to complete a considerable amount of useful work while Katherine commuted happily between the farm and my cottage.

'I've come across an incident which might be the basis of your song,' I greeted her one night, 'thanks to a librarian in Aylesbury.'

'Historical?'

'Yes. Apparently there was a young earl's son in the Hanoverian army which chased Bonnie Prince Charlie over the hills to Culloden. What made you think of that period? Did somebody tell you something?'

'N-no. Not that I can remember.'

'Then why did you pick on that period?'

'Romantic delusion, I should think,' she laughed. 'Is it what I said that made you look at that time? What happened?'

'Oh, the obvious. Some of the forces were camping near here and this young man met the farmer's daughter. I've just received some photocopies from the family archives in Buckinghamshire and it appears the young man returned to the north after the fighting was over. You were right. The girl did become pregnant and was obviously not of countess material.'

'So he dumped her?'

'Exactly, or was forced to by his family. Now I have to find out whether the title of the song means she was the Kilbaddy's daughter or became Kilbaddy's wife. You're right about something else too. The family name was Wishart at that time, or at least it was eight years later. There's a bill for seed corn in

117

the county archives.'

'Great! And who wrote the song? We need to know that too.'

'Mm. That could be significant. I haven't been able to find anything among local collections. The folk around here know the song well enough, but they all think your father wrote it.' She looked at me doubtfully, but said nothing. It warned me that she was still unable to encompass her recent traumatic experiences.

'Thanks,' she said quietly, looking suddenly very tired. I hugged her and sent her off to bed.

When the work on the farm permitted, Kilbaddy took Katherine walking over the fields and into the bronzing and purpling hills and woods around, not too far but often enough to bind the two of them together. It delighted me that she was able to experience my old friend's warmth and canniness. One afternoon, when the leaves were at their most brilliant, he came back alone. I had been out myself that day, reveling in the last warmth of the year and we met by the farm gate. I had a tub of brambles for supper in my hand. He frowned at me then at the brambles, looking puzzled, but said, 'She'll be doon when she's ready. She aye does come back.'

The significance of that was lost on me until several days later when, on a bright but much chillier Sunday morning, Katherine came walking with me instead of joining Kilbaddy and Matthew at church. I had a notion Matthew was not enamoured of religion but went to humour the old man. 'Up here,' she begged. 'I found such a lovely place the other day. But no matter what I said I couldn't get Kilbaddy to come with me. He insisted I should go up alone, then turned and left me. He was quite huffy about it too.'

A sharp chill of comprehension pulled the skin more tightly over my cheeks and my nerves began to sting. 'Show me.' We followed the burn upwards above the farm, climbing across rough pasture, along past another ancient drove road, then through a thicket of conifers and up over a heather and gorse-gold hillside. Eventually we reached a miraculously sheltered hollow where a smaller, even noisier stream met with our burn. Protected from all sides a thicket of birches and alders had established themselves naturally. Since I had first visited the wood, almost half a century before, a couple of the oldest alders had been blown over, one forming a bridge across the smaller waterway. Birches which had seemed fragile in their slender youth had grown sturdy guardians, their gnarled silver trunks beckoning us inwards towards the glade left free for new, young saplings fighting for their own space where the old had once stood.

'Isn't it absolute heaven?' Katherine sighed, slipping her arm through mine. When I failed to answer, having forgotten her completely for a moment, she spoke again, shaking my arm gently. 'Don't you think so?'

I sighed. 'Yes.' I sighed again, nodding to the fallen alder. 'We call it Kate's Corner. She used to love coming up here.'

'Ah! Mum said...' I tensed as she tailed off, but all she said was, 'I'm sorry. But how can I tell you without using the words? She did say it.'

'Say what?' Was I being foolish in asking?

119

'Oh, that her mother took her up here for picnics. And that sometimes you would come too.'

'Yes. Sometimes.'

'She must have meant Kilbaddy too. I expect she just didn't remember. She'd have been very little.'

'Kilbaddy and I used to take your mother up here too,' I murmured, 'after Kate died.' I prayed she would not realise that I had not told the whole truth.

'So why didn't he want to come up the other day?'

'Hm. It was here he wouldn't come?'

She nodded, beginning to frown. 'Doesn't he like it?'

'He does like it.' I bent to let the shallow water play around my fingers, hiding my face from her intent inspection. 'I expect he was just tired.' Take it or leave it, my dear. I was not prepared to share Kate's secrets that day. 'The last time we came up here, the two of us, it was just about a year ago. It was the day we discussed what should happen to the farm. In fact, this was where we decided that Matthew would make him a good successor at Kilbaddy.'

I looked up and found the girl watching me keenly. Then she looked down suddenly and sat examining her hands with that curious, intense concentration she had. 'My opinion doesn't matter, I know, but - I think you made a good choice.'

'Because of what he has done for Kilbaddy?'

'That's just ...,' she began to flare angrily then swallowed the tell-tale slip, '...a reflection, if you like. It's just another sign of what he's really like.' Neither of us took that topic further, but my mind was turning over some interesting ideas on the way home. I began to watch more closely when the two young people were in each other's company, chiding myself from time to time for being an inquisitive old romantic. Only occasionally.

At least twice a week Kilbaddy came to play chess, sometimes bringing Matthew with him. Quite often the boy came himself, perhaps thinking to please me, but he had no head for the game. We usually ended up chatting. If Katherine was not present she featured largely in the conversation but I kept my amusement to myself. That way I heard of the changes she was working on the house in between her caring and cooking.

'I thought she was a feminist,' I murmured.

Matthew laughed with a touch of fond malice. 'She swears she is! Her argument is that she's doing all this by choice, and because it's a job needing doing.'

'Which is true. I am in favour of women being free to choose,' I pointed out, wondering if he saw my insistence as a sop to modern thinking. 'I think. It's only when it comes to this...' I almost said free love business, but thought again. How was I to know whether she indulged or not? Or what she and Matthew were doing in the hours they spent together? Those had increased markedly, very often alone, for Matthew took to entertaining her on the evenings Kilbaddy spent with me. With the two old mongrels keeping each other's snouts out of the dish who knew what the young ones were scoffing? 'Well, her cooking is improving at any rate,' I finished absently to allay the distinct impression that the boy had divined my uncomplimentary thoughts. 'The evidence from my own kitchen assures me of that. No more 'toad' as tough as shoe leather.'

121

He defended her very smartly. 'It was Kilbaddy's fault that we ate it three hours too late!'

'I love the farmhouse, Bruno,' she confessed nearer the end of the year, very nearly the happiest year of my life. We had spent an expensive evening telephoning Kathy in New Zealand, regretting not a single minute. She told us of her translation work which had burgeoned with a continuing influx of government related reports in the wake of the Russian opening up. I hoped that was the explanation for no further mention of a trip to Scotland but had not dared to repeat my plea. Keeping our current closeness alive was far too important.

Bit by bit she was learning about her daughter's adventures, although I suspected she still did not realise that the motorcycle was in Scotland. That had been mended within weeks but Katherine rarely used it now, and it stood zipped inside a gigantic plastic bag in one of Matthew's sheds. Now and then she took it out and polished it, but whenever that happened it had an odd effect on Kilbaddy who began to mumble fretfully about 'the laddie with the big bike'. She had kept her hair cut short which might have reminded him of the first days of their relationship.

That apart she was extraordinarily like Kate to look at. More heart-pinching was her slipping away from the abrasive, defiant Kit qualities, swearing included, and the almost unnoticed acquiring of Kate's personality traits, a calmness which made her companionship delightfully restful and a gentle understanding of Kilbaddy's needs which left Matthew with an unmistakable longing in his eyes. In company

122

she treated the young farmer in an impersonal manner he was finding hard to accept, whatever she might reveal in private. In particular he was painfully unhappy when an occasional interested male from elsewhere came calling, including Lewis Allen. Always using the excuse of checking over the bike, Lewis was so much older that I laughed silently at the idea - and stifled as best I could the stab of worry I could not quite ignore.

On the other hand, she had several days of energetic ill temper after a very fetching female vet came to attend to a case of mastitis - and returned in the evening to check on the beast, dressed provocatively in a very short skirt of white leather. Matthew was not immune to the implied flattery, or perhaps he saw an opportunity to jerk a reaction out of Katherine. He was a long way off being a fool.

'I love this wee cottage too,' she reassured me, 'but it's a one man place and your personality is stamped most wonderfully on it.'

'You don't feel an interloper?' I asked anxiously. She hugged me out of the very idea.

'Just a well spoiled guest. Isn't that what you want? The farm's different, maybe because I know there have been families there in the past. And it was Mum's home, of course. It's so big! I had to bring in a double ladder to paint the hall ceiling and Matthew is going to set up scaffolding for the top of the stairwell. It's going to take a whole roll of paper to go from top to bottom.'

'It doesn't sound safe, my dear. Why not have it professionally done? I'll pay.'

'No fear! I'm responding to a challenge, don't you

123

remember? When Matthew told me to do something about it when I called the place a tip? Mind, to be fair, he doesn't want you spend, spend, spending on what will end up as his. I respect him for that. And I don't think the muck was all his. Kilbaddy couldn't have been much of a housewife and he let that wumman from the village get away with sweet f..., er, nothing. And it hadn't been decorated for so long that all it needed was a scrubbing brush to bring me down to bare wood. He wasn't as fastidious as you, was he?' I smiled and didn't argue. 'I haven't found the key for the door to the stairs to the top storey yet.'

'It's just as well. If I remember correctly, the place is half rotten. There's a ton of rubbish still up there, I think. Perhaps there's even stuff from Kilbaddy's predecessors. They were his two old spinster aunts, the last of a family of twelve. They only just managed to hang on until he came back from the war. I shudder to think what's up there.'

'Treasure!' The child in her glowed.

'Rubbish,' I repeated firmly. 'All it will be fit for will be a shovel and a bucket.'

When they finally broke open the lock I was proved more or less correct. They deliberately pushed the banister rails out of their sockets to prevent anybody leaning on them unawares, and I began making enquiries about having the whole area treated for woodworm, only to be told not to fuss because all old farmhouses were like that and were still standing after centuries without much harm coming to anybody. I compromised and employed a carpenter to erect a new, safe railing. The rubbish proved much more exciting. A couple of old tin trunks were packed with ancient linen spotted with age. When Katherine tried to wash a large damask tablecloth, however, it disintegrated in the washing machine.

'They're not even fit for dusters,' she said in sorry disgust. 'It's such a crying shame. The stuff in the camphorwood box might be okay. Oh, there are books and papers which should be looked at though. Is that a job for you, d'you think? The stairs is, um, are, a bit steep, not very safe even with the banisters but I could bring them down to the back parlour and put a fire on.'

'If the jackdaws haven't blocked the chimney there. I'll come up and have an initial look to see if they are worth the trouble,' I promised. Most of the books were badly wormed but a few letters and hand-written ledgers were set aside to be examined by an archivist.

'Such beautiful writing,' drooled Katherine. 'Must have taken ages to do.' With Matthew's help and Kilbaddy's disinterested permission we cleared the whole area, two huge rooms, where Victorian servants would have been well accommodated, on either side of a broad landing. Each had a fireplace, a door and a window.

A vacillating autumn of several Indian summers peppered between nasty storms reached its climax in a gigantic Guy Fawkes bonfire a month overdue. Old discarded mantle-shelves wormed through and through, broken chairs, books and linen went on the conflagration which all the local children came to enjoy, along with sausages and baked potatoes which Katherine and various mothers cooked in advance. The rest of the junk went in all directions.

'I'm keeping the old flat iron, so the rest of you can

whistle. Now, the gig lamps to the cottage restaurant with that red painting, the chandelier to the hotel across the road from the hospital, the box of buttons and shoe buckles to the wee antique shoppie,' she read out her delivery list one night. 'We got good hard cash for all of that - only we're arguing about whose money it should be.'

'Spend it on something for everybody,' I suggested.

'Such as?'

'Hm. - A trip to the theatre?'

'Ooh, what a good idea! - But what about Kilbaddy?'

'What about him?' I countered easily. 'I know he's always loved pantomimes.'

So all four of us went to see 'Tom Thumb' in Aberdeen and had a wonderful time on the proceeds of the junk. The journey there and back in the land-rover was hardly comfortable but none of us complained.

'Didn't he love it,' Matthew sighed over coffee the next morning, watching Kilbaddy poring over the programme. Then he glanced at me and I saw the reflection of a worry of my own. I nodded. My old friend was indeed showing more signs of reverting to his childhood. 'Kit has noticed,' he said quietly. 'If it increases, what shall we do? She already has enough on her plate, especially with what she's doing in the house. - Bruno, I never intended to make a skivvy of her.'

'As you said, she makes her own decisions about what she tackles. Er, have you ever tried to change her mind on anything?'

'Yes.' He answered stiffly.

'Have you succeeded?'

'No. Not yet.' I desisted, and went home to consult my imagination. When I had vanquished it I made an appointment to see Kilbaddy's specialist.

Chapter Eight

Christmas and New Year came and went. They were among the happiest I could remember, full of quiet companionship when I wanted it and good music when I was alone. Katherine seemed in no way to regret that she was not with her Antipodean family, although she spent half an hour chatting with her mother on both of the festive days, from my house at my insistence, and she telephoned each of her brothers on different occasions. I had risked inviting Kathy and the boys for the season and she had promised to try. It was more than she had ever offered before, but in the end she couldn't come. Or wouldn't. Brian and Jock merely sent apologies couched in cool, polite letters which told us little of their lives other than a brief outline of their activities. I contented myself with the growing trust I sensed in Kathy towards me. That would suffice in the meantime.

Matthew had invited his parents to stay, a charming couple just about to retire. His father was a banker and his mother a teacher of mathematics. Beneath exquisite politeness, however, their initial greeting was stiff enough for me to realise that they did not fully understand the odd situation surrounding us, or perhaps disapproved of it. Near the end of their visit I set about making matters plain after tea - or evening dinner, as Katherine was making a special effort in their honour. Having had a port too many I made an uncomfortably clumsy job of it.

'Sometimes your son fails to use two words when two are required,' I said frankly. 'I assure you there is no hanky-panky going on. Nor will there be while I am around.' Katherine's face flushed crimson as she turned on her heel and marched out to fetch a coffee-tray she had prepared, her back steel straight in outrage.

'Bruno! Sir!' That was Matthew, but when he saw I was toying with a smile of satisfaction, he grinned unwillingly himself. 'You are an old devil, and tipsy with it.'

'I'm not for one minute saying you wouldn't like some hanky-panky.' I wondered at my own effrontery and blinked at my glass with surprise. 'What I do know is that without your generosity and patience an old man would have had a very unhappy and very crazed ending to his life. And his old friend would have suffered almost as much along with him out of sheer misery.' I rose to my feet and took Matthew's hand in an emotional grip. 'My boy, there's very little I can do to thank you. But I have taken the liberty of raiding your desk and removing a few of your bills. - Now, don't argue again. What else is there for me to do with my money? I have made a good living over the years, you know.' He huffed and puffed, then told me I wasn't getting another drink that night. I was in my cups.

Later his father waylaid me. 'Do you mind me using the name Bruno, sir? Your surname defeats me.'

'Yes, I object to the sir,' I babbled, by then bloody well oiled as Kit had hissed when she caught me on my way from the bathroom. She was still bloody well ruffled with me, too. 'I am known everywhere as Bruno.'

'The last thing I want to do is offend you. But my son is very uneasy about your financial generosity, you know. If he is in difficulties he can always come to me.' I shook the fumes from my head, suddenly very sober.

'I see.' I looked at the man keenly and remembered my own warning to myself in the early days of Matthew's tenure. A man has his pride. Had I made a major error? 'I - see. Please excuse me, Mr. Grey. I think it is time for me to consult the stars.'

Now, exactly whose feathers were ruffled? Matthew's? Or his father's? The two were fond of each other. That was easy to see, yet I had sensed a tension between them exacerbated by a tendency in Mr. Grey to advise his son just a little more than his son either wished or required. I was not sure the advice was all good, for the father seemed to know less about farming than I had expected. Was this venture Matthew's attempt to establish his independence, perhaps against his father's judgment? He had sold a working enterprise in the West Country to move north, a long way north where conditions were much more taxing. His stock unit had been much smaller certainly but our investigations had confirmed it as a going concern which had encouraged Kilbaddy when he accepted Matthew's offer for this farm.

Only Kilbaddy and I knew that a higher offer had been received from Kindrum's second son, George Patterson. The oldest son, Patrick, would inherit Kindrum from his father. Married with two children, he

130

was proving a shrewd husbandman who knew the land and what it could give. Without the same security, George was plainly anxious to outdo both father and brother with a slightly bigger, slightly better property, an ambition which surfaced when we discovered that Kildrum, his father, had also put in a bid. Plainly Kildrum knew nothing of his second son's offer nor George of his, we supposed, which made it sound unlikely that either planned to run the two places as a family unit as might have been expected. I wondered about the relationships within the Patterson family.

I had never liked George. Even as a boy he had exhibited a jealous, slightly vindictive bumptiousness. Now nearing thirty, just a little older than Matthew, he was acquiring some of his father's dour and acquisitive suspiciousness. It had not missed my attention that he had begun to call on Katherine. So had Gareth, the boy who had helped with the barley roguing, but the youngest son was a happier character altogether. A decade behind his brothers he was the adored baby of the family with a blithe, cheerful nature and friendly good-heartedness. Often with a friend or two of either sex, if the sex could be hard to identify now and then, all Gareth sought was the companionship of another youngster. Kate was his own age and was just as fond of good fun.

This new, noisy camaraderie amused Kilbaddy but disturbed Matthew, anxious about the age gap which suddenly appeared to yawn between himself and Katherine. I left him to find out for himself that Gareth, with fewer of his brothers' brains, far fewer than Katherine herself, would not be entertaining the aspirations I suspected of George who was extremely shrewd. It was with some regret that I realised that I should, in fairness, also leave Matthew to find out about the other unmarried Kindrum brother.

Kilbaddy, George would be thinking, was old and surely would soon die. And Kilbaddy was rich, at least to the tune of the price of a successful farm. If he couldn't have the farm George may be seeing no reason at all why he shouldn't go courting the money. My money too, he might reasonably assume. And most assuredly he would do his best to ensure that the man who had beaten him to the acres should not end up with the siller as well. After all, everybody around knew even before the new settler arrived that he would have a fight on his hands to survive. George would not be lending a hand, I was quite sure, not a helping hand. Nobody could see into the future but George would no doubt be watching for a second opportunity to bid for Kilbaddy and with extra money in his hands his chances of survival would be radically better. Kilbaddy money to keep Kilbaddy farm alive? And Kilbaddy's Bonnie Quine as well? Poor Matthew. I wondered if he knew what was threatening. He may have divined the direction from which danger approached, but I feared that he had missed the individual who posed it.

Half an hour later, Matthew and his father found me in the farm garden, sitting shivering slightly on the old seat Katherine had renovated after a fashion and admiring the lights of Cromarty far away across the Moray Firth, and nearer, on the south coast, the great glittering boat which was Lossiemouth.

'Bruno, are you okay?' The young man had brought me a coat.

'Fine, my boy. The fumes were interfering with my thinking, that is all. And my tongue. Nevertheless I want you to know something. I'll say it once, Matthew, and never again. I want you to survive here. You are right for Kilbaddy, the farm I mean as well as the neighbourhood. I had no business to look into your desk but I did. You are undercapitalised – but so are most farmers nowadays. Your disadvantage is that you haven't even the hump of experience or local knowledge to fall back on and I think you could do with financial assistance. Where it comes from doesn't matter but I can offer some without any strain on me. I have no dependents and require no collateral or obligation. Your parents on the other hand have other children and each other.' His father had the sense to keep quiet this time. Perhaps I had misjudged him.

'One more thing, I have strong personal reasons, emotional reasons for seeing the right man in this farm. Not just my own need of a good neighbour, please believe me. I would never buy a thing like that.'

'Kate,' he said quietly. I sat stunned. Was I so transparent? Yes, Kate. And Kilbaddy too, I wanted to tell him, but the wine was still too near to drowning me. And there was Kathy, our precious, prickly, clever Kathy. 'I'm sorry, Bruno. I shouldn't have...'

'I - need to go home,' I muttered, patting his hand. 'Will you bring Katherine back?'

'Aye,' he said gently, teasing in dialect to lighten the air a fraction. 'I will that.'

Father and son came for coffee the next day, leaving Mrs. Grey to pack with Katherine's help. They

133

at least were enjoying each other's company. I laid the bills on the table with their cheques on top. 'Do what you like with them,' I said stiffly. 'I must apologise to you both for the condition I was in last night. I said far more than I should have done.'

'Don't you want a good neighbour?' Matthew demanded and I managed a twisted smile. He picked up the papers and slapped them against his wrist several times, avoiding his father's eye. 'Thanks, Bruno. But let's be plain about this. I regard every penny as a loan.'

'That'll do,' I agreed aware that Mr. Grey was not pleased with either of us. My first instincts had been right after all. 'May we forget about the entire conversation now?'

'No. Er, I think that not enough was said,' the boy said awkwardly. My stomach yawed. 'It's, er, Katherine, sir.'

'What about Katherine?' I demanded.

'If I make a go of it I - want to marry her. You must know that!'

'Hm.' What a possessive old fool I was. 'That's up to you and her,' I grouched, 'and Kilbaddy, of course. - Ah. Are you wondering what effect it would have on him?'

'Among other things. He still thinks she's Kate.'

'Hm. I wonder? Don't you think he just accepts her as Kate for comfort's sake? A wishful thinking? At the back of his mind he knows something is not quite right about that.'

'That's worse, isn't it?' Mr. Grey contributed at last. 'And if he thought his wife was being taken over by somebody else he could become very unreasonable.

134

Katherine told us he was occasionally violent in the hospital.' I looked at him then back at Matthew and sighed.

'I don't know. The specialist did say that senility can be very unpredictable. It can happen that personalities change.'

'You mean there's no guarantee that he won't turn on Kit one day?' Matthew demanded fiercely.

'There's no guarantee that any one person won't turn on any other, given sufficient provocation, is there, my boy?' I held his eye, summoning up the day of the accident and his gaze lowered. 'But what constitutes provocation who knows? His current behaviour may show crossness and introspection now and then, but he has never shown any sign of violence since he came home again. - Has he?'

'No. Not that I've seen. I'm certain that Kit would have said if anything awkward had happened. She's so blooming patient with him.'

'Just like Kate,' I said. I tried then to explain the terrible times when Jock Wishart had come home from the wars. 'She had barely managed to put him on his feet when I crawled into the valley and she began all over again. She was a wonderful woman, Matthew, and very, very like Katherine. - You didn't say what she thought of your plans for her future.'

'Sweet nothing, I should think,' he muttered, telling us he was a long way off broaching the subject. It was probably cruel, but I laughed.

'You should take care. She has no time for cowards. If you leave it too long you might find Lewis Allen has stolen a March on you, my lad.'

Not George Patterson? I wondered why, in the

135

sober morning, I had chosen one name and not the other. Katherine herself indicated the reason to me when next I saw her in George's company. She was cool and very polite, - and plainly loathed the very sight of him. Matthew caught my eye and I felt a touch of shame as he grinned, reading my thoughts. I really should trust the girl and stop being so ridiculously over-protective. Day after day she was proving that she had every bit as much common sense and sound judgment as Kate had ever had. Kate would have trusted her. Matthew trusted her, or at least as far as a subversive influence like George's was concerned. However many qualms he might have about his own position, at least he knew she was not foolish enough to be taken in by greed. It did me no credit if I filled my mind with such doubts.

That night before Mr. and Mrs. Grey left to catch the overnight train home I made my peace with them over a meal for everybody in my cottage accompanied by some of my very best wine. I felt sure they were still unhappy about Matthew's acceptance of money from me, whatever the conditions, but his mother at least believed that my intentions were benign. I was comforted, too, by their apparent approval of Katherine although no more had been said about Matthew's rash admission. He and Kate worked happily in harness, running the farm and the house and giving Kilbaddy both care and freedom in a manner which impressed the visitors. It made Mrs. Grey admit to me on her departure that she was now reassured that her son was a mature and caring man, not a boy in need of constant guidance.

The boy was working much more on his own initiative now, leaving old Kilbaddy indoors where he could be warm and dry. It meant that Holly had no option but to accept his new employer's dictum, which he had been inclined to ignore when his former master was around. I wondered what would happen on the day when Matthew and Kilbaddy gave conflicting orders. It was past time for the new regime to be instated. Katherine colluded by inventing indoor jobs for Kilbaddy, unearthing old papers and bills from several years past which she surreptitiously photocopied in the local solicitor's office. For a week or so he worked at them religiously with the same dogged disgust he had always displayed, earning Matthew's amused sympathy. Inspection of them, however, revealed a sad, messy muddle.

As Burns Night approached he was deteriorating rapidly, for no definable reason. For nearly a fortnight he had been rambling more and more each day and now some of what he said was beyond even me, probably referring to his early life before I knew him. Katherine told me several times that he had still been in bed when she arrived, something that had not happened before. Until then he had been up first, or Matthew had been able to wake him for breakfast and leave him to attend to himself assured that the old man would manage well enough.

Now that certainty no longer existed. Then one evening the problem was compounded when he refused to go to bed. It was only after Matthew came to fetch Katherine that between them they finally persuaded him to settle down for the night and reassure him that, yes, they could deal with the cow that was due to calve. In reality there would be no calves for at least another two months.

'I don't like it,' Matthew muttered on the way out after bringing her home again. 'What if he, er, lashes out at Kit?'

'He won't,' I soothed him. 'But I'll have another word with the specialist as soon as I can.'

It was on Burns Night itself that I had a telephone call from Kathy which filled me with delight.

'Of course you may! Oh, my dear girl, of course you may stay. - Never mind that. You'll have a bed of some kind. What about the boys?'

'They're not boys any more, Bruno.' Even from New Zealand I could hear the arid tone. 'I'm afraid they go their own way and I don't see much of them.'

'Is this because of the motorcycle?'

'Probably not. Just generations unknitting themselves the way they always do. - You've never actually admitted it but I take it Kit took the bike on her travels and landed up at your door with it. Yes?'

'Yes. It's still here.'

'Is she still taking the damned thing to bed with her?' I long ago ceased to be surprised at Kathy's cynical perspicacity.

'No. It's been shut up in a barn for months. She's been far too busy to bother with it.'

'Thank the Lord for that! God knows, Alistair has done enough harm to all of us. - I suppose she's told you?'

'A little.'

'I'll bet. Anyway, mustn't speak ill of the dead. I should get away some time next month if Russia doesn't blow up.'

'Can't you tell them that you need your leave?'

'I can. But being a civil servant has its drawbacks.'

'I didn't know you were a civil servant!' I cringed at the note of pique in my voice. 'I'm sorry, dear. I shouldn't ...'

'Don't apologise for something which is all my fault. I've served the Queen for nearly twelve years now,' she interrupted. Then added sadly, 'Bruno, I'm a silly, selfish, bad-tempered bitch. I don't deserve you at all.'

'Just come home, dear. As soon as you can.' It was all I could manage and crashed down the phone before I disgraced myself.

Ten minutes later I walked up to the farm through a fierce black night of stinging hail to tell Kilbaddy the news, not sure if it would mean anything to him. Matthew was not in the kitchen when I entered, my feet and fingers throbbing with cold.

'Mak's your cheeks rosy, Bruno,' Kilbaddy said cheerily enough.

'It does indeed.'

'It'll kill the piglets though.' I frowned. He had never kept pigs, I was certain. 'Kathy'll nae be pleased. She likes the piglets.' The only connection I could think of was that as a small girl she had had a favourite song about pigs with curly tails.

'She's coming to see us,' I announced baldly. Katherine swung round from the range with a steaming casserole in her hands. She was much later than usual with the meal from which I assumed she had just completed yet another decorating task.

'You mean that?'

139

'Yes. - Oh my dear, forgive me. I promised myself that I'd tell you privately first. My tongue ran out of control.'

'No matter,' she said quietly, turning back to her work. 'When's she coming?'

'Some time next month. She'll let us know.' I glanced at the girl and saw that she was looking weary and glum. It occurred to me that she had done for a week or so, perhaps longer.

'Since Kilbaddy began to be difficult,' Matthew confirmed when I mentioned it to him. 'In fact I'm not sure which came first. She hasn't been communicating with him as well recently but I can't figure out why.'

'When did it start?'

'I'm not sure. But I've noticed that as Kilbaddy has gone downhill so has she. Or possibly the other way round. If she's wrapped up in herself for some reason perhaps he is sensing it. She hardly seems interested in her mother coming, does she?'

'Hm. You're right. It isn't the estrangement. That's past, I'm certain. Do you think Kilbaddy has absorbed the news?

He shrugged despondently. 'Sir, I have a feeling we're going to need help soon. He - wet his bed last night. I've hidden it from Kit so far but if it happens with any regularity I won't be able to.'

'What have you done about it?'

'Nipped into town and bought another set of linen and a plastic sheet. I bunged the wet lot through the launderette. Unfortunately I ran into Mrs. Allen at the door and had to explain.'

'Ah. She's an estimable lady but keeping secrets is not one of her strengths, I'm afraid.'

'Damnation,' he swore quietly.

'Why keep it from Katherine?'

'Pure instinct. Heaven knows why. I just feel she's getting near the end of her tether.' I looked at him in alarm. Since I had seen no sign of any loss of patience I wondered why he had that impression.

The following night she came home immediately after tea, sooner than usual. 'You look tired, my dear.'

'I am. D'you mind if I go straight to bed?' Once she had gone I phoned Matthew but he assured me nothing new had happened. Perhaps she was sickening for something? There was flu in the village. I began to wonder. Before morning I began to fear. Was history about to repeat itself yet again? Oh, Kate, Kate. Why do you seem farthest away just when I need you most? Is there nothing I can do for those dear ones of yours, of mine? For your great, sad hulk of a husband and your unhappy, bewildered grand-daughter who is trying so hard to stand in your stead for him?

And the black dog was threatening to bite at the worst possible moment. I was feeling cold and dead. Every draught stung my skin and bit through my clothing no matter how much I built up my fire. Mercifully Katherine was not in the mood for touching or hugging these days. Not from me at any rate. But whatever she might think, she needed me still. I was certain of it but I could not divine why. And there I was longing for silence and privacy just when her need was greatest.

141

The next night Katherine came home having discovered about the bed-wetting, although it had not happened again.

'It may be an isolated incident,' I suggested, daring the irritation I felt to ring in my voice.

'Doesn't matter. I'm still going to move up to the farmhouse so that I can look after him properly.' she announced.

'In that case I shall come and protect your good name.' She looked taken aback then furious.

'What the bloody hell for?' And Kit roared back into existence. Was I being old-fashioned? I was still in the Stone Age, she assured me, at length and luridly. And what business of mine was it what she did in her spare time? Or any time for that matter? She didn't have to be here, or there, or anywhere else she didn't want to be.

'So be it,' I said flatly, determined that she should not realise how extremely reluctant I was to be dislodged from my own cocoon. 'I had no control over the era into which I was born, or the principles with which I was indoctrinated. You should at least remember that Matthew might not relish gossip and it is his house. Simple courtesy ought to make you consider his standing with his neighbours. It could mean a great deal to his survival here.' She glared at me in true Kit fashion, fired another volley which included several barbed comments on my being a typical hypocritical male and a bigoted Roman Catholic prude to boot. Then she retired early yet again.

'Very well, sir,' was Matthew's expressionless reply when I brought the matter up. 'I hope you will both be comfortable. I confess it'll be nice to have somebody else in the house. It's such a huge, rambling place that I sometimes feel thoroughly miserable alone with the old man. I suppose I don't have Kilbaddy's memories.' But was he, I wondered, already trying to create some of his own? Should I intervene? - Of course not. A lively, unpredictable vagabond was unlikely to look kindly on that. I forced myself to remember that however much she might look like my Kate, Kilbaddy's Kate, she was somebody else altogether. She also had a right to be her own person whatever I might want her to be.

I shut up the cottage the next day, taking my work with me to spread it over the acres of dining-room table in the farmhouse. It was never used for any other purpose except at Christmas. It was only when I was ensconced in the household that I understood how hard Katherine had been working. There were fifteen rooms, including the top storey which she had wisely locked up again and left after the sweeping and scrubbing. Long, dark corridors ran from end to end of the old house, which showed evidence of being built and added to in several separate eras. Each of the reception rooms could have provided Matthew with space for storing an excellent crop of hay, the kitchen being the largest of all. All of it Katherine insisted on keeping clean and polished, including the few gigantic pieces of furniture Kilbaddy had inherited with the house and left behind because they were far too large to fit anywhere else. I made a note to provide her with more than the aged vacuum and washing machines which seemed the only electrical aids she had.

Apart from touching up the worst parts of the kitchen she had not decorated there because of the inconvenience of moving all the food and crockery out. She had also left the corridors untouched so far, but elsewhere she had scrubbed, painted and papered, barring the door against us all until she had finished the room in hand then throwing it open for inspection. Matthew had no money, of course, and had been far from willing to let me buy the materials. About soft furnishings he had dug in his toes, but the heavy brocades and velvets which Kate had bought at second hand sales post-war had been carefully brushed to give an extra year or two of wear. The three ancient but good carpets had been shampooed and the linoleum on the rest of the floors polished to a state of high peril so that rugs had to have sticky tapes put on the undersides. In the six months since her arrival she had revitalised four bedrooms and the bathroom on the first landing, the beautiful square, high ceilinged drawing-room by the front door with its pair of bow windows, the ground floor shower-room I had chivvied Kilbaddy into installing some years ago and the dining-room where I now sat. It was little wonder the girl was exhausted. I did my best to help Matthew persuade her to leave the parlour alone.

The black dog on my shoulder weighed heavily during that particular visit. While I worked in silence during the next few days, my eyes glued uselessly to my papers, Kilbaddy came in and sat at the other end of the table. There he worried at ancient papers and bills and pored over newspaper articles on milking parlour designs long out of fashion or studied machinery leaflets from firms long gone out of

144

business. 'Jist tidyin' up ma desk,' he said each time he entered, otherwise leaving me undisturbed. I could not have said which of us was the more pathetic. At least we kept ourselves out of the hair of the young people. When I occasionally asked to eat alone in the room, unable to tolerate even the kitchen company, Kilbaddy simply nodded. It was Matthew who worried.

'For God's sake, leave him alone,' Katherine snapped irritably at him, barely checking Kilbaddy was out of hearing. 'He's only telling us he can't stand the sight of us for a bit.'

But still he hovered. When he came to the dining room to remove my plates he asked anxiously, 'Is there anything I can do for you, sir?'

'Yes!' I snapped, every bit as churlish as Katherine. 'In the name of patience stop sirring me!' Hurt flared in his eyes and, for once, someone else's pain stabbed through my own bleak misery. I dropped my face into my hands. 'Oh Matthew, I'm sorry.' He stood beside me in awkward incomprehension. 'I should have made something plain. I am a manic depressive.'

'I know. I understand. - Well, I suppose that's the point, really. I don't. If you could manage to tell me how to handle the situation I promise to do my best.'

'Nothing. Just do nothing,' I muttered. 'Leave me alone and it'll come all right.'

'Do what Kilbaddy's doing?' he asked tentatively. I nodded wearily then flinched beyond control as he put out his hand to lay it on my arm.

'Sorry,' I mumbled again, the sound thick in my mouth. 'I can't stand being touched.' He nodded and backed away, shutting the door behind him with infinite care. Dear God, what a hideous burden we were placing on this young stranger.

Chapter Nine

By the end of another week I was more or less better and Kilbaddy was marginally worse. Matthew had persuaded Katherine to stop the decorating for the moment, on the grounds that I - I, mind you - might find the smell of paint an affliction. She began to tinker with the few items of farm machinery instead. Since much of the heavy work was now contracted out this did not absorb her for long and she turned to the motorcycle, stripping it down and servicing it, oblivious of the chill, clear air.

Holly was driving Matthew to the limit of his patience. Kilbaddy wanted all the steading doors painted, for once choosing quite the wrong season. Holly proceeded to paint them. He ignored Matthew's requests, pleas, threats, and final towering rage. When Kilbaddy was persuaded to rescind his order, somewhat querulously, Holly still insisted that the job should be finished now he had started. We all explained that Kilbaddy was only there because he was sick, and that Matthew was now his boss, but his answer was devastating. 'If he's that sick we should dae whit he wints and keep him sweet. - That's what you're a' doing.' In the end Matthew gave up and did Holly's jobs as well as his own. By the end of the day he was very tired indeed. By the end of the week he was tottering with exhaustion.

'Sack the fool,' Katherine said unforgivingly.

'I can't,' he growled back, equally out of sorts. 'Nobody else would give him a job in the present climate, especially at his age. At least the barn doors will be done.'

'What he does do,' I dared to add, 'he does well enough.'

'You're a pair of soft headed idiots!' she stormed. 'What a way to run a business.' Yet she never raised her voice to Holly himself.

Her patience with Kilbaddy remained infinite, but I became aware of a change in its quality. Certainly she too was tired. Perhaps she was becoming afraid to let herself care too much and was withdrawing from the previous closeness she had had with him for fear of what was to come. Whatever the reason she was cool rather than calm now, indeed almost cold. During my bout of depression I had scarcely noticed the change, but what shocked me even more deeply was that she seemed to be withdrawing from me as well. The pain of that was wild and bewildering. Why? Tell me, Kate, why? I could not believe that the depression itself was relevant. It never was with you. Was it? If it was, you never gave the slightest indication.

Kathy promised to be with us by the end of February. My growing longing to see her ballooned into an urgent desperation when we came to Kilbaddy's next turning point. He had been quiet and submissive for a week or so, obedient to everything Katherine asked of him but saying less and less each day. What he did say made less and less sense and Katherine was becoming almost as silent as he was. It might have been tiredness, for the old man was again showing signs of incontinence and not only at night.

148

When he needed to be changed he would allow only her to administer to his needs, refusing help from me and positively rebelling against Matthew who, in any case, was rarely indoors unless in his office, and was more than ready for his own bed when the time came. Whatever had been blossoming between him and Katherine seemed for the time being to have wilted, if it was still alive. Occasionally they exchanged hard words which left Matthew bleeding the more visibly, although I thought I knew fragile Kit well enough by now to suspect that her pain would be poured privately into her pillow.

George Patterson had not given up hope of making trouble. He appeared at Kilbaddy or at my cottage about once a fortnight on all manner of oddly plausible excuses. His appearance at this particular point, however, was most inopportune because he caught Katherine at a low ebb and persuaded her to go out with him one evening when she was near to breaking point. Worse still he somehow managed to be pleasant enough to bring her back with her spirits a little higher. Matthew spent the evening on the other side of the fireplace as still as stone and the next few days in almost speechless politeness.

It was on the second Tuesday of February when Katherine returned to the warm kitchen after taking Kilbaddy upstairs to bed. To appease Matthew's fretting over my paying the heating bill, we rarely used the drawing room. She entered quietly, closed the door then leaned against it chewing the corner of her lip. It took Matthew and me a few moments to realise that something was badly wrong.

'He - wants me to go to bed with him.' Her eyes were wide with distress making her look unbearably young. The cold carapace she had grown in the previous weeks had vanished.

'Good God Almighty,' Matthew swore quietly. We both stood up and I went to steer her to the fireside, willing myself to be the calming influence which was required.

'How did you handle it?'

'I - said I'd just finish off a few things downstairs.'

'Good. I'll check up on him in half an hour and no doubt he'll be sound asleep.'

'But...' she fretted. 'He couldn't...? Could he?'

'He's far too old,' Matthew contributed flatly.

My control disintegrated in an undignified snort. 'That, if you forgive my saying so, is the blind wisdom of ignorant youth.'

'Then that's it,' Matthew burst out. 'I'm not having Kit exposed to this.' When Katherine and I remained silent, absorbed in each other, he almost shouted, trying to command our attention. 'In the name of all that's Holy - and I mean that - it would be incest!' There was silence in the room for a minute or so and Katherine looked at me, her eyes wide and wary, holding mine with deliberation. Matthew grabbed her arm and shook it till she looked at him at last, sighing sadly. 'Kit, oh Kit, my darling.' His voice dropped to a despairing whisper. 'You can't. You simply, positively can't. I won't let you. I couldn't. Apart from anything else it's illegal.'

'She has no intention of going to bed with him,' I said briskly. 'She is wondering where we go from here.' Immediately he drew away, thinking he had insulted her unforgivably. 'Don't turn on yourself either, my boy,' I said to soothe him.

'You'll have to take her home again,' he replied woodenly. 'Now. Tomorrow first thing I'll phone the hospital.'

'My cottage will be as cold as charity. There has been no heating in it for weeks.' I thought for a moment. 'There is another solution, I suppose. Then again...' I looked at the weary girl who was being forced to carry the bulk of the burden, and would continue even if I hired professional help. She was gazing at her hands lying lifelessly in her lap, her face now freed of the cold mask which had been hiding utter misery. She had seen this day coming. How could I ask more of her? It would be grossly unfair. 'No. Forget it.'

'Can I have a say?' She looked up. 'I'm not a thing on the wall,' she added with more asperity than I had heard for days, except when she was sniping at Matthew. 'I'm not having him put back into hospital. And I'm not having him drugged all the time either.'

'And I'm not having you in the house with him overnight,' snapped Matthew, matching her growing belligerence. 'Nor am I having you alone with him during the day. Not for one minute.'

I had to cool this soup before it boiled over. 'You're over-reacting, Matthew. What happened tonight was perfectly natural. While Kilbaddy sees Katherine as Kate, what could be more normal than for him to expect her to sleep in the same bed? She always did. Sooner or later he was bound to wonder why she isn't doing so now. It was the first complication that entered her mother's head.'

151

'Did she say so?' Katherine flared.

'She didn't have to.' An arid answer avoided the suggestion that her mother was likely to know more about married life than she. Or me, an ironic voice jeered inside my head. But still my resolve disintegrated. 'Now it has cropped up, I'm sure we can deal with it just as naturally.'

'How?' Matthew growled.

'Exactly the way we are doing tonight. I'd be very surprised if there's any trouble from him.' He gritted his teeth and I leaned forward in my chair. 'Look, Matthew, Kilbaddy's room is up the back stairs. The rest of us use the front stairs. All we need do is lock the adjoining door separating the two landings. He would never come down one flight then up another. To begin with he would have forgotten why he was doing it by the time he arrived. On top of that he would have no reason for imagining that Katherine would be where she is. Kate never was. I don't think he even realises that either of us is sleeping here.'

'He knows she's around during the day,' Matthew said doggedly. 'It must be on the cards that he might wake in the night and go looking for her. Can you guarantee he wouldn't?'

I couldn't, of course. Nor could I guarantee that if he were feeling amorous he would not force his attentions on her. I was positive beyond any doubt that he had never forced Kate. But I was equally sure he would never have needed to either. He had probably been able to take whatever liberties entered his head with her. On the other hand the specialist had warned that personalities can change, disintegrate in senility. And Kilbaddy had shown signs of violence

152

in the hospital. That had been totally out of character. I made another bleak resolution. Matthew read my expressions avidly, sitting back in sad satisfaction as he noted my conclusion.

'I'm still not a thing on the wall,' Katherine moaned, her face beginning to crumple. Matthew dropped to his knees beside her chair, slipping his arms round her.

'No, my darling. You're not. Things would be a thousand times easier if you were.' And he held her as the tears came. I stood up and laid my hand on his shoulder before swathing myself up against the cold night.

'Bring her down in an hour or so. I should have the fire lit by then.' Yes Kate, I was wrong even to consider the easy way, easy on my conscience, that is, for wanting him at home. The burden would not have been mine. You are right again. Kilbaddy would go looking for you. Sooner or later. After all these years I still do, don't I? I am doing so now, if only in spirit. As I told them, it's only natural. Kilbaddy was not out of line. Wasn't he even less out of line than he knew, my dear? But what is disturbing me is that Katherine might know better than he does where that hidden line is drawn. Is that it, could it be possible?

The first thing we tried was a home help, at Katherine's insistence. First one came, then another but Kilbaddy rejected each with a vehemence which bordered on viciousness. The doctor suggested tranquilizers but Katherine fought against such "animalizing" as she called it. I waited for Matthew to put his foot down but all he did was shrug and let her have her way.

153

He did have his way over where she slept and back in the cottage she and I settled into our previous routine. It had worked joyously throughout the autumn and early winter but now was a dark contrast. The glaciation in our relationship had not dissolved. She was still cool and cautious and there was no more physical contact, no more kneeling with her head on my knees or quiet talking by the fire. There was nothing I could do but live with it as calmly as possible, hiding the hurt of it as completely as I could. Her burden was great enough.

It was soon clear that if Kilbaddy were to remain at home he had to be medicated to make him sleep at night, if only to preserve Matthew's health. In the end I commanded it. The boy desperately needed a good night's rest to enable him to keep the farm running. Holly was still obtuse on occasion, although Kilbaddy now rarely gave him any orders.

The side effect of the drugs was increased incontinence. That resulted in constant bathing and laundry. Matthew insisted, now with my support, that the bathing should not be done by Katherine, and it usually fell to me. But the laundry she was determined to do herself and she was not content with mere tumble drying in the new machine I had imported. For the old man's comfort she insisted on ironing every sheet, every stitch of clothing. With that on top of the housework and home cooking to keep the huge new freezer stocked, adamant about rejecting convenience buying, all of which she refused to skimp, in no time at all she was exhausted.

Suddenly, on the twenty second of February, everything changed again. Kathy phoned to say she had to postpone her visit. Jock, her younger son, had had an accident at work and would be bedridden for at least three weeks with a back injury. There was nobody else to look after him.

Within an hour of my bringing that news up to the farm, Matthew came rushing in to telephone for an ambulance. Holly had slipped on a sheet of black ice by the byre door and broken his leg.

'Oh, preserve us!' Katherine muttered in a fury of frustration. 'What's the third thing going to be?' She looked into my eyes and saw it right there. 'Oh f... hell! Not again.' I turned and walked out and away from her without another word. I wished I were dead. Truly I did.

A third home help came in the unlikely form of Lewis. Mrs. Allen had been hovering and worrying over the sad situation in the Kilbaddy farmhouse but so far had restrained her strong instinct to interfere. She herself would have been quite unfit to help. Now, however, she must have concluded that Katherine and Matthew could no longer manage on their own, especially when the infallible grapevine confirmed that the black dog was on my shoulder again. No doubt the village was aware that I was back home and no doubt Mrs. Allen's Presbyterian principles also saw the need of a chaperone in my place, although Lewis was hardly the one I would have chosen. Kilbaddy had known Lewis all his life, of course, and at first accepted help from him, relieving the physical burden on the young people.

Tom Allen waded into the back-log of farm jobs unasked. At the next mart day he muttered it around with some surprise to an inquisitive audience that things were 'nae as bad as ye'd expect. Nae for a white settler. He can graft, I'll gie him that.' To Matthew's discomfort Peems Patterson from Kindrum, a grumpy character at the best of times, turned up one evening and gave him the low down on the two hundred rule and where he could buy the best bargains in cattle feed, 'clean stuff, noo, wi nane o' your crushed carcasses in it. I dinna hold wi' cannibalism.' He even mortified his new neighbour by offering to order fertilisers for him along with his own. 'Pay back as an' when. I'm nae in a hurry.' Almost in tears Matthew accepted. Patrick would not mind but I could imagine George's fury when he heard of his father's unlikely altruism.

'What's the two hundred rule?' Katherine asked me in dull tones several days later, seeing the light begin to reappear in my eye. Perhaps because this bout had been so hard on the heels of the previous one the depression had not been quite as deep or as long as usual. She herself had come home with a grey tinge in her cheeks and her own blue eyes were over bright. Her hair had lost all its lustre too. Perhaps she did have flu.

'It's a sophisticated theory, though simple enough to put into practice. If you measure the soil temperature each day after New Year - in centigrade - and add up the degrees above freezing until you reach two hundred, that is the time when sowing should commence. The strange thing is that whatever the variation you might think there has been in the weather it almost invariably happens that sowing time is in the same week each and every year, according to your area. Down in the Laich around the twenty something of March. Up here perhaps a week later. Of course the weather conditions may not be right for sowing just then but the point is that a farmer should wait for the next suitable spell *after* the two hundred and not be tempted to steal a March on winter. - That could be the origin of the saying, come to think of it,' I pondered.

'Just as well there's some way of deciding,' she said, her voice dull. 'Kilbaddy's no help any more. He's just not making any sense at all.' Only when she had let it slip out did she glance at me as if regretting the admission.

'Matthew will develop an instinct for it,' I soothed her. 'In the meantime his neighbours will keep him right.'

'If he sticks it.'

I sat up in surprise. 'What do you mean? He surely isn't thinking of giving up so soon?'

'Well, we haven't exactly helped him to a good start, have we?' she snapped. 'No wonder he wants to get out from under and away to somewhere where there are no hangers-on.'

'Hm.' I eyed her closely. 'Did he say so?'

'Not exactly. - Oh, if you must know we've had a hell of a row. He probably said a whole lot of things he didn't really mean.'

'As you did?'

'Oh, bugger off me, Bruno!' I sighed. The return of the swearing was not a good sign.

'You need a break,' I said flatly. 'I think Kilbaddy should return to hospital, at least for a few days.'

'No way. They'd never get him to eat now.'

157

'They would, you know, one way or another.' She shuddered. 'My dear girl, don't you owe anything to yourself?'

'I owe myself damn all. And damn all to you, before you try that one.' She stood up, suddenly deeply angry in a manner I had not sensed before. It wasn't the childish, hurt defiance which had raged and spat in brief periodic flashes. Nor was it rebellious grief and a general despising of the world. This was far inside her and stretched a long, obscured way back into the past.

'Katherine,' I began, feeling my way through the last mists of my miseries. 'My dear, I know there's something badly wrong. Is there - anything I can do?'

'Make Kilbaddy better?' she taunted, flinging the rejection in my face. 'What the hell can you do? Or anybody else? Sweet nothing. Not now. It's too late. Oh, I'm going back up to the farm,' she announced defiantly. 'And if you're worried about what Kilbaddy will get up to, don't. I'll be safe enough in Matthew's bed.' She laughed roughly when she saw no surprise on my face, just pain. 'What the bloody hell did you think we were doing all those evenings the two of you were playing chess? Might as well make good use of the guy while I can.'

'What makes you so disgusting at these times?' I demanded, sour with rage.

'Well, you made good use of the ladies of the Polish aristocracy when they were available, didn't you? You told me so yourself. And if you say, if you dare to say this is different I'll... I'll...' She was beside herself with fury by now.

'It is,' I said coldly. 'You can't deny your gender. Whether she likes it or not it is the woman who bears the child.'

'What damned child? What the blue blazes are you sticking on me now? D'you think I'm wet behind the ears? I knew all about looking after myself before I was into my teens.' She slapped around the room, picking up her few personal possessions and stuffing them into plastic bags. 'Nowadays there's more risk of AIDS than additions, or has that bit of up to the minute info passed you by? Doesn't come over on Radio Three, that's for sure.'

'Katherine...!' She slammed through into her bedroom to pack her clothes, continuing with a tirade about juvenile experience being the best preparation for life and the only place kids learned proper sex education was in the streets. 'From each other! Or from any other fancy guy or gal on the street willing to show us. Sure as hell it's not from our parents. They don't know the half of it.' The taunting became so ludicrously outrageous that I burst into her shrieking.

'This is utter nonsense. I don't believe a word of it.'

'Tough, tough, tough. You ask Matthew how good I am. Think I'm pregnant, do you? Well, my Mum may have had to lump it, but nowadays things are different. For a start abortion's not illegal any more. No girl has to keep a child she doesn't want. If she's stupid enough to... Oh, Jesus Christ!' She suddenly stood still and threw her head back in pained disgust. 'You're a ruddy Roman Catholic, aren't you?' She looked at me as if I had crawled out from under a very unsavoury stone. 'So that's why...'

159

'Yes,' I said quietly. 'That's probably why she became pregnant in the first place. Because she took my advice instead of Kilbaddy's. He at least realised that the permissive age was upon us.'

The silence throbbed around the room until she said in a voice devoid of all expression. 'And you've never forgiven yourself, have you? Or never forgiven your God maybe?' Then she laughed, a hard, bitter laugh. 'Simple story, isn't it, as old as time? And people like you, - oh and Kilbaddy too no doubt, for all his sound advice - were still stuck in your old, bigoted thinking. Couldn't swallow the new ideas of the sixties, could you? The new respect for the individual, huh! - What you did to my Mum was no better than was done to Burns's Jean Armour. You pilloried her, didn't you, till she ran away in misery and terror. When she did escape she refused to come back, didn't she? So you were done out of your chance to say sorry. Well, serves you bloody well right, the both of you!' By then the tears were streaming down her face.

'It wasn't like that,' I said dully, my abominable throat clamping so tightly that it choked me. 'Not remotely.'

'Wasn't it?' She spat it out. 'Wasn't it! By heck it was! Remember I saw the results. I had to live with them, the shouting and the screaming, the bruises and the beatings and the puke to be cleaned up afterwards.' I closed my eyes on her twisted, agonised young face but I couldn't shut my ears. In craven self protection I walked away, fearing it was the cruellest thing I had ever done. I walked straight across the living room, across the kitchen, through the lobby and out into the blessed stillness of the freezing night.

She won't let me reach her, Kate. She won't let me through all that disgusting debris. I shall never be able to comfort her from this distance. Oh Kate, my dearest, what have we done that such suffering should come to this fine, lovely girl? None of this was intended. In the name of my demanding but forgiving God whom she despises so virulently, such wretchedness was never, never on our minds when we let our Kathy go. It was what she chose. You know that, don't you? You believe that? She chose it long after the tears and confessions were done, after the coming to terms and quiet examining of the options, the swearing of our constant love, Kilbaddy's and mine, and support for whatever her decision might be. She couldn't have thought otherwise, could she? She stayed with her man to have three children, after all. She stayed until the youngest was twelve years old. And she has never been out of touch. Not completely, however much she hid from us.

But what about Katherine? What do I do about her? Forgive me, my dear Kate, I am thinking such terrible thoughts right now. When she came to me, I let myself believe in the night that you had returned, that she was Kilbaddy's Bonnie Quine reincarnated. When Kilbaddy saw it too and responded to it, the dream took on the dresses of reality. We were all so happy during those months before the turn of the year. With you. Even Katherine. Especially Katherine, with your wonderful spirit growing within her. Now, oh now, my dear one, I am praying I am wrong, that it isn't your spirit incarcerated in that tortured being. Oh, Kate! Even your God, harsh

161

Puritan though He be, would not visit such foul misery on a child, the child of your child. And surely not on this child who was giving almost her last drop... Ah. Is that it?

I blundered on through the darkness, shivering, but thinking fiercely until I had sifted and sorted things in my mind. Then I turned for home again, sensing Kate helping me, gentling me away from distrust and disgust, shepherding my thoughts towards the wisdom of loving, always her way to cure.

By the bridge I heard my name being called.

'Matthew?'

'Oh, Bruno! Thank heavens. Kit's nearly crazy with worry over you.'

'I needed to think,' I said apologetically, then wondered why I was doing the apologising.

'You'd have done it better with your coat on,' the boy said quietly. 'Come and get warmed up. She's built up the fire.'

'What about Kilbaddy?'

'He's with Lewis. I'm afraid we... had a bit of a rumpus tonight.'

'She told me.'

'Did she? She said she didn't.'

'Ah. Perhaps she didn't tell me all. Tell me again.'

'We've had a devil of a job with Kilbaddy. He took it into his head that somebody was coming after him with a gun and he went careering round the house trying to lock the doors and windows. - It's a heck of a big house for chasing somebody around in. And since there are no locks he started blocking up doorways with furniture. Lewis and I managed to get some tranquilizers into him but for once they didn't work.

162

Then he caught sight of Kit and wanted to insist that she should sit with him in the front room so that he could protect her. He was so belligerent, so unlike himself and she was terrified. To be blunt, so was I and kept myself between them. She insisted that she'd be okay and just grew angrier and angrier till...'

'The swearing began?' I sighed. 'Yes, I'm afraid she's been at it here too. Matthew, don't turn away from her just because of that.'

'I won't. I - think I know why it happens.'

'Do you?' I failed to keep the surprise out of my voice.

'Come on, let's get you into the warmth first. She's up at the farm. - No, no, don't worry. Kilbaddy's out for the count now. The story of tonight's tantrums is not finished, I'm afraid, but I'm going to get something warm inside you before you hear any more. I insist.' I was unexpectedly glad of his ministrations, and even more so for the kind, simple way in which he told the rest of the story and answered my questions.

'Without hesitation or deviation.' My commendation was wry. 'So there's Lewis with a broken nose and a loose tooth, and Kilbaddy pumped full of sedatives. I'm afraid I didn't hear the doctor's car go by.' I recollected Katherine's sour jibe about Radio Three. 'I agree with you. I think she is - do you call it freaking out? - because she cannot accept the inevitable.'

'We've kept him at home just as long as we possibly can,' he said miserably.

'And you told her so?' He looked at me bleakly. 'And that was when she, er, disagreed?' I sighed. 'And you tried to insist that she sees sense and she fought back, and so on till you were both saying terrible things to each other that should never have been said?'

'She did tell you.'

'Just enough. Matthew, - if you walk out after I say this I will quite understand. If - the pair of you are lovers, or are likely to become so, please will you, er, take care? I mean...'

'Take precautions.' He looked uncomfortable but resigned. 'We are, and we do. Please believe me, the last thing I want for her is one burden more and right now that is precisely what a baby would be, however much we might want it.' His frankness startled me into silence. 'It - started, just before my parents arrived.'

'Oh my goodness!' Even in such misery he began to smile at my horror.

'You did rather put your foot in it, sir. But we forgave you. We never did, er, sleep together when there was anybody else around in the house. No, not at all since you came up to stay, not since Kilbaddy began to go downhill. She, er, seemed too tired, you see.'

'So - are you saying she's not pregnant?'

'No! Of course she's not. Did she say she was?'

'Hm. Not exactly. And you think the frenzy of lying and swearing is just because she feels she has failed Kilbaddy?'

'That yes, but not just that. You know what psychiatrists say about abusers having sometimes been abused as children? And that sometimes abused people choose to be abused.'

'Good heavens, you can't really mean...'

164

'No, wait. I'm not saying either is the case with Kit, more the other way round. But I have had the weirdest feeling that she's - testing us.'

'Hm?' I sat and looked at him. 'Explain.'

'Well that first day I met her, the day of the accident. Remember? She sounded off like a fishwife, didn't she? She pushed and pushed and pushed - then gave up. I don't suppose she has any idea why.'

'She probably saw that instead of striking her you had crushed your wing mirror in your fury and cut your hand.'

'Precisely. If I had clouted her she'd have been over the hills and away by morning. I wouldn't have had a chance.' I looked at him dubiously. 'Don't you see, Bruno? She grew up in a home...' He realised at that point that his words might hurt me atrociously.

'Where there was violence.' I put my hand on his arm. 'I know, my boy. Bit by bit it has been creeping out. Kathy never said a word,' I added wretchedly. 'Are you saying that when there is a situation of stress Katherine tries to push us towards the edge of our patience? Over the edge, in fact?'

'Yes. She wants to know if either of us would ever reach the point when we would actually clout her. Or reject her maybe. She's only going to trust us completely when she's completely sure that we never will.' I had stood up and he looked up at me, cradling an empty coffee cup in his big hands. 'Am I way off beam?'

'If you are not, do you realise what you are suggesting?'

'What?'

'That Kathy might have taunted Alistair in the same way. That the children absorbed the scenario and learned their own responses from their, um, role models. I wonder how the boys have been affected?'

He looked down, then dared to ask, 'Where would Kathy have learned to taunt like that.'

It took me a moment to realise what he was implying. 'Ah. Not here, young man. Some people might well say Kathy was abused in a manner of speaking. But the abuse took the form of thorough spoiling. I never ever spanked her and I'm fairly sure Kilbaddy never did either. - Mind you, I wouldn't want you to think she wasn't required to toe the line. She was. We set fair standards and expected her to reach them. If she felt she couldn't we would expect her to explain why. And we listened to her explanation just as fairly. If we felt she had made her case she was excused.'

'Sounds highly civilised,' he murmured. 'Did she never try to play one off against the other?'

'Oh, frequently! But within half a day we had always caught up with her. - I think. Where does that leave your theory now? That she had no idea what the big wide world was like and she was woefully unprepared for the evil therein?'

'What do you think, sir?' His eyes were downcast.

I sat down again, leaning forwards to say softly but distinctly, 'Matthew, don't sir me.' When he frowned I added, 'In England it is a routine expression of respect, frequently empty. It didn't take me long to realise that things are different in Scotland. On the one hand Lewis uses it in awe, because he is under the thumb of his mother and his mother is an extremely

166

formidable old lady with a will of iron and very old-fashioned ideas on who should be addressed in such a manner. The laird, I know. The minister, *if* his sermon has met with her approval. Maybe the Chief Executive if he belongs to the right political party, - but only if he is 'nice' and belongs to a 'good' family. And *me*, heaven help us! The rest of the time sir is used as an expression of scorn or mockery. Oh, very underplayed, I grant you, but I recommend you listen very carefully the next time you hear a Scot use the address, especially a rural Scot. If he uses the word sir to somebody, rest assured he doesn't think much of him.' At last Matthew's face lightened into a smile, but only for moment. He was not to be diverted.

'What do you think, Bruno? Had Kathy been too well protected? Had she no reserves? No defences?'

'She must have had some,' I said sadly, 'or she would not have succeeded as far as she has done but, no, she was woefully badly provided. It is a desperate pity she didn't have somebody like you to walk with on equal terms through life. Instead she had to do the leading and the managing, just as we feared, and her weak, charming, addicted husband couldn't accept it. That is my guess.'

'So violence was his way of being dominant?'

'Possibly. I imagine it would have taken very little taunting to push him over the edge. I'll give him the benefit of the doubt by saying this. I do believe it was the addiction which caused the violence. What caused the addiction is another story. - Matthew, forgive me, my boy, but I am very tired.'

'Of course. You will be okay, now? I made sure that Kit was safely in bed before I came hunting for

167

you. Er, her own bed. I wouldn't want Lewis jumping to the... well, to conclusions.'

'No, that wouldn't do. In the morning just tell her - oh, say her grandmother Kate says she loves her.'

'No matter what?' His eyes were moist.

'No matter what.'

The young man put out his hand to lay it on mine then hesitated, looking deep into my eyes to see if he was going to be rejected again. I turned mine palm up to receive his swift, warm clasp. 'Good night, Bruno. Sir, in Mrs. Allen's sense. - I don't ask you to stop calling me my boy, now do I?' he teased. 'And I'll be twenty nine in May!'

Grimly I promised, 'One day I'll tell you what that means too.' I had a feeling that day was none too distant.

Chapter Ten

'She's still in bed,' Matthew told me when I went up to the farmhouse to share a morning coffee.

'So's Kilbaddy, Mr. Bruno.' Lewis had slept in the little room adjoining the old man's bedroom. He swore he was a light sleeper and would have heard Kilbaddy every time he turned over far less if he got up and went downstairs in the dark. 'The doctor gave him a real big injection. It'll nae be too much, will it?' he wondered anxiously.

'I'm sure it won't. But - I'm afraid we have reached the end of the road.' I felt wretched, loathing myself for the treachery in voicing the words yet dreading the agony another would suffer if forced to say them for me. 'Don't you agree?'

'The lassie'll gae spare,' Lewis muttered. 'She's tried that hard.'

'I know. But her health is beginning to be affected. And Matthew's, and he owes none of us a thing.' Matthew threw me a frown and headed off to do battle with a cattle-cake salesman. I turned back to Lewis, examining the broken nose. 'How is it?'

'Sair, but it'll mend. I'll wait afore I get my teeth done. Jist in case, like.' He cocked an expressive eyebrow.

'What if Katherine is hurt next time?'

His nonchalance took a painful tumble. 'Aye, weel...

'And what if Kilbaddy suddenly comes back to normal for a bit? He sometimes does, you know. How

169

would he feel about what he has done? Besides, in hospital he will be cared for by trained staff. He has reached the stage of being utterly disorientated. And last night he was also terrified. I gather he remained that way until the doctor turned up, and that was over two hours. If he had been in hospital he could have been spared that, Lewis, and been treated within minutes. Wouldn't it be cruel to keep him here any longer?'

'Yes.' We whirled to see Katherine standing in the doorway. Her hair was still dull and tousled and her face was chalk white but her eyes were more calm than I had seen for weeks. 'Oh, Bruno...' Her voice cracked. I held out my arms and she walked straight into them, turning her face into my shoulder to weep in despair and shame. In utter, total relief I rocked her quietly for a long time until the pain of the last accepting was over.

'The doctor is coming in again this morning, isn't he?' I asked gently.

'Yes. We'll ask him then. It...' She glanced over her shoulder at Lewis's battered face. 'It's better over and done with now.' Her head went down again in weary submission and I kissed her temple.

'This difficult stage might last just a few weeks, days even. But, my dear, we must accept that Kilbaddy could be like this for years yet. Physically he is strong and healthy. But we are simply not equipped to care for him in this state of mind any longer. Shall I suggest that we all take him in after tea tonight?'

She shook her head. 'Just you and Matthew. I can't bear it. Not...' Her voice rose in distress. 'Not when I know he won't be coming back. Can you

170

manage, just the two of you?'

'I'll be there,' Lewis butted in. 'Jist in case be.' She turned to him, struggling to produce a smile, and kissed him on the cheek.

'Thank you, Lewis. I don't know what would have happened if you hadn't been with us last night. It could have been...'

'It wasn't,' I said hastily. 'I think I see the doctor's car coming. Do you trust me to deal with things, my dear?'

'Of course. But - can I vamoose? I've got no courage left.'

The arrangements were made before the doctor went up to check Kilbaddy and pronounce him none the worse. He did warn us that the old man would probably be groggy when he woke. That happened just before dinner time but he did eat a little and remained quiet and biddable all through the afternoon. He said very little, and very little of that made sense.

At tea time, not even he was able to eat much but suddenly, after his short nap, he asked, 'When div we leave?' He frowned at our startled faces. 'Are we nae going oot the night?'

'It's very cold,' I managed to say, turning his eyes from Katherine's swift tears. 'You'll need to wrap up.

'You and all,' he replied, with a jaunty scorn I had not heard for weeks. 'We want nae mair o' yon black moods. Ye've had too many this year.' Katherine began to shake. Even Matthew and Lewis were visibly distressed by this sudden return to lucidity, if that was what it was, tonight of all nights. I stood up with him and the pair of us went out to the draughty hall where I made a slow job of getting our coats on. When we

171

returned to the drawing room the two younger men were hunching on thick jackets and Katherine had taken shelter by the fireside, bending over to add some logs to the blaze with her back to the only light she had left on. Her entire body was quivering and I guessed that her face was awash.

'We'll have them in for a bit o' supper when we come back, eh, Kate?' the old man said to her and she nodded vigorously. Picking up the poker she stabbed blindly at the scorching flames. Kilbaddy was satisfied and turned to the door. There he stopped suddenly and turned to Matthew, tapping him on the shoulder.

'And a wee word, laddie. It'll be a grand day the morn but dinna believe in it. It's too soon for the spring corn. We're nae up tae the twa hundred yet, nae till next week. Forby, if ye sow the morn the gales will blaw it all away. I'm telling ye, they're comin'. On Sunday, maybe Monday.' Matthew looked wildly at me, then at Lewis who nodded seriously, well aware of Kilbaddy's ability to tune into things natural.

By then we were by the front door, out of sight of Katherine although she would have heard every word across the hall. Matthew jerked his head at me behind Kilbaddy's back and I slipped back to her for a moment. She had her hands flat against her cheeks, one palm clamped across her mouth, and the tears were pouring over her fingers as she fought to keep the sound of sobbing in check.

'Phone Mrs. Allen, dear. Ask her to come over and sit with you.' She shook her head. Kilbaddy was calling and all I could do in persuasion was push my handkerchief into her hand and kiss her brow fiercely.

172

The old man's voice was continuing with a calm strength, broadening with every sentence, which came desperately near to undermining the rest of us. 'Ye'll have sandstorms ower the weekend if ye touch the plough. There'll be nae soil, nae seed nor nae fertiliser this side o' Huntly and ye'll hae it a' tae dae again. Are ye hearin'?'

'Yes,' Matthew managed to say. 'I'm hearing. The middle of next week then?' He had begun to use the Scottish meaning, next week being the one after this one just beginning, that is after the coming weekend about which Kilbaddy was making dire predictions.

'That'll dae fine,' he agreed, 'if it's nae rainin' by then.' And that was the last thing he said, indeed the last any of us said during a journey of searing misery. When we reached the hospital Lewis remained in the land-rover. I was thankful for that when Kilbaddy turned earnestly to Matthew at the ward door and tapped him once more on the shoulder.

'Ye mustna blame Bruno, ye know. That was nivver the way it was meant. Kate would tell ye that.' He shuffled towards the bed where he had originally lain, stopping to frown uncertainly when he saw it was occupied. Suddenly I was angry, fiercely, irrationally furious. Why could the hospital not have ensured even the tiny dignity that his own resting place might have offered? Why was there not a nurse to meet us and warn us of the change? Why had I not checked at the desk first, thoughtless old fool that I was? And why, why, why, oh God, do You permit such a travesty of Your Grace to be made manifest in the senseless degradation of senility in old age?

173

'Oh, Jock!' A bright little sprite of a nurse broke into my ranting. 'It's good to see you back. Look, I've put your bed over here by the window. You'll be able to see right down the garden to the street.' She fussed around him, comforting him if not me. Matthew stood stolidly by, his expression forced into a blank mask but his eyes dark with pain.

'Tell Kathy,' Kilbaddy turned back to him, ignoring the fussing. 'Kate'll explain it wasna anybody's fault, least o' a' Bruno's. An' I nivver saw it that way. Ye will tell Kathy now? Ye winna forget?'

'I won't forget,' the boy mumbled. The message, surely, was for me. A final grasping for reality before the curtain closed? A desperate hankering for truth to be declared? Or was that my evil self-interest declaring its presence? Kate, help me decide. Please, dear girl, where do I, we, go from here? What is it Kilbaddy really wants?

'I don't suppose we'll ever know,' I tried to deflect Matthew on the way home, after dropping Lewis off at Balbeggie, there confirming that Katherine had not summoned his mother. Matthew had more sense than to open his mouth except to suggest we should all stay at the farmhouse for the night. Our beds were still made up. I left Katherine with him, beyond caring how they might seek comfort. For once I wanted to be at home alone with a new bottle of full strength port.

The next weeks were silent as I had never known them. In various combinations we all went to visit the hospital at least once a day. Sometimes Kilbaddy was bright and relatively lucid. More rarely he was quiet and uncommunicative. Perhaps we all hoped just a little that he would abscond again and return to us but it didn't happen. I felt lonely, too, as I had never felt before, a strange and painful experience for one who revels in solitude. Katherine seemed to feel the same, spending a few hours up at the farm, a few in the cottage, quite a number striding over the fields and moors and the bonny Banffshire braes growing green with approaching spring, always alone. She had a loose-limbed walk more reminiscent of her mother than her grandmother and I found myself longing fiercely for Kathy's return and spent the sad hours of the night teasing out my problems with Kate. For once, however, my dear one could not help, though for that she could not be blamed. How can one use the therapy of love when the sufferer is not willing to accept it?

I thought the girl avoided me whenever possible and wondered if Matthew was being similarly neglected. I doubted that he was receiving or giving preferential treatment. For one thing, she had come back to sleep in the cottage and they did not see a great deal of each other. For another, neither of them looked in any way happy. The only perverse flash of brightness on the horizon occurred when George Patterson dared to show his face. Eager to fill a non-existent gap, he must have been shaken by the fierce rejection he was given by both of them.

A few days after Kilbaddy left Katherine took herself in hand and stripped the cover off her motorcycle. While Matthew, still struggling along without Holly, drove himself hard to get ahead of the routine work before sowing, including bringing his paperwork up to date, she dismantled the machine completely. After detaching a bewildering array of pieces, she cleaned

175

and oiled each single item one by one, spending days over the task. When the promised gales did come, almost exactly on the equinox for once, she covered everything up with a thick tarpaulin topped with a couple of old blankets. In spite of her care, the silt still made its way inside and she merely stripped the entire machine down again, anxious to remove every single grain. Her attention to detail was bordering on the fanatical.

'I must admit,' Matthew confessed over the fence one coffee break, having refused to come in with the coating of sand he had covered himself with during sowing, 'I've never seen such a beautiful bike in such perfect condition. I suppose it should really be in a museum.'

'Are you going to tell her so?' I growled, knowing he would not dare. 'I am just a little surprised that she has not ridden it at all.'

'Maybe she is thinking of selling it,' he pondered, rubbing the sand out of the grooves beneath his eyes. 'Elgin Motor Museum would pay through the nose for it, I shouldn't wonder.'

Neither of us asked the obvious question. Why would she want to sell it? Why now? Was she thinking of returning to New Zealand now she could do no more for Kilbaddy? It was several days since he had even recognised her and we could see that maggot burrowing into her heart.

Without intending to she created another sharp shift in the old man's equilibrium when she did take the cycle out one sunny day right at the end of March and rode it down to town. Parking it outside the ward she went in still wearing her leather outfit, unwittingly

176

swinging the old man's crazed memory back to the previous summer when the 'laddie wi' the big bike' had visited him. Somehow he managed to associate that incident with the subsequent return of Kate although that was not immediately apparent.

'He didn't say a single word during my visit,' she fretted to me on her return. 'Not one. Just stared and stared at me. It was spooky.'

When I went down that same evening Kilbaddy was far from silent with me. He talked incessantly about Kate, Kate of long ago certainly, but also Kate who had seen him through the joyous autumn of the previous year, about the pantomime and Christmas, the clearing out of the loft and a hundred small memories. A few of the events were clear in his mind, but most were sadly confused and inaccurate. The disturbing element was his constant plea to me to bring her in to see him. He wanted to know where she was, how she was.

Unwisely I said she was at home and she was fine, realising immediately that his poor brain was latching on to the words with frightening tenacity. It was inevitable that he began to search for her. By this stage his mind seemed unable to guide his body out of the hospital. Instead he began searching inside the buildings, wandering into other wards and invading offices at all hours of the day and night. At first he would allow the staff to guide him back to bed, but there came the day when he resisted, a day when Katherine had again arrived by motorcycle. Almost immediately he became aggressive and unpredictable obliging the medical staff to act.

'You mean that he's to be sedated all the time?' Katherine demanded, aghast.

'I'm afraid they have no choice, my dear. He - came near to molesting a woman patient this morning.' I saw no need to mention that the patient had looked a little like her.

'Is it worse when I've been to see him?' Her voice was harsh and ugly.

I sighed and turned away.

'Is it? For Christ's sake tell me!' she gritted and grasped my arm, jerking me round to face her, an ill-usage she had never dreamed of before. Bracing myself for a return to Kit's tirades I admitted that I thought it was. Her visits which had once been a blessing to the old man now constituted a curse.

'The doctor asked if I could suggest tactfully to you that...' I swallowed hard. She merely nodded and went to her room without a single word. The hard anger in her eyes and the grim set of her chin made me wish for once that she had given way to her usual foul language.

Next day I went in to the hospital with Matthew, returning around four. Kilbaddy had been doped into near oblivion which had sickened both of us.

'I see why,' I muttered as I gave the boy a drink before he headed up the hill. 'I think.'

'If he's unsafe I don't see they have much choice. But I don't think we should tell Kit. I hope God will... Oh, hell,' he moaned miserably.

'I know, my boy,' I said gently. 'It's so very much against all our instincts to say it but I agree. I hope God will be merciful and not prolong this misery much longer. I suppose she's off walking again,' I sighed,

178

looking out at the bare hillsides which looked even more empty and devoid of hope than they had after Kathy's departure. Kate, my dear, dark girl, I am going to need you again in these darkest hours. Several times, just when Katherine was at her lowest ebb, she had spent the night at the farmhouse. Tonight would be another.

'She feels - exiled in a way,' Matthew tried to comfort me. 'Forbidden.'

Four hours later Kathy phoned. 'By the weekend? That would be wonderful! But, my dear, things are becoming very sad here now. It won't be the happy home-coming I wanted for you.' After I had explained it all to her I telephoned Matthew with the news for Katherine.

'She's not here,' he said, startled. 'I thought she was with you.' After a moment's thought he swore softly. 'Hang on, Bruno. I'll phone you back.' Five minutes later he did. 'The bike's gone. The lot, including the tools and the panniers. She wouldn't need them just to nip down to the hospital, would she?'

I felt bile rise in me. 'No. She wouldn't. Let me check her room.' That took seconds. 'Matthew? Yes, my boy. She has gone. And there's no note of any kind. Have you found one?'

'Nothing. Not a damned thing. God, when I catch up with her I'll...'

'You won't, you know,' I countered. 'History doesn't repeat itself quite as often as people suggest. May I suggest you do as I am going to do? Have a stiff drink and put yourself to bed. Perhaps things will clear themselves in the morning.'

They did nothing of the kind. After breakfast I dealt with the few essentials of mail requiring my attention. Then I overcame my reluctance and invaded the privacy of her room. It was mine, after all. What I found drove me to put on my coat and boots and head for the solitude of the hills. To exhaust myself I deliberately chose a swift pace. I walked for hours, heading uphill to the south until midday then sweeping westwards to pick up the valley of the Beggie Burn, following the little stream homewards until it finally reached Kate's Corner and joined our own stream. Miserably I sat down on the fallen tree by the bank, leaning over to dabble my fingers in the icy, peaty water. Gradually, very gradually, the amiable chatter of the little watercourses at their confluence began to sooth me. It had worked its magic often enough before. Why not now?

Well, Kate? How much of this lies at my door? I could hardly expect to escape as easily as I had thought. Retribution was bound to arrive eventually. We should be honest now, even if just between us two in this special place of ours. It was more my doing than yours, wasn't it? Of course it was. What you did was for Kilbaddy. Mostly. But what I did, I did mostly for me. A little for Kilbaddy, and more for you, perhaps, but...

From where I was sitting I had a commanding view down the hill towards the valley while remaining hidden from anybody approaching. I suddenly realised that far below Matthew had driven into the farm and, instead of heading for the house, had walked quickly round the steading and was climbing the hill, plainly following the course of the burn towards where I was sitting. All I needed to do was wait. He was almost into the glade before he saw me.

'Thank God I've found you,' he said lamely. I frowned at the odd note of caution in his voice. He stepped closer to look into my eyes then sighed with relief when he realised they were still alive. 'You okay?'

'Yes,' I said bleakly. 'Under the circumstances I'm fine. I take it she has not returned.

'No.' His eyes were darting all over the clearing in a curious manner.

'In Kilbaddy's words you came up that hill at a gie lick.'

'On his instructions,' he told me carefully. He ignored my gesture that he join me on the log but came to stand nearby and put his foot on it, leaning over to look down on the other side.

'Hm? You've been to see him this afternoon?'

'Yes. I took a chance and said you had gone missing. He told me exactly where to find you and exactly how to get here. Clear as a bell. He also said...' He looked down at me, again searching my eyes. 'You sure you're okay?'

'Quite sure.'

He seemed satisfied for he went on. 'He warned me to be careful because - he thought you had a gun. He was very worried. He was so sure, so definite. I couldn't take the risk that he was havering. He was, wasn't he?'

'No. He wasn't. As you say, he was clear as a bell. Just forty three years out of date.' Even the trees seemed to hold their breath. Matthew certainly did. I

181

reached up and touched his wrist. 'Sit down, my boy, and I'll tell you a story.'

He sat. 'I'm not sure I want to hear it.'

'Then let me give you a piece of advice.' He wasn't going to like it. 'Forget Katherine. She's not right for you. Let her go.'

He turned and stared. 'Of course I won't! Why should I?'

'You think she'll be back?'

'Yes. I do. We won't have long to wait either. I'm dead sure of it.'

'So you do know why she went?'

'No. But she's not answerable to me,' he said stolidly.

'Very loyal.' He was beginning to anger me. 'If you don't know then I surmise you suspect why she went.'

'I haven't the faintest idea. Have you?'

'I think she has gone to have an abortion,' I said bluntly. 'Let her go, Matthew. Let her take her filthy language and her contaminated ways out of our lives.'

He was instantly on his feet again. Of course he was. 'What the... For the love of Mike what brought that on?'

I swallowed the bile once more. 'I - think she's unstable, Matthew. Like her father.'

'Perhaps you'll tell me why you think that.' His voice was cold. 'I am positive she's not pregnant.'

'Are you? Do you remember when we talked about your relationship with her? You told me that you had made sure that she was protected against pregnancy. Did you think of protecting yourself, I wonder?'

'For crying out loud, Bruno, what the heck's got into you? I know she's not pregnant.'

'Hm?'

'Look, believe me. She isn't... What on earth did you mean, protect *myself*?'

'I may be old and out of touch, but even I have not been immune to the publicity about AIDS.'

'AIDS? For... Bruno, - you're the last man on earth I'd have imagined going lulu. What the hell are you talking about?'

'Katherine. Kit. Something she told me in one of her rages. She may be nothing like as clean as you imagine.'

'Balls,' he said rudely. 'You don't really believe that, do you?'

'I wish I didn't.' I plunged both hands into the burn and splashed my face with the icy water, suddenly trembling and hiding my face in my hands in disappointment and self disgust. Why was I visiting my misery on this fine young man? He already had his own suffering to deal with. 'I'm sorry, Matthew. I should not have told you these things.'

I was aware of him watching me for several minutes before he spoke. 'You must have had a reason. What did she say?'

'She - implied that she was - experienced sexually, that she had been promiscuous from a very young age. - I hate to think about drugs. If you remember, she has not been well since the middle of January, has been going noticeably downhill in fact. It could be pregnancy. I prefer to think that. But it could be something more permanent.'

'But - Bruno, you've got things wrong. Horribly wrong. Forget AIDS, if that's your drift. As far as the promiscuity - believe me, there hadn't been anybody

183

before me.' He read my sour expression correctly for he went on. 'Probably I shouldn't be saying this, not even to you, but - well...' He rubbed his mouth awkwardly with the back of his hand. 'We tried three times before we succeeded. On different nights, of course. She was hurting. I - didn't want that. I didn't want her frightened. And she bled when we finally did succeed. Oh, not that much, but - you can't doubt that, surely. It was days after her period had finished so there couldn't be any confusion. - And, well, we used double protection every time.' He was becoming thoroughly embarrassed now, and I could hardly blame him. 'I mean she was on the pill but she had only been on for a week or two and wasn't used to taking it regularly. So...'

'I understand.' I sighed. 'Very well. I'll go along with your assertions.'

'And I'm certain there's no baby. Apart from anything else we haven't - I mean, not since the middle of January... Oh, heck, why should I have to tell you all this?' I deserved that little flare of resentment.

'You don't. I'm sorry, Matthew. The last thing I wanted to do was invade your privacy.' We sat in silence for a little.

'Let's forget it and go home,' he said quietly. 'If she's not back by the time her mother arrives I'll go looking for her.'

'She doesn't know her mother is coming,' I pointed out.

He shrugged despondently and put out a hand to pull me to my feet. I shook my head.

'Just leave me here. I'll be down in half an hour.'

'You're still not convinced?' he asked, sitting down again. 'Why not? What else?' When I remained silent he persisted. 'Please, Bruno.'

'Yes,' I sighed. 'Yes. You have been undeservedly honest with me. It's only right that I should be as honest with you. She - took money from my desk. I make a habit of keeping some notes there. She knew that. Since she also knew that I'd have given her anything she needed, the only reason I can think of to explain why she did not ask is that she wanted the money for something of which I would not approve.' I added a sardonic comment. 'She was forever taunting me with being a Roman Catholic. As such, of course, I was expected to disapprove of both contraception and abortion.'

'And do you?'

'Hm. Yes and no. But that's another matter.'

'Well, how much money has gone?'

'Three hundred pounds.'

'But Bruno... Look, whatever your opinion might be, if she needed an abortion she could get it for free nowadays.'

'Only with the proper medical approval.'

'Well, if she did go private it would surely cost a heck of a lot more than that. So what else?'

'She has taken only the clothes she arrived in except for a couple of pairs of new jeans. All her dresses and skirts and nice shoes have been left in the wardrobe. Everything I bought for her she has left.'

'They wouldn't be much use on a bike,' he pointed out sensibly. 'What else? Come on, Bruno, tell me.'

185

'Well, I don't know what to make of this but - she left empty contraceptive packets on top of the chest of drawers where she knew I could not fail to find them. It was as if she were - taunting me.'

That silenced him for some time. 'I still don't see why you're in such a stew about this, you know. It could have been accidental, leaving the bits around as she rummaged. Don't you think? She probably meant to throw them away just so that you wouldn't find them, then laid them down for a tick and forgot. We all do things like that. Look, Bruno, let's get home now before the dark comes down. You're freezing. And I have every intention of going after her if she doesn't turn up.'

'Then what?'

'We'll talk.'

'What if she doesn't want to talk? What if she doesn't want to see you again?'

'Then she'll tell me so. That's a separate question.'

'Matthew... Dear God, I wish I didn't have to say this, but there is more. She - left with someone else.'

That shook him as nothing else had done. 'Who? Don't say George Patterson because she's got more sense. She can't stand him.'

'No, not George. It was Lewis.'

'Lewis! Lewis? But - he's...'

'Even Kilbaddy told you Lewis was daft for her. I must admit I never thought he had it in him to elope with a hen far less a real, live woman.'

'Who said he has? Where did this information come from?'

'Mrs. Allen told me today. Lewis had planned a couple of days ago to travel south with Katherine. They left yesterday while we were at the hospital. She picked him up at Balbeggie where he was waiting with his bag all ready packed at his feet.'

'And Mrs. Allen said they'd eloped?'

'She said she had high hopes of seeing one of her sons married after all. What else could she mean?'

'She might have hopes, but that's not the same as saying it's going to happen, is it?' I ached at the bravery with which he was protecting his love. Then his spirits plummeted. 'Oh hell. Oh, hell, hell, hell!'

That she had gone off with another man was more than he could tolerate. He would also remember the date she had had with George too. Both brought the abortion question back into play, of course, but I would never have said so to him. Who was the fool who said history does not repeat itself?

Chapter Eleven

I saw nothing of Matthew the next day until he knocked on my door around nine in the evening on his way back from the hospital.

'I thought you needed time to yourself,' he said lamely. 'Without seeing Kilbaddy, I mean.'

I pointed to the empty chair on the other side of the fire then at the bottle of port, a rare white one this time which was already half empty. 'Sit down and tell me why.'

'I don't know why. I just felt there were complications. What, for instance, am I supposed to be telling Kathy?'

'Come, come,' I used scorn to cover my dejection. 'You are not normally either lacking in intelligence or stricken with self delusion. Put it into words and be done with it.'

'Why me? Isn't it your job to tell her who her father is?' I opened my eyes then and saw the grim anger around his mouth.

'I fancy she already knows,' I said sadly, turning back to the fire. 'Has done for many years.'

'She didn't tell her children.'

'For Kilbaddy's sake, I imagine.' We sat listening to a mediocre Bach performance, each enclosed by our own bitter thoughts. When the threnody had woven its final pattern the silence crept back between us, stiff and sad. 'Would you believe me if I tell you that I love Kilbaddy? Not in any untoward way, just as a man loves a true and caring friend. It was he who first took me under his wing you know, not Kate, although Kate soon took over. He recognised another soul in torment, one who had been brutalised as he had been. That gives people an affinity. Nobody can really understand what it was like, not without experiencing the sheer horror and helpless degradation of war, the inexorable, hysterical uselessness of it all. Trauma is a good name for our malady.' I topped up my glass again.

'Kate understood part of it, of course. She could hardly fail to, nursing us through our black depressions the way she did. But she hadn't experienced the terror, the rage... oh, all the destructive emotions that war engenders. You've never been in that situation, my boy. I pray you never will be. But it makes things so hard to describe to you. Words take on different meanings, have different implications. They create pictures for us which you cannot even begin to see. Films make images, but the reality is barely touched, not the way it really was. Kilbaddy and I - we can use the same words and they mean the same to us both.' I laughed wryly, 'Even if one of us is saying them in a foreign language.'

'You speak it better than any natural speaker I know.'

'Rather out of date, I gather.' More than once he had heard Katherine tease me for my old-fashioned delivery. 'I loved Kate too, of course. You guessed that some time ago, didn't you? You could say that was in an untoward manner. She was Kilbaddy's wife, after all.'

'Kilbaddy's Bonnie Quine? Sorry. I know Mrs. Allen told Kit that her father had written the song but she's convinced that he only adapted it and that it's quite old.'

'It is. Remind me to tell her - if she comes back.' I sneered at myself silently as I went on. 'It appears to be the sordid story of an unfaithful wife who was spurned by her lover and eventually returned to her husband.'

'So the song would not have been written by either?'

'Unlikely. The lover was of Scottish descent with a Scottish title but he was brought up on his father's English estates, somewhere in Buckinghamshire I believe. The local records mention the incident, implying that she was not the stuff of which countesses are made, or so his family insisted. He would not have known the Scottish dialect in which the song was originally written.'

'Not the husband either, I shouldn't think.'

'Highly unlikely, in the circumstances.'

'In other words,' he said in a hard voice quite unlike his usual, 'the lady was no lady.'

'Profligate with her favours, I would say. Hm? More wine?' He had more sense than I and refused.

'Why port?'

'I'd be in a sorry state if I drank vodka like this,' I growled. 'Don't you like it?'

'I do. Surprising really. I'm a beer man, and I don't drink much of that.'

'Did the girl tell you she's a little afraid of her alcoholic heritage too? You want to consider that.'

He sat up, leaning forward with a frown. 'Look, Bruno. Until we have proof of your wild ideas I flatly refuse to believe them. In the meantime - please back off. I want to help you. I - have come to value your company but I'm not staying to listen to one jibe after the other about the girl I've grown to love.'

'She's wrong for you,' I said solemnly into my glass, defying him.

'How would you like it if I said your Kate sounds too good to be true?' he snapped. 'When all she was was an everyday adulteress who deceived her husband with his best friend?' It was like a rapier slash across my face. I was so shocked that my glass went flying. 'Oh, hell,' he muttered and dashed out to fetch a towel with which to mop up the sanguine spillage. 'I'm sorry, sir. Really I am.'

'No, you're quite right. I have been carping. You're right about Kate too, although I can never see it that way. And, my boy,' I knelt beside him to reach for the glass, 'believe me, I hope with all my heart that you are right about Katherine. I hope I will be proved to be grossly unfair and unjust to the girl. God knows, I have come to love her enough.'

'Because of Kate?' He helped me back into my chair more kindly than I deserved, realising at last just how much alcohol was inside me.

'Yes, certainly. And for Kathy. But also for herself alone. She's a... she's a...' To my utter shame I began to weep. 'Kilbaddy called her a grand wee lass on Friday. I'm sure he meant your Katherine, not Kate.' He left me alone, returning in ten minutes with a black, sweet coffee which he let me drink in silence.

191

'When I was bathing Kilbaddy,' he ventured at last, 'I saw the scars where the war wounds were. All over the lower half of his trunk and legs.'

'Inadvertent vasectomy,' I agreed. The caffeine was reopening lesions which the alcohol had anaesthetized. I let him fill up my cup again before adding, 'You are a farmer. You should understand a farmer's mind more easily than most.'

'In what way?'

'Kilbaddy had six years of his working life torn from him. He was exiled, cut off from all he had worked for as a boy and a young man. Think of it. When he was your age he was fighting in the desert somewhere in North Africa. He hadn't seen his home, his farm, his family, his girl for something like two years. He had no way of knowing whether his girl was being faithful to him. Some girls were. Some were not and every soldier knew it. His farm was in the hands of two old ladies, grand-aunts who had neither the strength nor the knowledge to do what he wanted done with it. Their best efforts could do no more than keep things ticking over, or so he thought. In fact Kate was working it with them, with occasional help from a number of neighbours who had avoided conscription. In some ways she was every bit as good a farmer as Jock was himself. It was partly out of respect for her that his neighbours hesitated to give him his soubriquet for so long.'

'Kilbaddy?'

'Yes. When he finally came back shot to bits there were those who thought he couldn't survive. I mean they thought he wouldn't recover at all, far less succeed in farming. Even I was afraid at one stage.

So was Kate.'

'Are you talking about physical recovery? Or was it his mental state which... You did say he suffered from depression early on.'

'He did. Appallingly. I gather it was only when he found I too had visits from the black dog that he began to believe that he could survive, when he realised he was not unique. Long afterwards Kate told me that he had been suicidal several times before I arrived.'

'Oh! So - it was on his account that guns were banned here?'

'Hm. No. You're jumping ahead. For the first year or so after I crawled into the valley Kilbaddy improved. Physically he grew stronger each day. He was inclined to drive himself beyond his strength but every time he did he recovered a little more quickly. His neighbours helped where they could, but slowly their help was needed less and less. And they noticed this, my boy. They noticed and respected his struggles. They respected Kate too for the work she put in on the land as well as in the house and in the community. She even kept an eye on the two old ladies. They retired to a cottage in the village when their Jock came back and married his bonnie quine.'

'Where does a farmer's thinking come into this?'

'Can't you see? What is the main drive of your life? Why do you do what you do?'

He shrugged. 'I do it because... it's all about life, I suppose.'

'Exactly. You sow the seed in order to reap the harvest in the next season.'

193

'You breed the cattle so that the young will be improved in vigour and health in the years to come?' he murmured.

'You establish the conifer plantation for timber in twenty years. - Don't you see? It's all about the future. If you wanted no more than the current crop you wouldn't spend good time and money ploughing back your profits and efforts into the land.'

'You mean it's being done for future generations,' he said bluntly, 'and Kilbaddy knew that there wasn't going to be one.'

'Not at first. Once he was well enough he and Kate began to try. - I didn't know at the time, of course. But I soon realised that something was going badly wrong when month after month Kilbaddy became more and more morose. Before that his depressions had been growing milder and had almost disappeared. Mine had been the reverse, unfortunately, but perhaps that had actually helped him. As he nursed me through my black times with Kate it gave him reassurance in his own growing strength, of mind as well as body. However, when Kate consistently failed to conceive he began to plunge downwards. At first it was gradual, then after about a year his own depressions became increasingly severe. Instead of allowing Kate to help he tended to shut her out.' I grimaced. 'That wouldn't exactly have helped his plan forward if he had been fertile. My guess is that subconsciously he had already accepted the reality but in the meantime was blaming his wife. Strange how unacceptable that particular truth is to men the world over, hm?'

194

'Only through ignorance,' Matthew pointed out. 'Nowadays we know enough to accept medical fact and not drive out a barren woman.'

'If your wife continually failed to conceive, whose fault would you suspect it to be? Yours?'

'Uh, - not until I'd been checked out,' he confessed.

'If your doctor told you tomorrow that you could not have children, how would you feel about it?'

He opened his mouth then closed it. 'Pretty damned disappointed I suppose.'

'Quite. Mind you, I don't think they ever stopped trying.' I eyed the last inch of liquor in the bottom of the port bottle. Realising I was coming to the most difficult part of the story Matthew stood up and poured it into my glass. I suppose he knew that I had to tell this to somebody, that it had never been told before. 'Kate came to me for comfort, you understand. Nothing else. She must have known I adored her. She knew that because of my shattered face and hands I was convinced that there was no worthwhile future for me, no more concerts with their fame and fortune, certainly little chance of any, er, relationships. Maybe she even thought she was safe with me for that very reason. At first.' I twirled the glass, watching the eddy become a whirling golden glow in the firelight. 'We had one short, glorious, precious season. That was all. Hm.' I smiled to myself. 'She was surprisingly innocent. Kilbaddy didn't know much about the art of love at that stage. Maybe she went back and taught him more. When a child was conceived there was nothing but joy. For all of us. Pure joy.'

195

As I emptied the glass I looked surreptitiously at the young man opposite. He looked straight back and waited. 'Of course the child, in theory, could have been either Kilbaddy's or mine. I knew very well that after she had been with me she had to return to his bed. It may seem odd to you, perhaps even slightly twisted, but it was something we accepted without disgust, without even resentment. We cared for him, you see, both of us. It was almost for him that we were trying... Well, no, not actually trying but we were at least willing to let it happen. And we were mortally afraid of the risk of his committing suicide even while we were continuing our love affair.

'When he heard of the child he became wildly excited. I don't suppose you can imagine the Kilbaddy you know like that, hm? But suddenly everything he lived for took on more meaning. Everything he did had greater purpose. That alone delighted Kate. And it comforted me, please believe that, especially as my conscience was searing my soul like the flame of hell. I - am not a very good Catholic. I have never confessed to this particular sin. In a way I made my own penance. You see I knew that I could never claim the child. It was enough just to know it would be mine, however Kate represented it to Kilbaddy. We talked about that, of course, and agreed that she should just accept it as his. Her own happiness was an odd topsy-turvy double doubt and joy mixed.'

'And the gun? That's what you set out to tell me about.'

'Hm. Yes. Well, as soon as Kate suspected her pregnancy she told Kilbaddy because she knew how desperately he wanted it. But for a while she and I continued to "meet and marry" until about the fifth month. By then it was obvious that Kilbaddy was well on the way to recovery. He never did regress after that. By then I was also beginning to realise that the affair had to stop, if only for the sake of the child and its future. Kilbaddy was still not entirely secure and I shuddered to think how he would react if he discovered. Sooner or later he would, I felt, no matter how discreet we were. Kate and I agreed to stop. That was that. It was over - although spiritually it never did end, hasn't even now. In my heart Kate has never died. But we had no doubt that the decision to end physical relations at that point was right. Whatever the morality of any of the other actions. Whatever the pain of separation.'

'Leaving you to plunge into depression instead of Kilbaddy?'

'That's about it. Not immediately. About two months later. Early autumn it must have been. The pattern of my depression was less obvious then, but that particular bout was very bad, very deep and long. It wouldn't shift no matter how I scourged myself in private or tried to hide it from the others. In the end I fetched Kilbaddy's gun one day while he was at market. I told Kate I was going to shoot pigeons. She knew I often did. But she must have doubted me because when Kilbaddy came home she sent him after me.'

'She knew where you'd be?'

'Oh yes, she knew. It was where we usually met, almost always met. It's a lovely place, isn't it? A place of peace. A sanctuary.'

197

'Kit loves it too. She's been going up there quite a bit this last fortnight.' I scowled to combat the sudden rush of emotion his words produced. He must have misunderstood my expression because he sat forward again.

'Bruno, she was hurting abominably. It was the only place where she could find any comfort at all after she was banned from looking after Kilbaddy.'

'Yes.' I put out my hand blindly. 'Yes, I wasn't doubting that. If she found peace there I'm glad. - Kate would be too.'

'Sorry, I thought... Oh, never mind. What about the gun? Kate didn't tell Kilbaddy the truth before she sent him up, did she?'

'I've no idea. I doubt it, but I didn't know then and I don't know now. I never dared to ask.'

'So what happened?'

'I saw him leave the farm and climb up by the burn exactly as you did yesterday. I realised instantly that Kate had sent him and I simply sat and waited. The gun was loaded and cocked and I was sitting with it between my knees. There were no fallen trees then so I was sitting on the big, flat stone by the burn side with the water just touching the toe of my boot. Kilbaddy came and looked down into my eyes to see what kind of condition I was in. As it happened I was just beginning to recover from the black bout. Since he was still alive he must have felt sure that at least I did not intended to shoot him, or not there and then. He had just given me a far better opportunity as he climbed the hill. Only - I didn't even know whether he knew that I might have a reason for wishing him dead. He reached for the barrel and pulled the gun out of my

198

hands. I made no attempt to prevent him, just held his eye.'

A half burnt log fell into the grate and I left Matthew to replace it before I continued. 'I had no idea whether he would shoot me, or shoot himself, or shoot both of us. There wasn't a vestige of expression in his face. And, do you know, I didn't care. I really didn't care what he chose to do. If he had chosen the second option I would have completed the job by making it the third. In the end he did none of them. He walked to the middle of the wood, broke the gun open and emptied out the cartridges. Then he took the thing by the barrel again. I remember he held it so tightly that his great knuckles stood out like white bone beneath the skin. He looked back at me for a moment then swung the stock with all his might against a tree trunk, smashing it to matchwood. Since the blow bent the barrel as well it was rendered quite useless.' I closed my eyes as the scene returned in vivid detail. For some reason the strongest memory was the smell of thyme crushed beneath his feet. Ever since then the smell has been a warning, like a sniff of hell.

'He - threw the thing down and came back to me and said, 'We'll nae bother wi' guns aboot the place again, eh? We dinna want Kate to be upset, nae wi' the bairn sae near.' When I - began to weep he got down on his knees in the long grass beside the burn and just held me.' I laughed weakly, miserably. 'How's that for a twist in the tale? I know he never went back to that glade while Kate was alive.'

199

In the morning my head was anxious to split in two and spill out its loathsome contents. Before I reached the bedroom door it opened. Matthew entered with a glass of water and a packet of pain-killers.

'Oh, my. Did you put me to bed?'

'I did. I hope you don't mind but I used your sofa-bed as well.' Later, when I was feeling more sane, he suggested taking me down to see Kilbaddy in the afternoon. 'If you feel more like it now?'

'After the catharsis of confession? I'm sorry, my boy...'

'Don't go apologising,' he said irritably. 'Are you coming?'

The old man was again drugged, but not as heavily as before. He recognised me, though not Matthew, and held out his hand. I took it and sat on the edge of his bed.

'Bruno, lad, ye should tell Kathy.' It was shockingly apposite and I heard Matthew draw in his breath. 'She should ken jist how much we care.'

'She does know. She always has,' I insisted, willing him to believe. 'Are you remembering she'll be back the day after tomorrow? You'll be looking forward to that, hm?'

'You an' a'. She's yours as weel as mine, Bruno lad.'

'Of course she is. She's ours and she's very, very precious.' From there he began to ramble. The only other relevant comment from him was an odd one, right at the end of the visit.

'The lassie'll be awa' hame, eh? The young quine? Will she be back, d'ye think?'

'Could he be right?' Matthew asked on the way home. 'Is it possible that she couldn't stand the misery any more and wanted to go home to her mother?'

'Not realising Kathy was in fact on her way here?' It was a possibility both of us could tolerate more easily than any other. When we searched for her passport we failed to find it. Neither of us made any further comment.

'I've been thinking, Bruno,' Matthew said tentatively, 'about the way Kilbaddy keeps returning to the business of telling Kathy. At first I thought he meant you, but - I think he knows perfectly well whose child she is. And I think he realises somewhere in his muddled mind that it would be almost impossible for you to tell Kathy yourself. Not after all this time. Not after letting her believe something different all through her childhood. It just might come better from somebody else, somebody outside the situation.'

'Certainly somebody will have to tell her.'

'And before she visits him otherwise he'll say something himself.'

When Kathy arrived, however, I knew immediately that there was no need to tell her anything. She had insisted that she wanted to complete the journey alone, vehemently forbidding me to meet her at the airport for which I was cravenly grateful. As a result, the first I saw of her was when she came to find me, striding up towards the farm from the cottage, her long legs covering the ground with a familiar purposeful ease which made my heart stand still. For a moment I thought it was Katherine but, when the

201

amber setting sun drifted to the left behind her as she came aslant up the road, I saw that this girl wasn't dark but tawny, her hair burnished by the golden light of evening. Her entire outfit was tawny, with a smart tan jacket and boots and a tawny tweed skirt swinging about her knees.

When she saw me her head reared and her pace quickened to match my own. Within seconds I was running for the first time for years, reaching out to her in joyous yearning, eager to take my beloved daughter in my arms. She had been right, right for both us when she decreed a private greeting. We laughed and cried together there on the chilly hillside, our tears mingling as we stuttered out queer, broken words of welcome and regret, comfort and forgiveness, none of it making much sense but all of it meaning everything in the world

'Come home, dear,' I pressed at last, turning her downhill again. 'The fire is lit and the dinner in the oven.'

'Wonderful.' She sniffed hugely. 'Is Kit there? How is she? - Oh, blast, she's gone AWOL again, hasn't she?'

I felt wretched all of a sudden. 'I'm afraid so. We don't really know why. And we have no idea where.'

'Didn't she leave a note?' her mother demanded, angry that our reunion should be spoiled by an inconsiderate child. When I shook my head her crossness turned into dismay. 'That's not really like her, Bruno. Honestly. Even when she - well, when she defied me and went to look after her Dad she always rang me or wrote to me just to say things were okay. And all the time she was on her grand tour I was getting postcards from Auckland. They told me sweet nothing, of course, because she'd pre-written them and got somebody to post them at regular intervals just to stop me worrying too much. - It's no wonder the police couldn't find her.'

As I hefted her case from the doorstep I wondered how soon she intended to leave again. It felt disturbingly light.

'Is she still being sought by the police?'

'No, of course not. As soon as we knew she was safe and sound with you... You don't think Brian really shopped her, do you? He laid a charge because it was the only way he could get the police to take an interest in a missing person.'

'He didn't want the cycle then?'

'Well, I wouldn't say that but - ooh, lovely. Nobody can track down a good port like you do. - Look Bruno, Brian was worried sick about what his little sister was up to. So was Jock.' She rattled on. 'Oh, he's not so bad. On his feet again, though I've persuaded him to start looking for another job. I hate the idea of him clambering around on roofs again and maybe taking another tumble. As it is he can't hump heavy loads for months so... Anyway, to return to the bike. Neither of the boys has actually said so, but I think they were hurt that Kit got the bike and not either of them. Not because of its value, not even because it was a bike and bikes are meant for boys. They already knew she was a good mechanic. It was because it was their father's pride and joy and, well, it meant something.'

'Were they in touch with their father?'

203

'Not as far as I know. But I think there might have been brief meetings. They operated a conspiracy of silence for my sake, I suppose.'

'Did Katherine, er, Kit know?'

'No. I'm sure she didn't. It's Jock I think saw more of him. You see, Jock's a singer like his Dad was. Didn't Kit tell you? I think he's pretty good, too. Fortunately he doesn't drink, so I don't get too bothered when he sings round the clubs. Brian's not much good, but Kit is, when she tries. I expect she... What are you smiling at?'

'You. The way you are rushing through all your news as if...' I stopped short. Surely time was not that short? 'As if you were your daughter. She has the same rapid speech delivery as you have.'

'I always was a blether, as you never ceased to tell me.' She said that slowly. 'Bruno, we need to talk turkey. I can't stay long. I'm involved in preparing for a big conference at the end of April.'

'Conference?' I fought to keep the disappointment out of my voice.

'In Sydney. It's on international food trade agreements, including some with both Russia and Poland. I'm fairly high up the ladder now and it means I don't have the same freedom to tell them to get stuffed. They need my linguistic skills and they need the information I have stocked up in my head after a couple of years of reading documents.'

'Of course, dear. - I'm quite delighted to hear you have done so well.'

'Are you?' She looked at me anxiously.

Astonished I laughed, 'Of course. I've always known you have a fine mind. It's only right that you should use it for the good of others. I am very, very proud of you, my dear.'

'So you should be,' she said archly. 'You were the one who put my brain into gear and set it running. It really riled you that I upped and got married instead of going off to college, didn't it?'

'I was - a little disappointed, I admit.'

'Whereas Kilbaddy didn't really care. He would have been quite happy for me to be a contented little Hausfrau like my mother, wouldn't he?'

'Your mother was far more than that,' I said, unintentionally sharp. Kathy smiled, her mouth twisting sadly.

'But she was hardly an intellectual, was she?'

'No. Not that.' I was wary. 'Immensely practical. And sensitive and caring. Wise.'

'Kilbaddy wasn't an intellectual either, was he?' she persisted. 'Just - immensely practical. And sensitive and caring. Maybe not quite so wise but utterly reliable with a great knowledge of Mother Nature and her wily ways. I'm not denigrating any of those qualities, Bruno. Heaven knows I benefited beyond measure from them but... Well, isn't it time we faced the truth? I got my brains from you.' I closed my eyes for a moment. When I opened them again she was gazing at me in anxiety. 'Shouldn't I have said it? Is there any good reason for wanting to cover it up any longer?'

'No, my dear one. Not any more.'

'Not even for Kilbaddy?'

'He was always more of a father to you than I was and he knows that. He was a hundred times more capable of caring for a child and giving her a secure background and a sound grounding in human relating than I could ever hope to give. I realised that long before your mother died. A reclusive, blighted intellectual with no real heed of the hours and inclined to disastrous black moods was in no way fitted for fatherhood. Mind you, it was a painful process accepting that.'

'Does he know?' It piqued me slightly that she should accept my judgment of the relative values so automatically.

'I don't know. No, truly I don't know although recently he has said one or two things in his ravelling that suggest he might. If he does, I have no idea at which stage he discovered.'

'I suppose it's pretty nearly irrelevant,' she said glumly. 'Suppose we eat, then go and see him. I'm dreading the first meeting. Would your protégé up at the farm lend you wheels?'

Chapter Twelve

Kathy's meeting with Kilbaddy must have been just as painful as she feared. She went in alone leaving me to reflect that she had always done things that way, on her own with her tawny head held high. The more serious the challenge the higher she held it. That night it almost touched the ceiling. She stayed for twenty minutes then came out, her face bleached and lined.

'Do you have to go in?' she asked very quietly.

'No. Let's go home.' She wept on the way silently and privately in the dark, at one point stopping to wipe her eyes clear enough to enable her to drive. Back home I gave her a last port, hugged her and packed her off to bed before phoning Jock to tell him she had arrived safely. It was the first time I had heard his adult voice and was pleased to hear it was jaunty and attractively modulated. There was no trace of reserve or criticism in it.

'Tell her I've got a new job,' he added. 'She doesn't need to worry any more.' Before I could ask what it was he rang off cheerily.

'Gee whizz, Bruno!' I almost laughed at Kathy's use of the comic book phrase, making a note to keep its utterance as ammunition for the verbal sparring I knew would entertain us soon. 'Why didn't you wake me?'

'I tried. You snore abominably. Come and have a late lunch then we can...'

207

'My shout. I'm the visitor. We're going down to the village. Please? I want to visit my rose bush.' Her smile twisted. 'But if you'd rather I go alone I'll...'

'Of course I'll come. I often go down there, you know.'

'And up to Kate's Corner? Do you go up there?'

'Yes. I took Katherine once a little while ago. Matthew tells me she has been back rather often recently.'

'Good,' her mother nodded, her eyes suddenly full of tears. 'That's good.' She looked at my sombre expression. 'Don't you see? It means she'll come back. It's not dead, is it? My rose?' The expression in her voice was so exactly that of the anxious nine year old that it was my turn to blink.

'Wait and see,' I said, managing a smile. Since there was a W.R.I. sale of work being held that Saturday we ran into dozens of people who knew Kathy. Every one of them greeted her with surprised delight, telling her she hadn't changed a bit. It took her almost two hours to chatter her way along the street, past the post office, - which had survived, - and the school, - which had not and was now a house, with three more bungalows in the playground, - and up the kirk road past the manse to avoid the tightest of the throng by the village hall, past the old grey kirk itself, stark in its simplicity, and down to the kirkyard at the other end of the village. When they saw where we were heading my neighbours tactfully withdrew. The entire wall both to the north and the east of the corner by Kate's grave was embellished with a network of new shoots each sprouting tiny reddish green leaves.

'I can hardly believe it! Is it the same one? Spread all that far?'

'The very same.'

'It must be the bonniest bush in the village. Appropriate, I suppose. It can't be natural, surely. Not the way it grows with so much discipline.' She poked about among the stems. 'Somebody's pruned it. And there are staples in the wall. Somebody must be looking after it.' She looked at me, realised it was completely beyond my competence and shook her head, her face reflecting wonder.

The gate creaked as we pushed it open and went in. 'I can't really remember Mam, you know. That hurts a bit.'

'Nothing at all?'

'I remember picnics. Up in the wood. I remember her looking pretty with the sun behind her making her hair shine in a circle like a halo. But I can't quite catch her face, except for once. She's looking at you and laughing. - It's always you I remember up there. Never Kilbaddy.' She looked at me. 'Is that how it was?'

'Yes.' I was silent, debating whether I should say more. You think I should, Kate? 'We always told him we were going there. In fact we always invited him, but he never came. It was as if he... Well, I think he was giving me that time to be with you both without his interference. Whether that was a deliberate act done out of knowledge or just an instinctive kindness because I would never have any other family I don't suppose we'll ever know.'

'Either way it was pretty wonderful, wasn't it?' she said sadly. 'I wish... Oh, what's the use?' She gesticulated fiercely at the grey sky before turning away to walk among the other gravestones, leaving me by Kate's. Within a few minutes she came back to slip her arm through mine.

'I'm sorry. There's nobody to talk to down under. Not anybody I can really share my inner thoughts with. I had for a year or two when I went to Al Anon, but that dealt only with the one specific problem. Kit told you?'

'She said a little.'

'Apart from that I've had to work like stink so I haven't had time to seek out any like minds. I've kind of got out of the habit of sharing my innermost thoughts. I've been so used to bottling everything up... It's not going to be that easy to rekindle our old open honesty.'

'It doesn't have to happen in five minutes, dearest.'

'Suppose not.' She began walking me along the inner path which took us all the way round the graveyard. 'If you must know, I wish... I wish that I'd come back sooner. Soon enough to make some contact with Kilbaddy at the very least.'

'You have, surely?'

'Nope.' She sniffed unhappily. 'He had no idea who I was last night. I don't think anything has ever hurt me as much as that. Not even Alistair's leaving, not even his death.'

I didn't dare probe there. 'He may recognise you yet.'

'Even so - it's so late. Oh, heck, why don't I just admit it? I should have come back twenty years ago.

At least for a visit. And I should have accepted every single suggestion you made for you to come to us. Accepted and be damned. It should have been worth the risk. Love will out, won't it? Wasn't that Mam's philosophy? Only, I suppose, it did out and... Oh, God, I'm maudlin.'

'No, dear. You are hurting. And still very tired. Let's go home again.'

Once she had recovered from her jet-lag Kathy and I began to communicate properly, reminiscing, exchanging news of events in our discrete lives. It concerned me that I learned no more about her marriage and its difficulties but we returned swiftly to our old, masochistic entertainment of sharpening our wits on each other. Suddenly I was aware that we had never done so in Kilbaddy's hearing. It would have smashed the conspiracy completely. Had she sensed something even then?

'This is great,' she said to me at the end of one evening's sparring. 'You're as sharp as ever. I don't think I've met anybody else of your acumen in all my travels.'

'You have developed your own mind immensely. I really am glad that you are able to put it to good use.' She sat drowsing in the first silence of the evening. 'Do none of your children enjoy the dialectic art?'

'Haven't you tried Kit out?'

'No!' I was surprised. 'I was much more aware of her grandmother's qualities. She has a serenity about her which I find extremely comforting. And she's a good listener. To music, I mean.'

211

'Yes.' Kathy looked at me sideways. 'She's all of that. Jock is a happy-go-lucky character with no time for anything but straight conversation. And music, of course. And football and bikes and pals. He has a good enough brain but nothing like the others. It's Brian who is the real deep discussion merchant, when he's not down in the dumps.'

I sat up sharply. 'Tell me,' I said anxiously.

'Oh, I don't think he's depressive. Or not in quite the same way as you. But he's blooming frustrated.'

'Why?'

'Because he has a dashed good brain that's being badly underused.'

'In the surveyor's office? Is he still there?'

'Yes. He's no more than a glorified clerk and it's driving him mad, but he won't take the risk and try for something more ambitious. Instead he's slogging through evening classes to get himself further qualifications.' After a moment she added, a shade guiltily, 'You know he left school as soon as possible. I didn't want him to but at the time there was little I could do about it. Did Kit tell you?'

'An inkling. That your husband left home about that time leaving you in debt with three children to support.'

'Mm. Ah well, all that's water under the bridge. What it meant for Brian was goodbye to a college education he'd have sailed through. He left school with nothing but a teacher's recommendation expressing regret that he hadn't stayed to sit his exams. What good's that? Now he has a giant chip on his shoulder and won't even consider becoming a mature student although I could just about afford it

212

now.'

'Come now, he's not even old enough to be a mature student, if my calculation is right.'

'We know it's spot on,' she said darkly, the first oblique reference to the circumstances of her departure. Then she suddenly asked, 'You've no idea why Kit has lit out?'

'Not really.'

'And even if you had, you have no intention of elaborating. - You haven't changed a bit.' But her exasperation was not so great that it stopped her from the next move. She slipped to the floor before my chair, folded her arms on my knees and laid her head on top, turning it slightly to meet my fingers as they began to caress the brown gold tresses. Though the colour was more muted they were just as warm and heavy and silken as I remembered.

'I've missed you so much, Bruno,' she said sadly. 'I've hated the breach, every single minute of the whole twenty five years.'

I dared then. 'Why didn't you come back? You must know you would have been welcome.'

'I couldn't. Not once Brian was born. You see, he's very like you to look at. I know you think you're hidden behind a wall of plastic surgery but I'm perfectly certain that anybody who saw the pair of you side by side would instantly make the connection. It's in the bone structure, those high, handsome cheekbones. Alistair never gave it a thought but by the time Brian was six months old I knew for sure you were my father because his eyes were already the colour of yours. Mam's were blue like mine. Kilbaddy's were grey. So were Alistair's. So... If I

213

had brought the baby home Kilbaddy would have known at once. Everybody would have and...' She sighed. 'However much you both might love me, I knew you two were sort of permanent props to each other. I couldn't bear the thought of the pair of you falling out, not over me. Each other *was* really all either of you had.'

'We would have weathered it,' I dared.

'I thought perhaps you could. After all, in a way you were the winner. But I wasn't nearly so sure about Kilbaddy. Even if he wasn't my genetic father, he...' She lifted her head and examined my face, frowning in the intense way she had always had, as if trying to see inside my mind.

'He was in every other respect,' I helped her out. 'For what it is worth I think, *I think*, he has always known. But until you were gone he simply would not accept the truth. Whatever Kate said, if she said anything at all to him, he preferred to think of you as his child.'

'And when I did leave?'

'We had a bad patch. There was no point in telling you about it. But for several months we found each other's company very hard to tolerate. However, we persisted and gradually began to relax again into our old understanding. Now he is no longer around I miss him abominably.'

'I don't suppose you would consider coming back with me next week?'

'No, my dear. For Kilbaddy's sake. He can still communicate with me just a little. I thought he would have responded to you but since he hasn't that makes me the only link he has left with reality. As your Kit

214

puts it, I'm the only string he has to hold on to. And there's Katherine herself. If she does return I want to be here for her. She was very disturbed before she left.'

'If? You mean there's some doubt?'

I wished I had said less. 'Well, she did take her passport. She might be on her way back to New Zealand.'

She laid her head down again as I reached over and set my old radiogram going. 'Mm. It's as splendid as ever. Jock just wouldn't believe that an old thing like this could sound so good.' A few minutes later she asked drowsily, 'Am I hearing a touch of anger in you? With Kit, I mean?'

'Hm. I regret that she is not here to be with you.'

'Cautious, aren't you? What's gone wrong? You seemed to be getting on like a house on fire.'

'Fire burns. Oh, forgive me my dear. Katherine and I have had our ups and downs. Why she has taken herself off now I've no idea. Give her the benefit of one doubt. She didn't know you were coming so soon. Let's just leave it at that shall we? Tomorrow I shall take you up and introduce you to Matthew. He's been a singularly good friend and I am beginning to feel guilty at neglecting him.'

'Will you mind if I leave Bruno to show you round, Mrs. Sanderson?' he apologised with a polished politeness which I could see amused Kathy. 'I'm working without a man and I'm behind with the jobs.'

Matthew was cool in his greeting.

At first I thought he was cross with me again, then I realised he was simply shy, not at all sure how to handle this brilliant, beautiful woman with her sharp eye, sharp dress sense, exceedingly sharp wits and, on occasion, sharp tongue. All he could see of Katherine in her were the blue, blue eyes. Even the lashes were different, for Kathy had inherited Kate's dark-edged sleepy look.

'Sounds to me as if Holly's swinging it. Time you told him to get off his lazy backside. Even if he can't walk the fields I'm sure there are some jobs you could find for him.'

'He's coming back the week after next,' he replied frostily.

'Tom Allen said something about fences when I met him this morning,' I mentioned. He looked embarrassed. 'He wasn't complaining. He just asked if he could mend that one in the field where he's had the sheep. It's his fault he let them rampage over your land after all.'

I knew perfectly well that he had no wish to impose any more on his neighbours, especially the Allens. Lewis was never mentioned except for one harrowing day when George Patterson came over and announced maliciously that he had had a phone call from someone in Moffat. Apparently this someone had mentioned that he had seen Lewis with a beautiful lady friend. George pointed out that Moffat wasn't far from Gretna Green, was it? And had we noticed who else was missing from the parish?

I glanced at Kathy and waited.

216

'It's up to him to put up a fence that's fit to keep the dodgy blighters in,' Kathy said firmly. 'He knows fine that hill sheep are expert escapologists. I'll just go over and remind him.' It was just what I expected of her and I grinned at the boy's horror. When he saw me he grimaced, barely appeased.

'You're being an old devil again, Bruno. I ought to turn the stirks into your garden one day.'

'They'd starve.' Kathy's taunt was withering. She sounded quite like Kit. 'He's no better a gardener than he ever was. By the look of your demesne it looks as if his grand-daughter takes after him.' As he drew in his breath she cocked a frank eyebrow at him and turned towards the front door. 'You're sure you don't mind me tramping all over the house? It is yours after all.'

'Go ahead,' he said weakly. Then as she disappeared he turned to me almost gasping. 'Phew, that's quite a lady! - You might have warned me you'd told her.'

'She told me,' I admitted, bemused. 'Yes, she's quite a lady.'

'No news?'

'No news. Do you think I wouldn't have told you, my boy?'

A couple of days later there was news. Odd news. Brian telephoned. 'Your mother is down at the hospital.'

'Oh. Well, could you tell her that Kit has phoned? I've no idea where she was, somewhere with traffic in the background but she seemed to want Jock and myself to go to Scotland. Do you know why?'

'To come here you mean?'

'I think so. She spoke to Jock and he's as clear as mud about what she wanted. Just something about time running out.' I thought for a moment.

'All I can think of is that she wants you to come and see Kilbaddy before...' How could I explain this?

'Is he dying?'

'Not exactly. I don't know how much you have been told but Kilbaddy is unlikely to leave hospital again. It isn't his physical condition which is concerning. I'm afraid it's his mind which is dying. I fancy your sister wants you to come and try to make contact with him before it goes completely.'

It was his turn to think. 'Do you think that's wise?'

'Wise?'

'I mean - won't a crowd of strangers bursting in on him just make things worse? My mother said he didn't even recognise her.'

'He didn't at first. But there have been brief moments when he most definitely has known her. And moments when he remembers your sister.'

'She hasn't come back then?'

'No, not yet.'

'Will you let us know if and when she does, please?' The request was stiff with animosity but also real concern.

'Of course I shall, immediately. Hm.' I gathered my thoughts. 'Will you be at home for the next hour?'

'I can be,' he said cautiously.

'Then I shall call you back.' I gave him no time to argue. Forty minutes later I had finished my business.

'Brian? Ah, good. Now I want you to listen carefully. Have you a pencil to hand? Take note of

218

this number.' I gave him the name of a bank in Wellington and an account number lodged at it. 'That account is in your mother's name, her married name. The manager has now been instructed to permit you and your brother to draw from it up to a certain limit, your sister too if she returns. The limit will easily cover travel costs if you should decide to come to Scotland. There will be no need for you to use your own funds or your mother's from elsewhere.' I ignored his attempts to break in. 'It's something I offered to do years ago but your mother refused. I think it's time for you to make the decision for yourself.' I added emphatically, 'If it's your mother's tender conscience you are worrying about, don't worry. I'll handle her.'

Less than fortuitously, Kathy chose that moment to make her presence known behind me. 'And Brian, if the limits I have suggested to the bank manager prove too tight, please let me know and I shall have them extended, provided I deem the need reasonable. - Brian? Are you still there?'

'Yes.' The voice was stone cold. 'I would like to speak to my mother. Is she there?' Without a word I handed the phone to Kathy, daring her with my eyes to countermand my instructions.

'Bossy old blighter, isn't he?' was her weak comment to her son. 'I missed half of what was said so I'd be grateful if you'd repeat it.' As he did so I laid my hand on her arm, partly in warning, partly in pure, desperate pleading. 'Well, if that's what he wants we might as well let it ride. - I don't know. I haven't seen her and I've no idea where she is. Nobody has. - That's up to you. If you want to come, come. It just might do the old man some good.' She looked at me slyly, recovering her acerbity. 'I'm certain sure it would do Bruno good.'

I took myself off to the kitchen, thoroughly annoyed with her as I had been on so many occasions in her childhood when she stepped just a little too far. And as always she crept in with a penitent expression and tapped at my arm until I turned and hugged her. Nothing more was said. Just like long ago.

For some reason I found sleep elusive that night, perhaps kept at bay by the gale thrashing among the trees at the side of the house. When I thought of Kate I realised that she had been absent since the night of my jumbled indiscretions to Matthew. Alarmed I became deeply afraid that I had driven her away, that she felt betrayed because I had shared our secrets with another. Oh, Kate, I was only trying to do what was best. Truly. He's a fine boy, and I wanted... Oh, if I'm honest I was drunk. But I wanted him to believe in you because you were Katherine's grandmother. It's so important to him that he should believe that she is good, and that she came of good. She is good, isn't she? And were we so very bad in what we did? Kathy doesn't seem to mind. Surely I don't need any more punishment, not at such a cost to that fine wee quine with the big bike. Kilbaddy misses her so much. Please, God, where is she? Out there in the storm somewhere?

It was Kathy who came to me, hearing me stumble around the living room. She didn't say anything, just came to me, alive and warm, and hugged me, rocking me as I had Katherine. When I had calmed down she

220

led me back to bed and said the only thing that was worth saying.

'Go to sleep, Bruno dear. It's going to be all right.' I was not coming out of a depression at that time, not a clinical one at any rate, but the simple words comforted me just as much as they had when she had used them long ago in similar circumstances. Her mother had used them too when I had most needed comfort and I often wondered if the tiny girl had overheard them and had repeated them instinctively when the need arose. She had always known when that was.

She kissed my brow and left me alone. But - not alone. Suddenly the comfort of Kate's presence was there again as I drifted off to sleep.

'Wake up, dullard! It's Saturday again. And there's a tree down across the main road.'

'I hope to heaven Katherine isn't coming that way,' I mumbled, feeling thoroughly thick-headed.

'What?' Kathy was startled. 'Is she coming?'

'Oh, - it's just a stray thought. She terrified me the way she talked of doing a ton on that dreadful machine of hers.'

'Humph. Me too! Come and have some breakfast and tell me what got into you last night.'

'No. I mean, I won't tell you. It's between me and your mother.'

'Oh. Sorry. Did you - sort it out?' she asked cautiously.

'Yes, dear. Much of it thanks to you.' I had never spoken like this to anyone before and I wondered if she might suspect my sanity.

221

'Good. I thought we could do some shopping for the freezer before we visit Kilbaddy.'

'Mm. We have been eating rather well.'

Before we left, however, Matthew came begging a cup of coffee. He looked tired and run down. It was the first time he had dared to drop in unasked since Kathy's arrival, although he had come a couple of times by arrangement and had been exceedingly careful not to stretch his welcome. I was amused that Kathy's intellect terrified him. He was just about to leave when a car drew up outside. The door banged and it drove off as quick footsteps marched to the cottage and straight in without a knock. When she opened the living room door Katherine stood and stared at all of us, one after the other, as we all stared at her. She was white and dishevelled although her hair had regained a little of its lustre. Her eyes came to rest on Kathy.

'Hi, Mum,' she said lamely.

'Hi.' Kathy's answer was wry and she let her eyes run over the jeans and leather jacket. The cycle boots she had exchanged for a shorter pair which looked new. Everything else was crumpled, dirty even, including the woollen shirt and the single pannier bag she had slung over her shoulder. She looked at me.

'You okay?' It was a ritual greeting between us.

'I'm fine.' I watched her turn to Matthew as he rose slowly to his feet, neither of them at all sure of the other's reactions.

'You look shattered.' Unfortunately in his nervousness he made it sound like an accusation and the Kit personality came surging to the fore.

'You bet I'm f... shattered!' Kathy gasped with

222

shock. 'So would you be if you'd spent the night on a filthy train with the bloody British army. Half of it was bloody drunk and half was bloody amorous and half of each half was f... both!' Kathy would have moved forward in her outrage but I reached out to put my hand on her arm. Katherine swung the pannier to her feet with a thump, glaring at Matthew who merely bent down and moved it to one side where nobody would trip over it.

'We were about to go and see Kilbaddy,' he said flatly. 'Do you want to come?'

'I've just been.' The change in her was so swift that it was almost uncanny. Still gazing at Matthew she began to tremble and her face crumpled. 'It was so awful!' A moment later she was crying in his arms, crying as if her heart would break. I wiped my hand over my mouth then jerked my head to Kathy to join me in the kitchen.

'Well, well, well,' she said quietly, shaken but nevertheless sharply attuned. 'I bet those big hands of his are useful for other purposes besides farming.'

When I said nothing she laughed, but very gently. 'Come on, they've had long enough.' Only a minute and a half. What was she afraid of? 'I haven't seen my daughter for over a year,' she pointed out then announced loudly, 'We're coming back.' Matthew was still holding the girl and he looked over her curly head at Kathy with a calm challenge in his eyes which made Kathy grin broadly.

'Well, have you found out where she's been?'

He put his lips to Katherine's hair and said nothing at first. Then it burst out of him. 'Where on earth have you been?'

223

'Poland,' she mumbled.

'Poland!' Kathy and I reacted with identical shock, all amusement gone.

'Poland? Why?' Matthew put a hand behind Katherine's head, lacing his fingers among the curls which needed a trim by her usual standards.

'I went to fetch something.'

'On the bike?'

'Yes.'

'Well, where is it?'

When she gave a huge sniff then turned to take the handkerchief I offered, Matthew finally persuaded himself to let her go. 'I've sold it. I said I was going to in my note, didn't I?' The rest of us looked at each other.

'What note?'

'The note I left on the mantle there.' She pointed to where I had a heavy brass candlestick sitting ready for the next power cut. 'Hell. - I did. Honestly I did. Oh hell,' she said in weary disgust.

'Never mind that now,' I soothed, wondering if I had crumpled it up and burned it, thinking in a drunken stupor that it was one of the notes I occasionally wrote to myself. 'You're exhausted. Why don't you get some sleep? You can tell us everything later.'

'Might make more sense then,' her mother agreed sardonically. I expected a revolt but Katherine headed for the bedroom without a backward glance.

'You, er…' Matthew began awkwardly, rubbing the side of his mouth with a crooked finger, 'are going to have sleeping problems. Would any or all of you like to come up to the farmhouse? There's plenty of everything in the way of bedding, thanks to Bruno's generosity. I'll put the heating on when I go back up.'

'Tell you what,' Kathy said. There was a warning glint in her eye. 'I'll come. In the meantime I think just Bruno and you should go and see Kilbaddy. I'll stay and look after...'

'That's enough, my girl' I growled. 'You and I are going to see Kilbaddy.' Matthew's face flamed as he understood Kathy's grin. She didn't stay to see any further response, but she might have been pleased at the smile of chagrin which I was left to face. He was quicker than she was crediting. For all his nervousness of her, he was certainly tougher and more determined too. I wondered if even Katherine realised that yet.

Chapter Thirteen

By the time Kathy and I had returned Matthew was back in the cottage kitchen after feeding his animals. Or so I presumed. Kathy kept her face straight and said nothing, merely glanced at the closed bedroom door. There was now a faint furrow of anxiety between her eyes but it might have been caused by driving into the sun.

'Kilbaddy remembers Kit all right,' she told Matthew. 'He said quite plainly that she'd been in. And he told me to see she had a wash before next time.' She was so mortified that we actually laughed. 'What's more the damned traffic has multiplied a hundred times in the last twenty years.'

'You should try some of the European cities,' Katherine said blearily from the doorway. 'I went round a square in the middle of Bremen three times before I could find a way out. Did he really remember?'

'Yes, love. He remembered.' Mother and daughter looked at each other for a few moments then moved forwards into each other's arms.

'But - he just didn't make any sense at all when I was there.' She hugged her mother so tightly for a moment that she made Kathy gasp.

'Apparently that's the drugs,' Kathy reassured, patting her shoulder. 'They're disorientating. That's why they stick to giving them at night and recommending visits in the afternoon or evening when his mind is clearer.'

'Can't you ask them not to drug him?' Katherine begged. 'They'd listen to you maybe.'

'I'm seeing a specialist on Tuesday.'

'Oh.' The girl disentangled herself and looked down ruefully at her disreputable clothing, now more rumpled than ever. 'That's three whole days.'

'Clever. For heaven's sake go and clean up. At least you won't fall asleep in the bath now.'

'Yes, Mum.' Matthew and I blinked at each other. It sounded too submissive to be true.

Just a few minutes later the telephone rang. Since Kathy was busy in the kitchen and I had my hands full of cutlery Matthew answered.

'Oh no!' His tone stilled us both and Kathy came to the doorway. He listened, his face showing growing concern. 'And when was this? Yes, of course. In the meantime is there anything else we can do? They have been warned, haven't they? And told about the complication? Yes. Thanks for letting us know.' With his eyes on his hands he laid the receiver back on its rest. In the silence I deposited the cutlery on the table with a small symphonic cacophony. None of us wanted to speak.

'What complication?' I asked eventually seeing that Kathy's face had grown tight and drawn. 'I presume that was to tell us he has absconded again?'

It was to Kathy that Matthew elected to speak. 'I'm sorry, Mrs. Sanderson. The specialist was planning to tell you on Tuesday that they've isolated a heart complication in your - Kilbaddy. This time they're very worried about him being out wandering. They've made sure the police know that this time is different.' With touching gentleness he said again, 'I'm so sorry.'

227

Unable to reply she shrugged and took her emotions back to the kitchen to be alone.

'Hell, I'm sorry about that slip, Bruno.'

'She didn't notice. Who's going to tell Katherine?'

We simply looked at each other and waited for her to finish her bath. She sensed something the instant she entered, fresh and glowing with little curls clinging round her face and neck. She had chosen to wear a simple blue dress the exact colour of her eyes, surely to merit her mother's approval.

'Kilbaddy?' Her face fell as she turned to Matthew. He nodded, reaching out to grasp her upper arms to draw her closer to him. She was curiously subdued which puzzled me. 'Oh, well, I don't expect he'll be too long.' She glanced at the window. 'It's a lovely day, a real farmer's day so he shouldn't come to any harm.' By a common instinct we left it at that, praying Kathy would say nothing. 'And the longer he's away the more the drugs will wear off.' She patted on Matthew's chest then went to finish her self-improvement before lunch.

'You're daft, the pair of you,' Kathy scolded in resignation. 'She's bound to find out soon... Okay, I'll keep my mouth shut.' Then she blinked in mock astonishment as Katherine entered. 'My, what a transformation.'

'Bruno chose the dress. And paid for it.'

'Chalking up the debts, are you?' I was about to turn on Kathy but Katherine intervened.

'Not any more. I'm now in a position to pay them all back.' Her voice had at last regained the calmness reminiscent of Kate. 'And you mustn't worry about Kilbaddy, Mum. He always comes home again. He'll

228

be fine. Really he will.' She was willing us all to believe her.

She retained the soothing manner till well on in the afternoon. It comforted the rest of us as we made regular checks all around the farm. Matthew went about his jobs, meeting up with us several times to see if there was any news. Each time he found an opportunity to touch Katherine, her hand or arm or shoulder, just for a moment. And each time it happened the frown lines between Kathy's eyes deepened a fraction.

'Can't keep his hands off her can he?' she muttered to me. If she discovered the whole story she was not going to like it.

'She doesn't seem to mind.' My mild reply only made her narrow her eyes crossly. Katherine plainly did not mind but, on the other hand, she made no effort to either court the caresses or acknowledge them. Apart from moments of stress I had never seen her do so and she had never done so in Kilbaddy's presence. But neither had Matthew. I watched him closely the next time he joined us and saw that his eyes flickered first to Kathy, not Katherine and there was a challenge in them. Beyond question he had sensed her disquiet and was refusing to pander to it. Or was it something even more deliberate? The imp in me began to look forward to the moment when the buttons came off the foils. I began to wonder if the two of them were more evenly matched than either realised.

'Bruno,' Katherine broke into my thoughts, 'you know how Kilbaddy always seems to be tuned in to whatever is going on at the farm? What would you

229

expect him to be doing on a day like this? I mean in the middle of April?'

'Hm. Well, he'd have finished the bulk of the sowing. He'd probably have got rid of any sheep he was over-wintering. The rasps would be pruned weeks ago and the first of the calves would be coming. Hm. - Matthew? What are you going to do next week?'

'Check all the fences and hedges then start on fertilising if the weather's right.'

'So he could go anywhere,' Katherine murmured glancing at her watch. 'It's getting a bit late.'

'You stay here,' Matthew interrupted. 'I'll do the rounds and come straight back.'

'Don't forget...' She broke off and looked at her mother then at me. 'There's the little wood up the burn. Will you have time?'

'There's a full moon,' I murmured to him.

'Yes, and it's early. Don't worry, Kit, I'll check every inch of the way.' This time he put his arm round her shoulders and gave her a swift hug. 'You go round the farm again.' A moment later he turned at the gate. 'Have you tried the house?'

'Oh God! We are fools!' There was so much relief in Kathy's voice that at last Katherine picked up the fierce anxiety we had been trying to hide. Again it was to Matthew she turned, not touching, just looking, her blue eyes begging silently to be told. With infinite gentleness Matthew explained and Kathy delayed her search for long enough to watch the girl step into his arms for a few moments of comfort.

'Go and help your mother search the house,' he murmured. 'If he's there, use the gong to fetch me back.' It remained silent. There was nobody in the

230

house, nor in the steading when we searched one last time before nightfall, or anywhere in the fields, or on the plantation, or among the rows of raspberries. In growing panic Katherine searched up and down every single avenue checking the base of each stool and all along the maturing hedge planted for shelter around the entire planting. Matthew trudged back almost two hours later to say he had covered every possible route to and from Kate's Corner.

'The cemetery!' Katherine cried suddenly, giving him no time to sit down. 'Grandmother's grave. The rosebush!'

'Come on then.' He led the way to the land-rover, looking over his shoulder at Kathy. 'We'll check along the roads while we're at it. Could you phone the hospital and the police again, Mrs. Sanderson? Bruno, do you mind going up to the farmhouse again? At this time of night he's more likely to head for there than anywhere else.'

It was nearly ten before we all sat down to eat, in the farmhouse because that was where Kilbaddy would come if he came at all. We were all beginning to doubt that.

'I'm sorry,' Katherine apologised. 'Even best steak tastes like cardboard tonight. Who's having a bed here?'

Matthew looked at Kathy.

'Doesn't matter to me. Kit if you like,' Kathy shrugged, too dispirited to fight for the moment. Matthew was not.

'Not without a chaperone,' he said quietly taking a pile of dirty dishes from her. When Kathy's eyes widened I thought, one up to you, my boy.

231

'Will you two blighters stop fighting over me like a dog over a bone!' The sharpness indicated Kit in ascendancy. 'This bone has a mind of its own.'

'In that case would it kindly make up its mind to give a bit more help with clearing the table,' her mother interrupted.

'I did the cooking,' Kit flashed back. 'Cooks don't wash up.'

'They do when I'm around or haven't you noticed?'

'That's enough, the pair of you!' I snapped.

'You could all stay,' Matthew broke in quietly. 'I made up all the beds while Kit was sleeping this morning.' A second telling point, but that one had Kathy gritting her teeth. She recognised a smokescreen when she heard one.

'I'll stay in the cottage,' I proposed quickly, 'just in case he comes there, or in case someone rings.' That was the decision made.

I don't suppose any one of them slept any better than I did. At least I had Kate to share my fretting. The sky had hardly lightened when there was a tap on the door and Katherine walked in, dressed in boots and jeans and a big jersey of Matthew's.

'I thought you'd be awake,' she said flatly, coming straight to me for a hug. 'Is it too early to phone the hospital?'

'They must have somebody on duty.' We tried, and we tried the police. The people who answered were kindness personified but for once no news was the worst there was.

'He's going to die, isn't he,' she said quietly, her face drawn, 'after being out all night? It's still

232

blooming chilly.'

'He's a tough old bird,' I said firmly. 'Look what he has weathered in the last year.'

'That was before this new heart problem.'

'Who said it's new? It's only just been pin-pointed but he could have had it for years.' She looked at me wanly. 'Does Matthew know you're here?'

'He will when he reads the note on the kettle!' she snapped and I realised I had trespassed. 'What the hell have you been telling Mum about us?'

'Not a thing.'

'Then why's she behaving as if I'm a bitch on heat?'

'You're exaggerating. She is simply curious.'

'Curious my... Oh, Bruno,' she wailed and came back to be hugged again. 'I can be so blooming awful when I flip.'

'Don't fret, my dear. I know it's a blood-letting to relieve an otherwise intolerable pressure. It might be better if you can confine it to me and in private. Your mother is suffering at least as much and there's no sense in making it worse for her.'

'It's not fair on you,' she moaned.

'We'll survive. Now, I want to get up and start searching again.'

'I've been round the steading already...' She jerked round as the telephone rang and had grabbed it before it could ring again.

'Yes? - Oh, Mum, you're exasperating! Where the hell did you think I was? Bouncing with Matthew? Oh, b... off!' I pulled the instrument angrily from her hand.

'Kathy?

'What in heaven's name has got into her, Bruno?'

233

She sounded completely bewildered. 'I phoned to tell you that they've found Kilbaddy but she didn't give me the chance...'

'They've found him? How is he?' Katherine's hands flew to her face in shame and horror.

'Suffering slightly from exposure but otherwise okay. I - tried to persuade them not to use the same drugs. Even better to give him none at all but I'm not sure if they cottoned on. Will you tell Kit I tried?'

'Yes, dear. And be patient with her, dear. She didn't mean any of what she said.'

'Oh didn't she just. Okay, okay, I'll defer explanations. I'm going back to bed.'

'Maybe you'll sleep this time, hm?' I laid the phone down. 'Now, my dear...'

'I'll go and make my peace. Right now.'

'No. Just go to bed and forget it. She knows you're with me.'

'They've used different medication this time,' I told a disgruntled Matthew when he brought Kathy down some hours later. 'But they don't want us visiting today.'

'In that case I'd like to use the land-rover. Kit, do you want to come to Kingussie with me?' His voice was cool.

'Why?'

'To look at a dog.'

'What the heck for?'

'You frustrating woman! You were the one who said a farmer without a dog was as much use as a doctor without a stethoscope. I'll go alone.'

No...' Katherine's own ill temper began to waver.

'I'm sorry. It's just that - does it have to be today?'

'The wheels are free today,' he pointed out. 'Tomorrow you'll want them to go to the hospital.'

'What's wrong with taxis?' Kathy interjected, intrigued by the charge in the air between the two young people. They ignored her.

'But what if - something happens?' Katherine asked Matthew. 'If his heart gets worse? If...'

'Okay,' he capitulated although not as graciously as usual, 'we can go another day.'

'I've only got a few more days,' Kathy announced apropos nothing. Katherine whirled, her face filled with dismay.

'Aw, Mum! Why?' When her mother explained, the girl stood glancing from her mother to her lover, a picture of confusion and conflict.

'I am coming back again,' Kathy said quietly. 'And I didn't come to haul you home against your will, you know.'

'Oh.' She stood swallowing hard. Glancing again at Matthew's grim face she flopped on to the floor by the fire and stared fiercely at her hands. When Matthew moved to leave she said loudly, 'I'll stay.' More softly she added, speaking to him although looking at Kathy, then me, 'For Kilbaddy. He might need me yet.' She bounced to her feet again and began pleading, 'Oh, why can't we try just once more? He wouldn't be trying to get out of that place if he didn't want to be at home pretty desperately, would he? Oh, please! Please, Mum, will you ask them on Tuesday?'

'But Kit,' her mother shook her head, by now badly off balance, 'it's not our house any more, love. We can't...'

235

'He would be more than welcome, Mrs. Sanderson,' Matthew butted in, 'but I don't think the doctors will consider it for a moment.' Katherine took it to be a refusal, a rebuff, and simply turned and left the room, closing the door quietly behind her. Matthew looked at me. 'Would they?'

'We could always ask.'

'What's with you two?' Kathy hissed in anxious frustration. 'Why are you pandering to her like this? You know it isn't on. You know she's acting like a child. And a pretty mixed up, fanciful child at that.'

'Matthew,' I sighed. 'I think you should go and get your dog. Let me discuss this with Kathy.'

'Okay. But I really meant it. If you can swing it, and if you think it's right for the old man, I'd be more than willing to have him back in the farmhouse.' Looking thoroughly miserable he left then.

'A spat, I wonder?' murmured Kathy.

'You must not be offended by what I'm going to say, dear, but you are quite wrong about Katherine. She is deeply distressed about Kilbaddy. In some ways she has been able to understand him better than all the rest of us together.'

'Kate-like?' It was barely sarcastic.

'If you like. Whatever she was when you last saw her in New Zealand she is certainly no child now. I told you that she had been playing the part of Kate as well as her own self during the past months. It has taken a very heavy toll on her. From the way she behaved a few minutes ago I suspect she is still in touch with what Kilbaddy wants.'

She said slowly, 'I don't doubt that. What concerns me is the sheer impracticability of her suggestion. Crazy she might be but it just isn't like her to lose touch with reality. She must know things have gone far too far for what she's suggesting.'

'She nursed her father as he died,' I reminded her. It silenced her completely which was perhaps as well for Katherine returned to the room, subdued and dressed in warm trousers and jersey.

'Mum, would you mind if I did go with Matthew after all?'

'To work on him?' Kathy asked sharply. 'Your idea's daft, Kit, and you know it.'

Katherine shrugged unhappily. 'I won't say a word to him about Kilbaddy if that's what you want. There are other things that need saying.' She looked at me darkly. 'Bruno's got his clam look about him so he's not going to tell me.'

'Tell you what?' her mother demanded.

'Whatever evil imaginings about me are rotting their suspicious brains.' I remained silent and she glared at me. 'I'll tell you about Poland when I get back. In the meantime you'd better have this.' She handed me a roll of bank notes. 'With interest. You can count them.'

I took them silently and placed them straight into my desk still rolled, ignoring Kathy's stare. 'I'll telephone Matthew and tell him you've changed your mind. Don't worry, I won't let him back down. Have you quarreled?'

'No,' she said uncertainly. 'I - don't quite understand what's happened. When I walked in yesterday he, well, kept touching me as if he was glad I was back. But the minute we were alone he was as cold as charity and didn't want to be within a mile of me.'

'Does it matter?' I asked.

After long moments turning over the implications behind both question and answer she said steadily, 'Yes. It matters.' After a short silence I phoned Matthew.

'Kit,' Kathy said, more gently than I had ever heard her speak, 'think, love. It has to matter to him too.'

'I know,' the girl said quietly. 'Otherwise it would be a recipe for disaster. And - I know it has to come from him.'

'I have something to say, too, my dear,' I interrupted. 'I was the one who doubted you while you were away, not Matthew. He wouldn't budge in his faith.'

'Well what the hell's wrong with him now?' As a spurt of Kit-like anger it was heart-breaking in its weakness.

'Hm. I think the one thing which really shook him was that you left with Lewis Allen.' She looked frankly bewildered.

'I was just giving him a lift to Moffat on the back of the bike.'

'Moffat?'

'It's off the A 74.'

'I know that, but - why?'

'He was going to navigate for some woman friend in a rally. And then he was picking up a car for

238

somebody at, um, is there a place called Bathgate?'

'There is.' In spite of myself the sigh of relief was audible.

'What else needs explaining?'

'Sort it out with Matthew, my dear,' I grimaced. 'Then come back and scream at me if you wish.'

'I'd rather have your support over Kilbaddy.'

'Oh, Kit!' It was very near to a moan of pain from Kathy.

'Mum, please listen. Just for one minute. I know what I'm suggesting is way out, honest I do. But - oh, surely it isn't impossible? If we took him home I'd look after him. I'm sure he wouldn't be violent or afraid any more. He's...' She pulled down her lips to stop them trembling too much. 'He's got past that stage. I know he has. And - it wouldn't be for long, Mum.' Kathy stiffened. There was a compelling sadness about the girl's assertion. 'Not long at all. I don't know how I know. I just do inside me. Now I've sold the bike I can afford to hire a nurse if we can find a good one. Oh, Mum, please ask them on Tuesday? Try and make them understand that all he wants is to die at home. He knows it's near. That's why he's getting so distressed at being cut off from everything he knows.' It was Kathy who was in tears. Katherine stood frozen in composed desperation. 'Will you ask?'

'Yes, love, I'll ask.'

It was a silent, disturbingly withdrawn girl that Matthew carried away with him. Kathy and I sat thinking. Much later she asked the inevitable questions.

239

'It's none of my business whether they are lovers or not,' I answered smartly. 'Nor yours. Don't you remember the reply I was given twenty odd years ago? No doubt Kilbaddy had the same medicine.'

'Touché. Incidentally I've often wondered if you blamed yourself for what happened. You know, advising me to stay away from contraceptives. Did you think I'd obeyed and that was what landed me in trouble? I know fine you said it to try and make me stay away from sex rather than for ethical reasons. You're not that good a Catholic. Well, I didn't.'

'I know you didn't stay away from sex,' I dared.

'I didn't stay away from contraceptives either,' she said a trifle awkwardly. 'I just made a mess of counting. So you see it was Kilbaddy I obeyed, not you.'

'You seemed very confused about things around that time.'

'I'll say I was. Do you realise why? It was the first time in my life that I'd been aware of you and Kilbaddy being diametrically opposed to each other in the way you wanted to handle me. It was only when I had kids of my own that I realised what a wonderful job the two of you had done for me. It was no joke trying to keep an even keel without undermining Alistair in their eyes.' She chewed her lip. 'And I realised how blooming ungrateful I'd been.'

'Even allowing for the irregularity of your conception?'

'It made no difference,' she said quietly. 'To me you were both the most special people in the world. Finally tumbling to the truth didn't in fact change the facts which had always existed, including the

240

abundance of love and caring. I don't remember ever being surprised by the discovery. The only thing that kept me away - apart from Alistair's alcoholism - was that I didn't know whether Kilbaddy knew. I think he does, Bruno.'

'Yes, dear,' I said, sad because of the long exile Kathy had imposed on herself, 'I think he does.'

'I suppose I was giving myself a penance by staying away. I couldn't see myself as particularly loveable after the way I had behaved. Even if you were prepared to forgive and forget I couldn't swallow the shame of letting you both down so badly. On top of that Kilbaddy gave us the money to start up in N.Z. Did you know?'

'I guessed.'

'It got Alistair started in the garage in Palmerston North and things were okay at first. Now and then he would drink a bit too much, nearly always when he wasn't singing, but I wasn't really looking for trouble at that stage. Brian was a super baby, bright and lively and completely fascinating. I think the trouble began when Kilbaddy's cash began to run out and I realised that we had been living on that rather than on what Alistair was earning. The garage simply wasn't making much of a profit. Well, I waded in and took over the books, then the management of the workshop jobs. Immediately the profits began to improve - and Alistair began to drink a bit more. I didn't make the connection at the time.'

'What connection?'

'What do you think?'

'More spare money for his habit?'

'And?'

I frowned, almost afraid to voice my earlier fear. 'You mean he didn't like the fact that you managed things better than he did?'

'Spot on. And that, dear Bruno, was the trouble from start to finish. He simply couldn't wear having a wife who was more able than he was. He had charm, a good deal of musical talent, was a great guy in company - and more than enough intelligence to realise that he was a lousy manager. And I suppose he realised that I was miserable stuck at home with babies with no means of exercising my brain except by keeping him out of the red and out of the pub. He felt a failure, so he tried drowning the feeling. In the end he succeeded in a highly spectacular fashion.'

'Oh, my dear.'

'It's over, Bruno.' She laid her head on my shoulder. 'I do feel to blame though. In the first place I should have listened when you told me we were wrong for each other. I was most emphatically wrong for him, bad for him even. Secondly it took me far too long, years too long to tumble to the root of the trouble and by then things were too far gone for me to backtrack. We needed my salary just to survive. Thirdly, when it came to the last stage I hadn't the guts to face up to the challenge. My poor torn daughter had to do it instead. There's a hell of a lot more of Kate in her than there is in me.'

'You must have taught her a great deal of what makes her what she is.' She gave a strange, harsh laugh.

'The irony is that she probably learned much of her kindness from her father. Oh yes, when he was sober he was a surprisingly kind man. Forever doing people

242

favours, giving to charity, helping friends with loans then suffering torments when he realised that he had overdone it and his own wife and kids were obliged to do without. When he wasn't sober, of course, it was drinks all round. Every soak in town knew he was a soft touch. He soon saw the back of your trust fund for the kids. I'm sorry, Bruno. Somehow I couldn't bring myself to tell you why I didn't want any more gifts. When you opened that account for me he was genuinely cock-a-hoop. Thought it was the solution to all our problems and by that he didn't mean his drinking. He really did think it meant new clothes for me and the kids. A freezer that wouldn't break down. Our very first new carpet maybe.'

'Didn't it?'

'No,' she said gently. 'It meant another trip to the clinic and another go at AA and Al Anon. When you sent me that last cheque book, when I finally went to Wellington, I just - threw it on the fire. If he had got a hold of it or a note of the account details he'd have blown the lot in no time. And himself sky-high. When he realised what I'd done he went berserk.' Suddenly she stopped. Thus far and no farther. I knew my daughter even after all those years. I would hear no more. Instead she changed direction.

'What's this Matthew Grey really like?'

'Don't you like him?'

'Oh, don't be aggravating. Is he good for her?'

'I think so.'

'And is she good for him?' I was still for rather too long. 'Oh, God, not again.'

'I'm not sure yet,' I said cautiously. 'But don't underestimate Matthew. He's much tougher than you

243

are thinking. I hesitate because I feel their love affair has been developing under conditions of immense stress and I am not sure how either will react when the stress has been lifted. Your Kit has a streak of the wanderer in her, you must admit. She is very young yet and may not find it easy to settle down whereas Matthew needs a wife at his side right now.'

'Does it have to be Kit?'

'Well, I gather there was another girl several years ago. His mother hinted that he was badly bitten. But yes, I rather think it does have to be Kit for him. He's very much in love with her.'

'And Kit?'

'You know her better than I do.'

'And I'm just scraping the surface. Oh, let's forget it and go to evening service for the good of our souls. There's nothing much we can do about them or Kilbaddy except pray and hope to God there is a God. At least I'll meet half a dozen of the few religious apologists left in this old, grey land of the Puritans.'

Chapter Fourteen

'They're back,' Kathy announced as we returned. There was a light on in the farmhouse.

'Leave them to feed themselves.' It was after nine when Matthew brought Katherine back, by which time the furrows on Kathy's brow had almost met. They came in quietly holding hands. Their heads were held high but they were both tired and I sensed an indefinable strain.

'Did you buy?' I asked Matthew.

'Yes, a nice, little, white-faced collie. A bitch by the unlikely name of Jack the Lad.'

'Bruno,' Katherine came straight to the point. 'I really did leave a note. It said I was going to sell my bike and that I'd borrowed the cash to cover expenses. I'd have asked if you'd been here. Lewis told me the way to get the best price. After Kilbaddy went back to hospital I booked the bike into an auction down in England for last Friday. Then I had to advertise it in all the proper specialist mags to make sure all the right folk knew it was coming on to the market. Once I'd done that all I could do was wait so...' She shrugged.

'You went to Poland. I see now why you took the clothes you did.'

'Look,' Matthew said awkwardly, 'you don't want me around now. I'll just go and check that calving cow.'

'Please stay.' Katherine's voice was very small.

'But, darling,' he shook his head slowly, 'surely what you want to tell them is private? Whatever you found in Poland is nothing to do with me.'

'Please?' When he sighed and nodded she headed towards her room.

Matthew immediately turned to me. 'She's dreadfully withdrawn, Bruno. Even worse than she was before she left. Do you think we could bring Kilbaddy home? I'll chip in to hire help.'

'Will you?' I mocked. 'With what? Shirt buttons?'

'I'm sure Kindrum will wait for his money,' he snapped, very near the edge of his patience. 'For this he will.'

'Matthew, my boy, I know. Forgive me. And forgive Kathy for appearing to prevaricate this morning. She has already promised Katherine that she'll speak to the specialist about it. And you know very well we don't need anything more from you beyond your permission...'

'You've got it. You always had it.' The thread was one of defiance rather than anger. Kathy merely held out her hand.

'Thank you, Matthew,' she said quietly. 'That means a great deal to me.'

Carrying a battered envelope Katherine returned in time to see the handshake. She sat down on the carpet beside the low table I sometimes kept before the fire. Following her lead Kathy and I took the chairs on either side. Matthew stood for a few moments, looking down at the weary girl at his feet until she looked up.

'Are you sure?' he asked doubtfully.

'I'm sure. And Mum and Bruno won't mind.' He promptly sat down on the floor beside her, slipping his hand to her waist. For the first time she responded in public, leaning towards him slightly. I flicked a glance at Kathy. Both of us realised that the girl was yearning for his touch just as much as he yearned to caress her.

'I went to Treblinka. To fetch this.' She took a very small photograph from the envelope and laid it in front of me on the table. It was a cutting from a newspaper or leaflet and was spotted brown with age. 'I - stole it, I'm afraid. Well, borrowed it. From the archives they've built up on the victims.'

My hand trembled as I reached out for the scrap of paper. It showed a girl, a stiffly smiling girl with high cheek bones and hair cut so short that it gave the impression it had been pulled back into a plait at the back. I knew the hair would have been tawny gold and the eyes brown with flecks of green and yellow in them.

'She did die,' Katherine said hastily, to prevent me from even beginning to hope. 'And the other two. They died very soon after they were taken in. I hunted and hunted but I couldn't find out anything about your mother. I forgot to ask you her maiden name. Which sister is this?'

'Louise.'

'I wasn't sure if they'd got the right photo. When I asked about it the archivist told me that it had been handed in several years ago by a very old woman. He told me her name and I went to find her but she'd died. I eventually tracked down her grandson and he told me more. His grandfather had been some kind of kitchen orderly in the camp cooking for the officers.' She swallowed hard a couple of times and I noticed Matthew's fingers fondle her unobtrusively. 'You didn't tell me she was a musician too,' she finally burst out.

247

'A pianist,' I nodded.

'That's why she didn't die straight away. She was made to join a chamber music ensemble and had to entertain the officers. It's - oh, its so f... disgusting, isn't it? They spend all f... day doing despicable things, wiping out fellow human beings and then they come in and... and sit down and listen to music. It's like...' Matthew held her tightly to him till she recovered. 'Sorry. It just seems to debase the whole thing even more, doesn't it? Mozart and all his buddies sullied because they appealed to monstrous devils who made a hell on earth for millions.'

'Louise?' murmured Matthew to deflect her from her own horror.

'Yes.' She wiped her nose with the back of her hand. 'I gather she stuck it for about nineteen months playing at after dinner concerts in the officers' mess. Well, one day there were visitors, some foreign deputation. I couldn't find out exactly who, some charity I think, but she must have thought there was a chance that the foreigners were in the dark about what was going on. So instead of sitting down and playing Louise got up on her hind legs and told them. Just flipped and let fly.' She palmed more tears away. 'I can understand that all right. She told the visitors where to look for the evidence. Apparently everybody was so surprised and she spoke so quickly that she managed to get a whole lot of damaging evidence out before she was shunted off. She - went to the gas chamber the very next day.'

When I was able I murmured, 'With her head held high I should imagine.' Kathy was locked in her own silent shock.

'Anyway, this lad from the kitchens was so impressed with what she did that he snaffled the programme - and that's where the photo came from. It's been hidden among his own family photos all these years.'

'You said you went to fetch it. That implies...'

'Yes. I first saw it last year. I knew your name, of course, and naturally when I was coming through Poland I went to try and find out anything I could about you. I started with your father. Mum had said something about him being shot by the Russians but his name wasn't in the memorial role. At least I couldn't find it when I looked last year. I - didn't want to upset you by telling you that. But last week I went to the local government department and a woman took me back. I'd looked on the main list but she pointed to the top. Or second top. He was the second in command. And he had more decorations listed after his name than anybody else in the whole blooming tome, not counting his titles. You didn't tell me about that either.'

'Hm. It isn't easy being the son and heir of a hero.'

'Come off it,' Kathy broke in swiftly. 'You have medals from three different countries yourself so...'

'What made you go back to Poland?' I asked the girl. She looked at me soberly - and I wondered why I had been so foolish for so long.

'When I saw the picture last year it rang a bell. A faint one. I just thought Mum must have had a photo somewhere.'

She dropped her gaze to the envelope in her hands and we waited. Eventually, when Matthew again tightened his fingers on her waist to encourage her, she took out another item, this time a photograph entirely familiar to me.

'Remember that old box of photos we found when we cleared out the top storey? Dumped on the stair? I found this in it,' she mumbled. She looked at it, glanced at Kathy, and laid it down beside the cutting. The two faces showed an unmistakable family likeness.

'Your mother would have been about thirteen then,' I said quietly.

'I'd never seen her hair pulled back off her face. But...'

'When you saw this you realised why the other picture had caught your attention.'

'Mm.'

'When did you realise this, my dear?'

'Oh, middle of January I suppose. I didn't really have time to look through the box till after Matthew's Mum and Dad left.'

Matthew looked at me, startled. 'That fits.'

'It does indeed,' I agreed then turned to explain it to Kathy. 'That's just the time when the relationship between Kilbaddy and Katherine began to fall apart.' Katherine gave a loud sniff. 'Oh, my dear child, don't blame yourself for that. Of course you were confused.

'I couldn't help it,' she pleaded. 'On top of everything else I - just seized up emotionally. I felt so cold. Everything wasn't what I had thought it was. My grandfather was suddenly not my grandfather. And you were, and...'

'And now?'

She leaned forward holding both hands for me to take. 'It's just the same really. Now I've had time to straighten out my thoughts. Knowing or not knowing makes no difference to the real relationships, does it? We still love and care in exactly the same way. Only… Oh, Bruno, I didn't care enough, did I? Not then, just when he needed me most of all.'

'Now, now, that's nonsense.'

'I don't think it would have made the slightest difference,' Matthew confirmed. 'Nothing you could do would have stopped Kilbaddy getting worse.'

'Not even slowed it down? If I hadn't been so - blooming wrapped up in ridiculous feelings of being betrayed? And my Mum being a bastard and maybe not even knowing it?'

'You do talk rot,' her mother said acidly. This time we all knew she was trying to bring us down to a less emotional plain. 'Where's the port bottle, Bruno?' That also dealt neatly with any impending query about how her daughter might wish to address me.

'Katherine, my dear,' I asked a little later, 'it isn't guilt which is prompting you to want Kilbaddy home?'

'No. Not at all. I'm not that far through.'

'Then why?' Matthew's concern told us that she had kept her word and not discussed the matter with him.

'He just wants to die at home,' she said wearily. 'And I want it for him. Awfully.' He sighed and looked at Kathy and me.

'Then that's the way it'll be,' he said firmly. He stood up pulling, her to her feet after him. 'On condition that you spend the next couple of days resting all you can. Right now you're not fit to look

251

after a flea.'

'Mm.' Without thinking she tottered off to the bedroom, all thought of sleeping up at the farm gone from her head.

'Humph.' Kathy eyed Matthew. 'Do I need a duenna?'

'Not if you feel you can trust me, Mrs. Sanderson. You are welcome to come and go as you please.' Yes, my boy. Another point to you, if either of you is aware of it.

Katherine had her wish. Matthew and I brought Kilbaddy home to her on Tuesday. The rain had eased off and the evening smell from early grasses drifted into the big hall with us, mingling with wood smoke from the drawing-room fire Katherine had lit and the aroma of baking Kathy was creating in the kitchen. Kathy alone was unaware of the stark change in the old man's build since last he had stood in the lovely room. He was even thinner than when Katherine had first arrived and his skin had a bluish tinge which made him seem aged.

'Grandad,' the girl sighed, going to him with no inhibitions whatsoever and slipping her arms round his waist. 'I'm so glad you're back.'

'Aye,' he agreed, accepting the hug as his due. 'Six years is ower long for ony man to be awa. Ye've done a grand job here, Kate. A grand job.' With a smile she led him to his chair and he sat down and fell asleep almost instantly.

'Thanks, everyone,' she said softly, content at last.

This time her task was well nigh impossible. Try as she might she could not persuade him to eat more than a few mouthfuls at a time, though he did eat more often. Mercifully he slept well at night entirely free from drugs although perhaps the hospital regime had established a habit. I took the little room next to his, since night had less to do with sleep for me than the others. The expected nurse failed to materialise but we realised that we could manage after all.

'Better than before,' Matthew told Kathy. 'Both of them are so much more placid. And Kit's not tearing herself to bits to get decorating done as well.'

'That won't last long,' her mother warned soberly. 'She's hopeless at being idle. And at leaving jobs half finished.' The corridors were as dismal as ever, I remembered, and she had already mentioned pots of white paint and sunshine yellow paper.

'And I'm not depressed,' I commented. That was tempting providence but at least it was true for the time being. Kathy looked sideways at me, beginning to appreciate just how low an ebb we had reached. This last lap was turning out to be so entirely different that I didn't even try to explain it to her. There was a new calmness in the house, a quiet peace which seemed to flow from Katherine as we went about the business of running the household. By the time Kathy had to leave she could see that her daughter really was a capable, caring young woman, that the child, Kit, was being left ever farther behind.

'I must admit,' she admitted as I sent her off at the station on the first leg of her journey, 'I feel marginally happier about leaving than I would have been if Dad had still been in hospital. She's certainly got a good routine up and running in double quick time. But I'm glad I'm coming back soon.'

'She's a fine, fine girl, my dear.'

'Er, she and Matthew work well together. I mean they - make a pretty good team.' I felt my mouth twitch.

'They do, don't they.' Since the tiny frown was back I risked an indiscretion to reassure her. 'They've been talking about the future.'

'What future? Together?'

'That was the drift, I think. But I had a notion Matthew was trying to extract a condition.'

'A what? What kind of condition? What kind of a man would...?'

'Now, now!' I glanced at the people who had turned at her shout of outrage. 'He wants her to go back to finish college first.' Her mouth opened then closed again.

'Oh. Oh!'

'Hm. Not such a bad lad, is he?'

'Well - maybe not. But I have a notion that the minute I'm gone he'll be in her bed. Especially with you up the back stairs.'

'Have you?'

'Yes.' She poked me gently in the chest. 'And so have you so don't play so innocent.'

'It's nineteen ninety, my dear. If they are taking care, is it so wrong for lovers to - love?'

'Are they taking care?' she demanded. I looked at her for a long moment as her train began to carry her away. Then I relented.

'Yes, my dearest, I am sure they are. Now don't worry. I'll look after them all till you get back!'

254

'Oh Bruno!' Emotion puckered her face. 'You really are the most exasperating... adorable, loving man.' Our fingers slid apart and we waved just once before each of us withdrew into the anonymity of self control again.

Matthew met me at a local hotel after finishing at the mart. When he saw my face he put his hand on my shoulder for several seconds. It was profoundly comforting.

Since Kilbaddy was plainly not requiring my services during the night I debated returning to the cottage. I had a notion that there was a strain between Katherine and Matthew which my presence may have been exacerbating. In the end, however, I decided not to scandalise my Presbyterian neighbours, the few who still bothered with niceties, settling for spending odd hours in my own little refuge before returning to the farmhouse for the night.

'No, my dear, I'm not slipping downhill,' I reassured the girl that evening. 'I'm just going down to do a bit of work. - And listen to a Radio Three concert,' I added, letting her see the light in my eyes. Satisfied she left me with Matthew.

'Have you an ulterior motive, sir?'

'Why should I have? - Well, the pair of you are just a little tense with each other. Not unhappy,' I pondered, 'just not quite relaxed.'

'There's no pulling the wool over your eyes is there? If you must know we - are having a few, er, difficulties.' He stood kicking gently at the grate, staring at the flames in discomfort and a certain amount of anxiety.

'Hm. I thought so.' Nothing more was said for several minutes. 'If you think I'm going to tell you what to do, my boy, you can think again. Failing all else visit a library. But I will say this. Make sure first of all that it isn't a simple medical problem. After that - talk. Be honest with her. Make her talk to you. I'd have thought there can't be much wrong that time and lots of practice wouldn't put right.' At that he threw back his head and laughed, the first completely relaxed laugh I had heard from him.

'Oh!' he sighed. 'You're great!'

'Well, another word. Time is on your side, you know. Don't rush things. It probably isn't working at the moment because one or both of you are ill at ease. Maybe you won't be fully relaxed with each other till after...'

'Till after we are married,' he said firmly.

'I'm not being prudish. I'm just reminding you that you are both the products of your upbringing.'

'You're probably right,' he agreed solemnly. 'Thanks. I'll come and fetch you up at bedtime. The forecast's lousy.' I grinned broadly at the adroit piece of management but he merely smiled back. After all, Kilbaddy would be with them.

Around the middle of the evening the storm hit the hillside. At its height a car door slammed, wrenching my attention away from a Couperin song cycle. Steps came to the door, a stranger's steps. When I opened to his knock I gasped. The face highlighted by the hall lamp came straight from my barrack-room mirror.

'Brian?' I reached to usher him in. 'Come in out of the rain. No wonder we couldn't contact you. Is Jock with you?'

'No. He's arriving the day after tomorrow. Kit's back then?'

'She came back last Saturday so your mother had a spell with her before she left. You knew she had a conference in Sydney?'

'I thought I might catch her.' By then we were in the living room and I reached for his wet coat, bringing my own face into full light for the first time. I was not prepared for his hiss and shocked expression. It was only when his hand strayed involuntarily to his own cheeks that I realised he was not reacting to the mask of repair work and I, in turn, looked at him in dismay. Was I really so recognisable? Alarmed I noticed something else. His eyes were a flat, cold brown. Stupidly we stared at each other. No, not stupidly. The young man's brain was clicking along like frantic clockwork. By the time I had recovered my composure he had reallocated his whole life, and his mother's, to accommodate a new and startling truth. And it was a truth he did not like.

'Where is Kit?' was all he said.

'Up at the farm. We brought Kilbaddy home on Tuesday and she is caring for him there. It's the only place where he feels at home.'

'She's alone with that farmer guy?'

'And Kilbaddy. Matthew's coming down for me in an hour or so. Let me feed you while we wait. I'm sure he won't mind if you use your mother's bed.'

'What about Kilbaddy?' There was a distinct roughness in his voice. The holier than thou attitude he was adopting began to irritate me.

'What about him? If you don't want to see him, stay here,' I added briskly. 'But your sister will be disappointed.'

'If Kilbaddy sees me it'll drive him crazy,' he said flatly.

'I doubt it. If you didn't come to see him, why did you come?'

'You knew?' he demanded, his voice rising. 'And you let her ask me?'

'She knew too. And your mother. And I didn't know what she had done. Brian, this is the last way I would have chosen for you to discover the truth. But as both Kit and your mother have learned, being aware or unaware of the details has made no difference to the truth.'

'That not only am I a bastard, I'm also a bastard's bastard?'

'In spite of what followed I have no doubt that you were conceived in love,' I said firmly, determined not to react. His provocative behaviour came out of pain, just as Katherine's had. 'The fact that the date of your parents' wedding was less distant from your date of birth than normal doesn't alter that fact one iota.' It appeared I was wrong to assume that such details no longer mattered. I took his coat into the kitchen and hung it up near the stove. 'Are you hungry?'

'No thank you.'

'Too many airborne meals and not enough sleep, hm?' He didn't even bother to answer. 'You are welcome to sleep here tonight if you prefer it,' I added quietly. 'I quite understand that anything else would be an ordeal under the circumstances. I didn't realise

258

I was quite so recognisable.'

'He can't not know,' he muttered, looking at me again, the deadness in his eyes beginning at last to lighten. 'Even Mum looks like you more than a bit.' He watched as I digested that. Did everybody in the parish guess? Had my whole life been a farcical facade? I wiped my mouth in consternation then sat him down by the fire and left to root out a bottle worth broaching. When I returned he eyed the one already sitting open.

'It's a low price Madeira,' I reassured him. 'Not even good for that so it will come to little harm if I cork it for later. This port's better.'

'I don't drink. - I'm sure you'll realise why.' This boy, too? Sadly I nodded and put both bottles back in the kitchen. 'Tea would be nice.'

'Then tea it shall be.' I indicated my collection of music records and tapes. 'Would you like to find something to your taste while I get it?'

A little to my surprise he chose Mozart, explaining that he was practically tone deaf but he could hang on to melodies as a colour blind person can follow lines. We sat listening, saying nothing. With my eyelids half closed I watched as his eyes ran surreptitiously along the bookshelves all round the room. He was using them as a gauge of my personality and interests and I found myself praying with peculiar desperation that I would not be found lacking. Another part of my mind, while marveling at his splendid good looks, regretted that his sallow skin had seen even less of the sun than Kathy's. And bitterly I saw that he bore the Middle European stamp, Hungarian or Slav perhaps as my mother had, but with not a trace of Kate in him. Like

259

Kathy and myself he had also inherited a large dose of the Jewish angst which seemed to defeat the gentle serenity and kindly wisdom of my quiet Scottish girl. Kate, my dearest love, I would have wanted it otherwise.

Suddenly, strangely, the boy rose to his feet frowning. He said nothing, just looked at me then away again around the room as if sensing something, or searching for something. After a moment he turned to the fire and stared into it, still frowning with puzzlement. Catching sight of the chessboard he looked back at me and raised a cautious eyebrow. We were still playing when Matthew arrived and blinked in astonishment at my visitor.

'How's Kilbaddy?' I asked.

'Okay. Off to bed.'

'And Katherine?'

'Likewise.' His tone was expressionless but his eyes were on Brian, wondering what effect this complication was going to have. 'You must be Kit's brother. Brian is it?'

'Yes.' Brian half rose, hampered by the chess table.

'Matthew Grey.' He leaned over to shake hands. 'I hope you're better at it than I am.'

'He's better than I am,' I admitted.

'Is he now?' A slight smile came to Matthew's lips. 'That's a novel experience for you.' He turned back to Brian. 'Would you like to use your mother's room up at the farm? You're welcome. Unless...'

'I'll stay here till I know how Kilbaddy will respond.'

'Okay. I understand. I'll tell Kit as soon as she gets up so she'll probably come and see you straight after breakfast. She'll be delighted.'

'And Kilbaddy?' The boy sounded genuinely anxious.

Matthew stood thinking for several seconds. 'I - think he'll be fine.'

'He'll know, won't he?' Brian was really addressing me.

'We think he's known for a pretty long time,' Matthew said quietly. Brian's lips compressed as he digested the fact that this stranger was familiar with every bone of the family skeleton. 'A few weeks ago he may have flipped. Maybe not.' He shrugged. 'But now I think he'll just be glad to see you, although he won't quite understand who you are. You mustn't let that upset you. Just watch Kit. Do as she does. Let yourself go with his whimsies and he'll let you into his mind. You can feel it's still his own mind even if it's a bit like a half made jigsaw puzzle, or half broken. It's a slightly surreal experience but - rewarding.' He shrugged again and looked at me with an embarrassed smile.

'My, my!' I smiled back. 'That's about as profound a speech as I've heard from you.'

'We can't all have brains,' he reproved, not in the least put out. 'Are you staying here with Brian then?' I hesitated for a moment.

'Yes, I think I will.' When I saw him to the door I said quietly, 'The boy's rather shaken.'

'I'm not surprised. Kit - Katherine's okay, you know, Bruno. I'm not leaning on her to do anything she's not fit or ready for.'

'I'm perfectly aware of that!' I said in surprise.

'It's just that, well, I thought I might have given the wrong impression earlier.'

261

'Hm.' I smiled a secret smile. 'Did you now? Go on home and get a good night's sleep. I suspect you're going to have some ditches to unblock in the morning.' I was perfectly sure I had not gained the wrong impression earlier. He was head over heels in love with my grand-daughter and was desperate to ensure that she was and would remain the same with him. That plus his innate patience and selflessness would make him a good lover one day, provided they didn't let unnecessary reticence interfere. Then he would look back at his current inadequacies and failures and laugh. I also thought he would be wise enough and tender enough not to snatch his pleasures in the meantime when she was not in either the right frame of mind or the right state of health to give. He did not need me to tell him that a far greater satisfaction would come to them both when the time was right. There was nothing wrong with his brain. Nothing at all.

Chapter Fifteen

'Is he flaming?' Katherine crept into the kitchen just after breakfast and gave me a damp kiss on the cheek. Jack the Lad was instructed to sit in the lobby which she did, steaming, with remarkable obedience for a dog in a strange place even for a collie. Matthew was a good judge here too.

'Attending to his jet-lag.'

'Silent as death while his brain goes into orbit, I know. Does too much thinking for his own good does my big brother. Phew, what a night it was!' She shook the raindrops off her hair. 'You okay?'

'I'm fine.'

'You're not cross with me for asking him to come, are you? It's just that, well, he could get to know you later but...'

'It's growing very near to the last chance with Kilbaddy?'

'And even if he's not our blood grandfather... Oh, Bruno, I don't want to hurt you'

I laughed and shook my head. 'My dear child, I feel exactly as you do, don't you realise that? Of course he needs to meet his grandfather. There's a great deal more to the making of a personality like your mother's than mere genes. She learned the bulk of what makes a worthwhile citizen from Kilbaddy, not me. Now,' I rose and began to unzip the sodden anorak, 'take this off so that I can hug you properly.'

'I just wish we'd always known you both,' she murmured. 'It's not very reassuring... Brian!' She flew from my arms to her brother's. 'My, my. You're really not at all bad-looking. I never noticed under all those stuffy office shirts.'

'And you're still a cheeky monkey.' He ruffled her hair the wrong way. 'What's not very reassuring?' She frowned.

'It's just that Kilbaddy thinks you might be the loon with the big bike.'

'Does he?' The boy sounded genuinely anxious. A moment later his head was on one side. 'And?'

'And what?' She glanced at me anxiously.

'He's no more a child than you are, my dear,' I advised.

'Well, Mum was so bottled up before she left. Oh, Bruno, I'd no idea what a mess she was in. Underneath, I mean. It wasn't just me, was it?'

'It wasn't your fault your note went missing.' Brian's face had grown blank at my words and I had the uncanny feeling that he was pulling on a mask - as I did. 'In fact she said she was very impressed with the way you were handling Kilbaddy.' Swift as she was in sensing my hint to change the subject I could see that Brian had been swifter. 'How is Kilbaddy this morning?'

'A bit tired, but fine.' Suddenly she was full of excitement. 'I birthed a calfie last night. Matthew knocked me up about midnight and asked me to help. It was big, you see, and he was getting worried because his hands were too big to get in and turn it. Mine fitted fine and it was easy with Kilbaddy telling me what to do.'

'Kilbaddy!'

He must have heard Matthew fretting earlier

because we'd hardly got back to the barn when he turned up. He was a Godsend. He calmed Matthew down immediately and told him he was doing exactly the right thing. No need for a vet.'

I kept my smile at bay. 'It's strange how anything concerning the farm survives in his mind.'

'Mm. It hung on for long enough to tell Matthew he was doing a 'nae bad' job on the farm, particularly with the animals. That gave him such a boost!' She flushed. 'Well, you can imagine, can't you?'

'Hm. No wonder the old man is tired.'

'But he's looking forward to seeing Brian.'

'Then I suggest a cup of tea while this squall blows over then a quick dash up to the farm.'

'Are you coming?' At last there was a trace of boyish pleading in Brian's voice.

'Of course.'

We had to bolster his spirits all the way there but in the end the meeting went very smoothly. The old man was intrigued with the 'bonnie lad' but for the first hour or two Brian remained almost totally silent apart from responding to his sallies. Eventually Kilbaddy accepted the new presence enough to turn his attention to Katherine, again seeing her as Kate, enabling Brian to observe his sister's technique and the strange new serenity she had acquired. By the end of the day he, too, had slipped into his grandmother's ways. It disturbed me deeply that behind the Cryckiewicz exterior there was something of Kate after all.

'It's taking a lot off Kit's shoulders,' Matthew told him gratefully, trying to break through the barrier of distrust the boy had erected the instant he had seen

265

the farmer and his sister together. 'Last time round she ended up in tears of sheer exhaustion.'

'Did she?' I demanded in surprise.

'Mm, I'm afraid so, several times.'

'While I was entertaining the black dog?' I confirmed glumly. Brian's eyes narrowed slightly as he pieced more of the picture together.

'It won't ever be that bad again,' Matthew comforted me. I knew what he meant. We had seen no need to tell the rest of the family about Kilbaddy's amorous interlude and there was little doubt that that danger or the violence were far behind us. It was a pity, however, that he had alluded to it then even obliquely. Brian's eyes were snapping with the awareness of something unsaid.

I was back in the cottage when Jock arrived almost exactly twenty four hours after his brother. He looked quite like Brian, and therefore like me, but he noticed nothing. This boy was Alistair's son, full of noisy fun and love of company, a character oozing with charm, more than content to accept everything at face value. Not stupid, I diagnosed, certainly not that, but intellectually lazy. When I had diverted his attention from my music collection I sat him down for an hour and explained the situation to him, quietly and carefully. However, Brian had understood more after a few terse sentences than this uncomplicated lad would ever absorb.

He was willing, however. Once he, too, had shaken off his jet-lag he was up entrancing Kilbaddy with his songs, making the mistake of choosing some his father used to sing but Kilbaddy seemed not to mind. An hour later he was out helping Matthew to relay some land-drains, heedless of his recent back injury.   At dinner time, however, he admitted to a twinge or two which made Matthew worry and suggest he help Holly feed the new calves.   The result was that the pair spent a jolly if not very productive hour exchanging symptoms.

Indoors again he was happy to trot around doing odd jobs for Katherine. He had a fund of stories, most of them humorous but many giving interesting reflections on life in New Zealand. Kilbaddy responded to a surprising number of them, taking particular enjoyment in the boy's company which left neither of his siblings in the least upset.   This brother was endowed with an abundance of bonhomie, but of the rare variety which did not lead to eventual irritation. That left me feeling a cautious relief.

'Bruno? A word?' Matthew came to me a couple of days later as I leaned on a gate watching a group of stirks galloping wildly but with doubtful bravery at an invading gorse patch. I had been aware of a growing worry in him. 'Do you know if the Sanderson children had a chance to take over the farm before Kilbaddy retired?'

'Ah, so that's it. Out of form they were asked, yes. But what do you imagine they could do with it? They are town children.'

'So was I, more or less.'

'But you went to agricultural college then had years of training in the hard school of experience. If you are hanging on with your fingernails what do you think would have happened to them?'

'Hm. I still feel uneasy.'

'Don't. It's all in order, you know. Kathy will inherit the money from Kilbaddy. And from me. Her children will come along after that.'

'If there's anything left.' He swung his stick absently at a skittish animal which had dared to nibble at his knee through the bars. 'You're spending money like water, Bruno. I don't like it.'

'Neither do I,' Brian announced behind us, his voice as hard as his eyes. So, he listened in like his mother sometimes used to. I saw Matthew's nostrils flair. 'Big debts all round,' he got in before I could say a word. 'We should be using the bike money now that Kit has sold the thing.'

'Isn't that up to her?' I snapped. Matthew turned silently on his heel and walked away towards the barn, very angry indeed.

'He's on to a good thing, isn't he?' Brian said loudly.

'Tell me.' My teeth gritted.

'Oh, come on Bruno.' His scorn was cutting. 'He's had three quarters of his barn of a house redecorated for free, loans for his fertilisers, a land-rover that is practically a gift, no end of electrical goods for the house and a constant refilling of his enormous new freezer. And he's making a heavy play for Kit, no doubt for her legacy.'

'That's quite enough,' I snapped grimly. 'Matthew is keeping a note of every penny spent. I didn't ask it of him. He insisted.'

'But it'll all be wiped off the slate on the wedding day, won't it?'

'There may never be a wedding day. And you're quite wrong to imagine that Matthew would accept that as a solution. Your mother failed to inform me that your motivation in life was greed. Or is it envy?' I was shaking with anger, which may have been why he had the sense to say no more. Forgive me, Kate, whatever made me think I might see you in him?

Later that day, however, just after Katherine had gone shopping I was again obliged to reassess the boy. He and Kilbaddy were deep in a difficult conversation, with the old man trying to explain how to judge when a crop of corn was ready for cutting.

'Ye chow it.'

'Chew it?'

'Aye. Tak a couple o' heads from a middlin' stalk, nae too ripe and nae too green. Dinna tak a bit where it's sandy. That comes on too quick...' While Brian concentrated hard on following the accented words I saw a familiar expression flit across Kilbaddy's face, the first time since he had returned. A moment later came the hot, acrid smell of urine. Still soured by the incident in the yard I made no move to help. For several seconds Brian hesitated, his back tense. When he did move his actions were swift and gentle, sweeping away Kilbaddy's incipient distress.

'Come on, Grandad. I'll help you change. So you'd go into the middle of the field, would you?' Ten minutes later he had brought Kilbaddy downstairs again, clean and dry, then he summoned Jock to keep the old man amused while he whipped the travel rug off his chair. We had instituted this over a plastic sheet when he began to be incontinent. By the time Katherine returned the wet things had been washed and tumbled dry. She never did discover what happened. She wouldn't have minded but Brian had

269

yet to realise this.   Not once did he look in my direction.

He did, however, come to spend the night with me in the cottage.

'I'm sorry.'

'So you should be,' I muttered, more in irritation than anger now. Why was the boy so grudging? 'It would have been better unsaid. Haven't you the wit to realise how precarious Matthew's position is? It was bad enough taking over a farm in the middle of a recession. He expected dour neighbours and he knew soil and climate conditions would be hard but he never imagined the millstone we have hung round his neck.' His face was stubbornly blank and my annoyance sharpened.

'And his own health is crucial. He worries about your sister but he's been near to collapse himself more than once already, all because of interlopers to whom he owes precisely nothing. He has taken on a large part in the caring as well, you know.'

The boy sat still as stone.

'Brian!' I snapped enraged, finally bringing his gaze to mine. His eyes were a frightening flat brown and at last I noticed an all too familiar whiteness around his mouth which made me take my ill temper in hand.

'Brian, my boy, try to understand. Even when he arrived here he was facing a very tough battle. The last thing he could have expected was Kilbaddy wandering into his life like a lost soul. Yet he took the old man in out of compassion alone and has allowed us to use the farmhouse as if it were our home. For that I have paid bills in lieu of our rent and paid willingly. I refuse to see him go down because of the burdens we have tied on to him. And I refuse to see the motorcycle money spent on this because Katherine is adamant that it should be spent on education, including yours.

'Incidentally, the land-rover is mine until Matthew can afford to pay for it. The kitchen items are for Katherine's use. You couldn't have worked your little trick without them so you must realise how crucial they are to her. But tell me, - how did you know about the fertiliser loan?' He remained stubbornly silent. 'Only Matthew and I know, and the person who... Ah. George Patterson called, did he?' He responded, hearing dismay and fury in my voice. 'I'm surprised he dared.'

'Why?'

I told him. 'Apparently he knew perfectly well who Lewis's lady friend was.' Brian was beginning to look uncomfortable which made me try harder to swallow my growing wish for solitude. 'What did he say to you?'

'Something about Kit being beholden to Grey,' he confessed.

'Hm.'

'He's stuck on her,' Brian burst out. 'It sticks out a mile! George said he'd got her into trouble and that was why she...' My face turned to ice.

'Please don't continue,' I ground out. 'Yes, Matthew is stuck on her, as you so elegantly put it. But he came to me some time ago and told me so openly and honestly. He is acutely aware of the danger that your sister might feel obligated to him and it is the last thing in the world he wants. He is very worried about

271

it. In fact he has made it plain that he wants her to finish her college course just as soon as she has the opportunity. He is as appalled as you and I at the situation in which your mother found herself.'

He digested that in silence.

'You should also know what Katherine was doing while she was away. It was a great deal more than selling a motorcycle.' I ignored the sudden moment of terror he displayed and outlined the visit to Poland. After some bad-tempered hesitation I eventually confessed to the suspicions I had nurtured and the determined loyalty with which Matthew had protested her innocence.

'Oh, heck,' he muttered.

'Forget it. Wipe it from the slate,' I said, fighting against an uncharitable inclination to prolong his penance. He looked at me doubtfully, then his eyes widened at something he recognised in mine.

'I've made an enemy of Grey now,' he muttered.

'I doubt it,' I said curtly. 'Try apologising first thing tomorrow. He will never raise it again.' I was dismally wrong to imagine he would leave the matter alone.

'Kit's very young,' he fretted.

'At her age your mother was heavy with her second child.'

'She shouldn't have been. She should never have been obliged to marry a useless husband then driven across the world with him. She didn't deserve to be thrown out the way she was.'

'She told you that?' I gasped, hurt beyond bearing. 'Is that what she believes?'

At last he had the grace to look ashamed. 'No. Oh, dear God, no! I'm sorry, Bruno. She loved my Dad and I know she chose to go with him.' Suddenly the boy stood up and left the room. When I heard him leave the house as well I swore at myself for my lack of sensitivity. The boy was still grieving for his father, and grieving in loneliness and frustration, worrying wildly about his beloved little sister and trying to come to terms with the past sins of two wicked old men who were not at all as they had been represented to him. It was more than an hour before he returned shivering slightly and I made a supreme effort to shrug off the black dog.

'Forgive me, Brian,' I said immediately. 'I have the kettle on.'

'No, let's clear this up first,' he said, curiously gentle. 'You're right. There are too many things which I should never have said.'

'And too many which should have been said long ago?'

'No. Yes... Heck, this is going nowhere. Look, I'll make the tea. Then we should just go to bed. I promise I won't interfere between Matthew and Kit. Maybe things are bad enough already.'

When he brought the tea I asked one last question. 'Did you believe George?'

He flushed vividly. 'No. I - hit him.' He swallowed. 'He just laughed.'

'Then you didn't hit him hard enough,' I grouched and he had the temerity to smile. A moment later he made to switch on the radiogram but caught my eye. 'No?

'I - prefer silence for the moment.' He merely nodded and we sat peaceably enough together. Just before he retired he said quietly, 'It must be the

Jewish angst I've inherited that makes me worry so. Like you and Mum do.'

'I do?' I felt dull and unresponsive but hoped he did not see.

He smiled a crooked smile. 'Very much like you. I'm not sorry, you know. In fact I think I'm rather proud you're my grandfather. I haven't got off to a good start with you, have I?'

'Don't talk rubbish,' I said irritably and he brushed his fingers lightly on the top of my hand. I didn't flinch, just raised the withered thing in the air. Immediately he slipped his own hand beneath it palm upwards but, revealingly, waited to see if I would clasp it. I couldn't. Miserably I closed my eyes. 'Dear God, that too? What an inheritance.'

'Not much just now,' he said calmly, withdrawing his hand. 'And probably not ever as bad as you. What do you want? Peace and quiet?'

'Please. Keep Jock away, will you? But - do it kindly. He'll never understand.'

Poor Jock didn't understand, just accepted his brother's command with apparent equilibrium. When the worst of the depression was over and I could once more tolerate noise, he came and sang for me which helped surprisingly. Up till then Brian and Matthew kept away too except for delivering or collecting Katherine. She came late in the evenings at the time she knew Kate used to come, and sat comforting me with her silent, soothing presence until I was able to face the terrors of the night. Once, only once, Kilbaddy was aware enough to come and play a sad game of chess.

'I told you Jock's good, didn't I?' Katherine enthused a few days later. 'But I don't think you should be paying for his music course. It should come from the bike money. And Brian must go to college too though I've no idea what he'd want to do. Anything he fancied I suppose. He'd make a good doctor,' she pondered.

'Good gracious, how much were you paid for the thing?'

'A hundred and three thousand guineas.' I stared at her speechlessly as she giggled. 'Guineas in this day and age. I told you it was special. The experts said there were only five left in the whole world and this one was easily in the best condition. It's gone to a big motor museum.'

'Such a price for a lump of old machinery!' I marveled at last.

'Bruno, I think I know why Dad gave it to me. I mean to me and not the boys.'

'Hm?'

'Well, I think he knew that in time I would be able to let go and sell it and that his family would get something out him after all.'

'You mean because you are a girl you regard it as a tool and not a toy?'

'Not even a teddy-bear,' she nodded solemnly. 'The boys are both terribly - sentimental. They say they hate Dad for all he did but it just isn't true. Some day they're going to have to face that and grow up.'

'They left home,' I reminded her.

'But on Mum's orders. I realise that now. She wanted them to learn to stand on their own two feet and not become - dependent like Dad I suppose. And

275

it was actually cheaper for her to let them fend for themselves when they were able. She wouldn't take money from them because...' She looked at her hands fiercely. 'I didn't realise how hard it was to make ends meet till I tried to sort out Matthew's house-keeping. The boys must have been living more or less hand to mouth on what they were earning.'

She looked up and I gestured to her to come and put her head on my lap.

'Dear Bruno,' she sighed as I brushed her hair with my fingers. 'Mum talked quite a bit the night before she left. She's in a real mess, isn't she? Psychologically, I mean, not in her general life. That's fine now and they think a lot of her in the office, I know that. But I'd no idea how guilty and uncertain she was under all her polished cleverness. All I'd seen was this marvellous, shiny lady with the glamorous job meeting glamorous people. And at the same time she seemed tough, tough enough to keep us all going no matter what. But under it all, oh, Bruno, she's blaming herself for everything, for Dad being the way he was, and for the boys not being given a college education. And most of all for the split with you and Kilbaddy - and none of it's true.' She brushed away tears. 'I just don't know how we're going to turn her around but we'll have to do it somehow, won't we?'

'Hm.' She looked up and caught my sad smile. 'I see you have been doing a great deal of growing up too.'

'Maybe,' she smiled back through a sniff. 'You're okay again? I haven't spoken too soon?'

'No, my dear one, I'm fine.'

'Well, we should talk. I've put thirteen thousands of

the bike money into a bank here and given the rest to Mum to invest for us all. It's time I paid my bills.'

'Shall we leave it for now? We are still on the edge of a precipice. And don't worry too much about your mother. The very fact that she was able to talk to you is a good sign, you know.' She looked doubtful. 'My dear, she is having to learn to face her own feelings too, her fears and hurts and a great many things she may never have dared to examine before, if only because circumstances simply would not allow her to dare. Who better to help her, share her innermost thoughts, than a loving, understanding daughter? Hm? If you are able.'

'Hm, as you say. I - did fall back on Matthew's support after that. I hope Mum won't mind that I told him a few things. And he told me some things too,' she blurted out. 'About Kate and...'

'I'm glad,' I broke in swiftly. 'I could never have told you but I did want you to know.'

'And I understand.' Just like Kate she slipped her hand into mine and smiled, her blue eyes completely free from censure. Ah, Kate. She's growing strong this grand-daughter of ours, perhaps even stronger than her mother. And wiser? Is it adversity which is teaching her? Or do you have a hand? 'I do understand,' she insisted, her eyes lighting up with something near to mischief when she saw my attention had meandered.

The twelfth of May was a lovely day, warm and calm after a fitful spring of bright blustery spells interspersed with grey drizzle and a couple of sharp, unwelcome late frosts. After his dinnertime nap the sunshine tempted Kilbaddy out with his stick, Jack the Lad at his heels. Matthew's little collie had taken on the same guardianship she had sensed in the rest of us and when the old man sat down under the oak tree up by the berry-field gate she ran barking for her master. The rest of us, my grandchildren and I, were gathering in the kitchen for an afternoon fly cup. The first warning we had that this day was different from all others was when Matthew's feet came pounding towards the open door. Before he came into view, however, the footsteps hesitated and he arrived to reach out and grasp the sides of the door frame, his eyes dark with emotion. He looked at Katherine, wondering wildly how she was going to react when he found the words he needed.

He needed none. Quietly she went to him and they held each other closely, her face hidden in his neck and one of his big hands cradling her head as he kissed her temple, his face tight with distress. It gave us all time to adapt. Even in that moment of finality I registered a spurt of amusement at Jock's expression of surprise.

'Do you want to see him?' Matthew asked her at last. 'He looks - beautiful.' She took his hand and they led a silent procession out of the yard, Holly and the little white-faced bitch tagging on at the end. Kilbaddy did look beautiful, as if in a deep and totally peaceful sleep. Katherine knelt and kissed his cheek, brushing the hair from his brow. In an unbearably Kate-like gesture she leaned over and, with touching gentleness, pulled his cuffs over his wrists as if to keep them warm. Again she brushed his brow then stood up and turned to Matthew. Oblivious of all of us

278

watching, she laid her hands on either side of his face and kissed him on the lips.

'Thank you,' she whispered. 'Thank you from the very bottom of my heart for letting me take him home.' Matthew could do no more than pull her into his arms again and hold her tightly for a brief moment while he regained control of his emotions. 'I must phone Mum,' she went on, remarkably calm. 'They'll let her come for this. If we'd known in advance...'

'We didn't,' I said firmly. 'It's best this way, my dear. For everybody.'

The day of Kilbaddy's funeral was yet another 'perfect farmer's day' as Katherine put it. Rain first thing had brought out all the late spring scents then left high scudding clouds in the warming sky. Crossing the yard with me after breakfast to check on another new calf, she stopped and looked at her boots which were crushing the tiny pineapple heads of mayweed, inhaling deeply. 'Kilbaddy said this was his favourite smell. I think it's mine too.'

'It came from Oregon last century. Did you know?'

'Know-all,' she teased very gently.

Kathy arrived with just two hours to spare, having been collected at Dyce Airport by Brian. As Katherine reached out to embrace her it was her mother who burst into tears and was calmly gathered close. When Matthew saw the boys standing by, frozen at their own inadequacy, he put firm hands on Kathy's shoulders and turned her towards the door, signaling to Katherine to take her upstairs.

'Mrs. Sanderson, why don't you rest for an hour? I promise we'll waken you in good time.' When they were out of earshot he turned to the rest of us and held Brian's eye, realising somehow that he was most in need of support. 'Now, we are all going to have a drink. For medicinal reasons.'

It was the largest funeral there had been for years. Mercifully Kathy did not know until the service was over. The minister was a man with a deep love for his fellows and a sweet turn of phrase, two good reasons to explain why he was one of the few who could call out more than a dozen parishioners on a Sunday. He gave a gentle and personal farewell to a man he had loved and admired and he spoke for all the others who crammed the pews and the gallery above. Some had travelled a very long way indeed, as Kathy saw when she faced the sea of sorrowing faces during the long walk to the porch and the harrowing greeting and thanking of the mourners. Throughout it all Katherine remained sad but composed by her side.

Perhaps it was a desperate need for respite that made Kathy finally seek sanctuary in the churchyard. Instinctively she turned towards Kate's grave although I knew she had not intended to be present at the actual burial. Katherine threw a startled look at me and hurried after her. Suddenly Kathy stopped, catching sight of the freshly dug earth. I waited for her utter collapse but curiously she grew calm. Somebody had raised the tendrils of the rosebush from Kate's resting place and laid them carefully along the top of the cemetery wall where the sun picked out the plumping of the green buds. Katherine reached her and slipped her arm around her waist. The girl whispered to her mother and guided her to one side. As the cortege passed they stepped quietly into the procession, the only women present. Not one of the men as much as raised an eyebrow, merely nodded condolences or touched a hand to guide or comfort them.

Katherine cried a little during this final farewell but I realised that much of her grieving had been done on that terrible winter night when we had taken the old man back to hospital, we thought for the last time. It was Kathy who plucked a fat rosebud and let it drop with a plop on to the coffin.

Among the mourners, I alone stood in shame. It had nothing to do with the covert glances I and my grandsons were receiving. It certainly was not regret that the old man had been returned to Kate at last. She was, after all was said and done, his Kate, Kilbaddy's Bonnie Quine, and that I had never disputed. I glanced at Kindrum and at his youngest boy Gareth who had held one of the palls during the ceremony and, base though the thought was, I thanked God, my God or Kilbaddy's or any God who might listen, for the quirk of fate which had kept his middle son away. However much I would have hated to see Kindrum offended, whether or not Matthew owed him a tidy sum of money, I could not have borne to see George Patterson at a handle of Kilbaddy's coffin.

Kathy had to leave again for Sydney the following day, aching as much as I did. 'I'll be back soon,' she promised, her face wan and white. 'Maybe there'll be a different kind of ceremony to fetch me,' she said thoughtfully then dropped her head on one shoulder.

'I have a notion Matthew did a bit more 'looking after' than you did.'

'Have you? Katherine's coming back to stay with me from tonight.' She poked my chest gently then kissed me goodbye, asking no more of me. Brian was going as far as London with her then flying to Warsaw before returning the photograph his sister had appropriated from the concentration camp records and, no doubt, exploring his newly-discovered family roots. I feared it would be a traumatic visit. Jock opted to head for New Zealand at the end of the week. I hoped that in the meantime he and the others would leave me alone. I needed to learn how to live without Kilbaddy. And Kate. My time was surely over now.

Days later, when Jock had gone, I wandered down to the graveyard after tea. Solitude had always been my preferred state, but in the week after Kilbaddy's death I found myself grappling with feelings of isolation and loneliness more positive and painful than I had ever imagined could exist. Yet, I could barely tolerate the kindnesses which Katherine and Matthew were anxious to heap on me. Is my own sanity going, Kate? Must I now consider that I had needed him more than you all these years? That Kilbaddy also had his part to play? Of course he had. Our friendship was long and deep, far beyond anything I had either expected or deserved. Dear God, how I missed the old fellow. And how I will miss you, my dear beloved, but surely it is time to give you back to him.

Time passed as the day faded among the quiet stones. A car drew in at the kirk entrance but I ignored it till footsteps sounded on the gravel behind me. I gritted my teeth, determined not to dispatch them with sharp words but when I turned it was to find Kindrum there, his face drawn and uncertain as he examined my eyes.

'Will I go awa again?'

'No, I was - startled.' He came and stood by me. 'They've put the bush back neatly, hm?'

It'll be a grand show this year again.' After another pause he said tentatively, 'Susan says would ye come for yer tea on Sunday? If the young anes dinna mind.'

'How kind,' I said, genuinely moved. I had been sometimes before but I recognised this as a particular gesture of compassion.

'George winna be there.' The sudden announcement caught me unawares and I turned swiftly, prompting a further outburst of distress. 'Ach, Bruno, I'm sorry for a' the trouble. And at such a bad time.'

'Trouble?' I asked cautiously. His crusty ill humour began to look paper thin. How much trouble was there in the Kindrum household, I wondered, which the outside world had never been allowed to witness?

'Ye ken fine what I'm at. George and his nasty meddlin' over at Kilbaddy. - Ye thocht I didna know about his offer for the fairm, didn't ye? Well, I did. And I knew fine he wouldna do. He wouldna do at a'. That's why I stuck in a bid myself. Tae warn ye, like. Mind, if ye'd ta'en it up I'd have had a terrible job paying the price, but it would have been better than having George in Kilbaddy. He'd have piled on the chemicals and cropped the ground tae death in five years. And he's the divvel himsel' tae the beasts. I canna abide that!' I was dumb-founded. I had known the man for many years but never had I imagined him capable of such frankness. Or such pain. 'Well, he's awa' now, and wi' more than his fair share, but I couldna tak more o' his lip.'

'We chose the man we thought was best,' I said lamely.

'An' by God ye were richt!' I blinked at his emphatic tone. 'I'm tellin' ye this, George would nivver have taken auld Kilbaddy back home like that laddie did. I respect him for that more than anything else. Mind,' he added sombrely, 'he's nae a bad farmer. Nae bad at a'.' Such high praise sent my spirits singing. If Kindrum thought that way, then so would others. 'And - ach, Bruno, George woulda been a hell o' a husband for that lassie o' yours.' My reaction to that was swamped by the heavy sigh he gave, recollecting that he had come to comfort me. 'I didna mean tae say a' this. I know ye're feeling...'

'Is Susan at home?'

'Na, she's sitting for Patrick's bairns.'

'Then come and help me decide if Kathy's Australian brandy is as bad as I fear. There's an hour of the day left.'

'But I dinna want tae intrude.' He glanced at the grave.

'Come.' I took his arm to lead him towards the gate. Then I stopped suddenly and smiled. 'Kate would approve your technique. I was wallowing in self-pity but you've given me something outside myself to attend to.'

'I nivver meant...'

'I know, my friend.' I propelled him forwards again. 'But it's working so ls go.'

Chapter Sixteen

'I want to be married in July,' Katherine announced the following evening. Matthew looked at her in astonishment then flushed vividly.

'This year or next?' he stuttered.

'This year,' she said quietly and his embarrassment vanished.

'Isn't it a bit soon after the funeral?' It did not seem to upset either of them that I was listening. Katherine looked at me.

'Kilbaddy knew,' she said. 'He said he didn't want us to wait just because of him so it doesn't really matter whether it's this year or next.'

Matthew sat thinking, his eyes on her. 'Is there something more?' he asked and Katherine dropped her gaze.

'Well, you know that I promised to go back to college?'

'I'm going to hold you to it, darling,' he said, and his tone was adamant.

'I'm not chickening out. It's just... Well I don't really want to do an arts course any more. I never did, really.'

'So what do you want?'

'Engineering.'

I laughed to myself, scarcely surprised.

'I won't say an engineer around the place wouldn't be useful,' Matthew admitted doubtfully.

'And look at the business Lewis gets. It's more

than he can handle. I'm sure I could start a wee business of my own or - go into partnership with him?' She said that with infinite care. 'And you know as well as I do that the farm's not going to stand on its own feet very easily the way things are nowadays.'

He frowned. 'It'll mean three years again.' I could hear him wondering what kind of marriage he was being offered.

'But three years in Aberdeen,' she persisted, 'if I can get in. It's better than going back to Christchurch and not seeing you for a whole year, isn't it? I could travel in Mondays and come back Fridays. Maybe even go in daily.'

'No!'

'No?' Her tone was one of total dismay.

'I'm saying no to daily commuting,' he amended hastily, seeing a multitude of advantages in her other suggestions. 'You'd be in a heap long before the end of the first term. And what about money? You'll have to pay every last bill yourself if you do it that way.'

'Mum's holding the cheque for our education. My Dad's legacy.' She tightened her fists on the solecism. 'She should be back home from Sydney now. I'll phone once Brian gets back from Poland. He's got to decide what he wants to study by then.'

'Well, if you're sure you can manage it, - okay.'

Katherine looked at him solemnly for a moment. Once sure he really meant it she let her face bloom into a smile which dazzled him with pure joy. It was meant for us both but, very naturally, ended up being a special gift bestowed on Matthew. He looked so bemused in his happiness that a stray thought flitted across my mind. Somewhere along the line they had begun to iron out their, er, difficulties.

'What do you think, Bruno?' Brian asked anxiously on his return. 'Do you still have doubts?'

'No, none at all. Tell me why you do.'

He shrugged awkwardly. 'I'm not sure if it's relevant, but I want you to know about something. I'm blooming sure Mum won't tell you.' I frowned. 'It's about what happened...'

'Something about your father? Are you sure you should be telling me?'

'Yes.' It was apparent that he needed to quite desperately. 'A lot happened that Kit didn't see and I'm not sure how much she knows or guesses. Dad used to get very drunk, you see, and when Mum wouldn't have anything to do with him he'd sometimes hit her. She was never badly hurt, not physically I mean, but usually Kit wasn't there. Maybe she thought it was worse than it was.'

'How do you know you saw the worst?'

'What do you mean?'

'Your sister mentioned incidents which sounded bad enough to me.'

'There was only one really bad one she saw. I think it might have been the only one of its kind. You see, one particular night Mum had said no - you know what I mean - and she and Dad were having a dreadful shouting match. Mum was really at the end of her tether by then. Kit got up out of bed and came downstairs and when Dad tried to hit Mum she got in the way. He turned on her then. - Bruno, he didn't know what he was doing. I know he didn't.'

'But?' I was sure I did *not* want to hear this.

287

He breathed noisily through his nose several times before he was able to continue. 'He started to rip her nightdress off her. She - was only thirteen but she knew what it meant and was absolutely terrified. I - I'm afraid I saw red and went for him. I'd done it before and always come off worse. I don't know whether he was more drunk than usual or whether I was at last strong enough to get the better of him but - I knocked him out. In fact I knocked him over against the fire fender and split his head open. He was in intensive care for a day and a half and the police were brought in to question me.'

'Oh my dear boy!'

'It blew over in the end,' he said at last, his face far older than it should have been. 'When he was well enough, while he was still sober, he and Mum had a long talk. It wasn't that she actually threw him out, you know. They decided together that he had to go. They were so scared that he might hurt Kit. I mean really assault her. He just didn't remember a thing about it, you see, and he really did adore her. He couldn't imagine he could have done such a thing to his wee girl. And I suppose they were scared to death that I might end up really killing him next time. Or the other way round. By that stage neither of them believed that even that fear would make him stop drinking.'

'Dear God,' I whispered, sick with shock. 'Presumably that's why your mother was so anxious when Katherine went to nurse your father.'

'I don't honestly think Kit realised that.'

'I wonder. She took care to keep you mother informed, didn't she?' He frowned at that. 'I presume you are wondering now if she, um, how shall I put it?'

'If she's screwed up sexually. What's this guy Grey really like, Bruno?'

'Hm. Possibly even more astute than I had realised,' I murmured to myself, wondering if he had discovered more than I had by the time he came asking for advice - and failing to get it. At least I could give comfort here. 'Brian, my dear boy, next time you see the two of them together just watch them. I think it will put your mind at rest.'

Katherine and Matthew were married on the fifteenth of July. The reason for the date became apparent when, early on her wedding morning, Katherine arose around seven and blew me a kiss as she passed through the living room where I lay still half asleep. Until the guests began arriving Matthew had been alone in the farmhouse, not out of any hypocritical pandering to public opinion, I was sure. Both of them had hinted that they were merely waiting and I felt sure they were not cheating on that either. The wait, after all, was not to be long.

'Jeans for a wedding day?'

'I've something to do. See you in half an hour or so.' She returned with an enormous basket of seductive, dark red roses which I recognised immediately.

'Ah. Is this the date the village gardeners agreed on?'

''Course it is.' Gently she laid her booty down on the table among the breakfast debris and came to kiss me and lay her hand on my cheek. Fetching a newspaper she used her new secateurs to snip off every single thorn, laying out the blooms in order of fullness and length of stem. With intense deliberation she chose the three most beautiful, most aromatic specimens and set them in a milk-bottle up to their necks in water. The rest were dumped in a couple of large buckets. Then she fetched the pair of brass ewers she had appropriated from the kirk.

'Stolen, borrowed or begged?'

'Offered. Mrs Allen and Susan and Betty Patterson are coming over to do the church arrangements because they think I won't know the first thing about them.'

'Are they right?'

'Uh, yes. They're not getting these though. Do you want your shirt pressed?'

'I did it yesterday, thank you.'

'Independent blighter,' she smiled. She stroked my parchment face again. 'I'm so glad you agreed to give me away, Bruno. It's *really* important to me.'

'Brian hasn't commented yet. I hope he's not offended.'

'He's not at all, I promise. He told me. You do realise what it'll mean, don't you?' She sat down and took my hand anxiously. 'People will see the likenesses between you and the boys. They're bound to, even if they didn't in May.'

I nodded. 'If that's what you want so be it.'

'It's more than that. I want you to know something. You know the way Kilbaddy used to suddenly come out of his dwam into clear sanity sometimes. Well, he did that once when we were alone about a week before he died. It wasn't for long, but that was when he said I should marry Matthew

290

and... become Kilbaddy's Bonnie Quine.'

'Ah, that reminds me! I have more information on that song.'

'You have? An extra wedding present.' Her spirits swooped upwards again.

'It isn't much. Just that one of Jock's new cronies came up with a scrap of the original song. It looks as if it was published in Elgin round about eighteen hundred.'

'Oh, that's too late.'

'Not necessarily. It may not be the first publication. Or it may have been published long after the events in the lyric.'

'Who wrote the song?'

I shrugged. 'This piece contains another stanza, something about helping her man to work the canny croft. It appears she went back to her husband. The author is somebody called William Morrison.'

'So yet another admirer?'

'Who knows? Unless Morrison was the name of her husband, not Wishart. It could be the name of the poet retelling the story, I suppose. - However, you were telling me what our Kilbaddy was saying.'

'He said he wanted you to give me away. It was only right, he said. And - he said he'd be fine just sitting in the front pew.' That thought made us blink at each other through tears. Then she sniffed and gave a shaky laugh. 'Fancy crying on my wedding morning! He also said he'd left a letter for Mum with his will telling her the truth. He didn't say what he thought the truth was, but he must have meant... you. I don't know if she got it.'

'She did. Apparently he had been guessing even before she was born, but it was only after she left here that he felt able to accept it fully. That's when he wrote the letter. He assured her that he had felt no resentment. Faced with Kathy or nothing he would have had her every time, whatever the implications.'

'It's more or less what you thought then? What if you had spoken about it openly?'

''What if' is a singularly useless start to any discussion,' I replied tartly. 'Now, do I have a bud for my button-hole or must I wear a carnation?'

'I thought you might prefer a carnation because of the Polish tradition but it's up to you.'

'I'll have this.' I chose a neat, fat bud and gave it to her to bind.

'For Kate?' She looked up at me, her shining blue eyes over bright.

'Yes,' I said quietly. 'Yes, my dearest, only granddaughter. For Kate. She would have been so proud of you.'

There was an echo of the rebellious, independent Kit in the wedding dress she chose. The silk was of the palest coffee colour, clinging smoothly to her slim figure then falling in a gleaming, flowing, whispering bell to within an inch of the ground. The neckline was simple and modest and each tight sleeve came to a small peak at the back of her hand. The startling thing was that it was completely unadorned, without a single button or bow, uncluttered by net or ribbon, embroidery or sequin, and emphatically free of all jewelry. Her curly hair was brushed into lustrous neatness and completely devoid of adornment.

292

Kathy's eyes widened when she saw it then grew moist as they met her daughter's blue gaze.

'He'll understand, Mum,' the girl said placidly. 'He gets me as I am and that'll have to do.'

'Yes, love.' The only other person who understood was, surprisingly, Brian. I had had so little time with my dear ones since their return the day before that I was not sure I had read his reaction aright. However, he caught my eye and leaned over to whisper to me.

'If the bridegroom can read unspoken messages like that, maybe he'll do after all, eh?'

'What are you two conspirators up to?' Kathy demanded.

'Just prognosticating,' came Brian's lofty reply. We turned and watched the bride's plan meet with a slight mitigation. Mrs Allen looked mildly scandalised at the stark simplicity of Katherine's dress, in particular the absence of headdress and veil. Without bothering to ask for permission, the formidable lady plucked a blossom from the mock orange which grew a few yards from the kirk door and tucked it into the dark hair. There it shone like a star, the only pure white item in the outfit.

'There now, dearie. That's better.'

All Katherine did was kiss the old dame and smile indulgently. I expected the flower to be removed at the earliest opportunity but it was left, as a kindness I was sure.

'That's Kate?' Brian breathed behind me before he left to herd the last of the guests inside, leaving me alone in the porch with my granddaughter. And my first love. It was strange that Brian of all people should be the one who had sensed her hovering presence. I wondered if someone would do the same for old Kilbaddy. I hoped so.

Matthew was surprised when he saw his bride, his eyes sweeping to her shining unadorned curls, dropping to the step on which she stood then rising swiftly to meet the anxious look in her blue eyes. His twisted smile told her he had understood instantly. He held out his arm for her then looked again.

Unadorned was not the correct word. In her hand she carried three perfect roses still with their leaves on, their stems bound in corn coloured ribbon intertwined with his slender gold chain and my string of delicate seed pearls. The enormous, rich heads drooped in undeniable voluptuousness, splashing almost blood red against the coffee coloured silk. Fantin-Latour could not have created a more striking effect. The intoxication of their perfume filled the kirk in a most un-Presbyterian fashion, their heavy fragrance caught up and tossed through the air along with the aroma from the huge displays on the altar and in the porch; there the door stood open to allow sunlight to flood the crowded, grey building.

I saw Matthew's eyes smile more deeply, then flicker at the emotion she must have shown when she noticed that he, too, had chosen to sport not a carnation but another little rosebud from her mother's bush. Her hand trembled as she instinctively reached up to touch it. Then, sensing the rapt silence in the watching congregation, he caught her fingers firmly and drew her attention to the exceedingly important matters in hand.

Afterwards there were the usual painful camera exercises. These I always found particularly distasteful because of my ugly, patched face and this occasion proved worse than I could have imagined.   I felt myself shockingly displayed with my two handsome grandsons on either side, feeling that I was surely courting scorn and contumely.   Jock was full of good spirits, however, and Brian did no more than murmur that I should not let my imagination run riot.   It was no help to my battered emotions when I noticed that dozens of the guests had followed the groom's lead and wore rosebuds, each and every one from the bush on the corner of the cemetery wall.   And still it was ablaze with bloom.

Before the gathering scattered to head for the reception Kit had one more silent declaration to make, the last before the child gave way to the woman.   She whispered to Matthew who led her to the churchyard, opened the squeaky gate and ushered her through. He touched Kathy's arm, spoke to her quietly and left her to follow her daughter looking slightly bewildered.

The gate was closed firmly behind them and he leaned on it to prevent anyone else from following. Nobody but the photographers would have dreamed of trying but even they were barred, though most of us saw mother and daughter approach the corner where the grave of old Kilbaddy and his Kate lay beneath a delightful sprawl of roses.   Hitching her shining dress Katherine crouched beside the mound and selected two of her own blooms, laying them together before the headstone.   Her mother bent and I realised she was placing the two necklets around the girl's throat.

A few moments later they wandered back hand in hand, a dark head and a tawny held closely together and gleaming in the summer sun. As Matthew swung the gate open again my heart took a sickening dive. They were coming straight towards me. In front of the whole parish Kathy kissed my cheek then stepped aside to let Katherine hand me, very deliberately, the last of her perfect roses.

Nobody seemed to mind. Perhaps they thought tears at a wedding were normal in elderly Middle Europeans. My neighbours and friends merely smiled, some of them less than dry-eyed, all of them surprisingly unsurprised, and began to head for their transport. Kathy and Brian linked arms with me to watch as the bride and groom drove off.

One last incident set the seal on my granddaughter's happiness. It occurred near the end of the reception just as the dance band arrived for the evening's revelry. Jock, of course, immediately gravitated towards them and Matthew, relaxed now the speeches were over, was chatting happily with his father and several younger guests with Katherine's hand tucked firmly in his. Kindrum came up to him, waiting ostentatiously until the youngsters faded before speaking loudly enough for us all to hear.

'Aboot that loan, Kilbaddy...'

'I can let you have it just as soon as the raspberry cheque arrives,' Matthew said hurriedly, missing the importance of what had just happened.

'Na, na. Jist when ye're ready, that's a' I wanted to say. Aye,' he beamed at Katherine, 'but ye've got yersel' a grand asset here, eh?' She was away ahead of her new husband and beamed back at their crusty neighbour, dazzling him. Her new father-in-law looked thoroughly bewildered.

Tom Allen appeared on Kindrum's heels.

'Weel, weel, ma lad, nae mair gaddin' aboot for you! But I'll keep an eye on the raspberry pickers till ye get back.'

'I really am grateful, Tom,' Matthew said, knowing that arrangements already made would be honoured.

'Ach, laddie, aifter a' ye did for the auld man we canna see the new Kilbaddy's honeymoon spoiled, eh?'

Comprehension and pure satisfaction slapped themselves at last over Matthew's face. He swung his bride into his arms and spun her round and round as the coffee coloured silk whistled about her ankles.

'The accolade!' she shouted in glee. 'Twice in two minutes!'

'Kit!' 'Katherine!' Brian and I laughed and shushed her at the same moment, with no success at all.

'Why don't we end this confusion,' Kathy interrupted from behind us, brisk and deliberate. 'Call her Kate and be done with it.'

Even Tom started at the suggestion and grew still with the others, unsure of my reaction. Anxiously Matthew swung the girl back on to her feet and I looked at her, this fine lovely quine who had inherited so much of the best of my beloved's wonderful qualities. Oh Kate, my Kate, should I dare to step towards the future now? This lass could take me forward. Couldn't she? Yet - I shall always ache a little when she turns that laughing, loving gaze, your gaze on me.

297

'Hm?' Slowly I nodded and savoured the gentle smile which trickled across her face, banishing the solemnity from her blue eyes. 'Maybe you're right, my dear. Kate does seem the best name for Kilbaddy's Bonnie Quine.'

Printed in Great Britain
by Amazon